I0747059

The Council

The Witch's Ambitions Trilogy Book One

Kayla Frederick

This is a work of fiction. All of the characters and events portrayed in this novel are either products of the author's imagination or are used fictitiously.

The Council

Cover by betibup33
Edited by Beth Agejew

ISBN: 978-1-950530-49-6
Library of Congress Control Number: 2024927275
Third Edition July 2025

https://authorkaylafrederick.com

Other Books by the Author

Voices
Flirting with Death
After the Devil
What I Did
Runners (The Core #1)
The Residency
Memento Mori
Dead by Morning (Rituals of the Night #1)

The Witch's Ambitions Trilogy

Book One: The Council

Chapter One
The Last Day

MY HEAD DROOPS as the guest speaker at the front of the class rambles on. It takes effort to keep my forehead from smacking the desk when I nearly fall asleep. I pop my eyes open as wide as I can and prop my head up, trying to focus. The speaker's an older witch from Mentis who is gushing about her telekinetic powers. Most of my classmates are enraptured by her words to the point where I can see the stars in their eyes.

I'm not as enchanted.

I've started developing telekinetic powers too, but there's a major difference between me and her—I'm from Ignis, land of fire.

Helena, my oldest friend, sits at the desk next to me. She must've noticed my lack of interest because she elbows me. I glance at her through unapologetic eyes and see the scolding waiting in her crinkled brow. She believed the teacher when she said the lecture would be important for our studies. Like me, Helena originates from UnEquipped parents. We aren't meant to have powers, but Helena still hopes hers will develop.

I haven't had the heart to tell her about mine.

I smack my pencil off my desk to give me an excuse to look at the floor. I scoop it up and reach into the folds of my robe for the thin, black chain hidden there. It's connected to a small, beautiful ruby—a present I received years ago from a family friend, Ambrossi. I'm supposed to wear it. He enchanted it with powers to lessen the aches from my childhood accident, but I've repurposed it. It brings me comfort when I'm nervous; it's something for my hands to fidget with to get rid of all the unwanted energy.

"And that's why you should always expect the unexpected at your Arcane Ceremony!" the witch at the front of the room states at the conclusion of her lecture.

Helena claps, but I don't. I put the amulet back in its hiding place and return to fiddling with my pencil.

"All right, class. I expect you know the etiquette and proper attire for tomorrow's ceremony. Last minute details will be handled by your Coven representative," Ms. Black says. "Before you go, does anyone have any final questions?" Her gaze sweeps across the room. Temporarily, it rests on me before continuing across my classmates. I usually ask more questions than anyone, but today, I can't think of a thing. I'm ready to be out of here. "No? Okay. Class dismissed!"

I grab my bag from its place under my desk and sling it over my shoulder, relieved class is over. I can't wait for the Arcane Ceremony and the break from the mundane life that comes with UnEquipped parents.

As Helena takes her place at my side, she hooks her arm across my back to help me out of the classroom and says, "You were so rude!" She smacks me with her notebook for effect. "Misty was pouring her heart out up there, and she could tell you weren't listening."

I shrug. "Sorry, but I wasn't impressed. Of all the presentations we've seen this week, hers was the weakest. I mean, both her parents were Equipped. It'd be more of a surprise for her to *not* have powers."

"Well, I think a good power origin story is inspiring."

"The girl with astral projection was much more interesting."

"Why do you have to be such a downer?" Helena asks, pouting.

"We've waited for this week for *years*, and that speech is the last one we get? That's disappointing. If Clio were here, he would agree with me."

"Doesn't make you guys right." She pauses, considering. "Where is Clio anyway? I thought everyone had to come to class today."

"He's the Adept. You know they have special privileges. He mentioned something about getting coached from the Council for tomorrow." I could picture the shining excitement he'd had in his eyes when he'd told me the day prior. "They're gonna put him in charge of training our Equipped classmates."

Helena arches a thin, orange eyebrow. "Do I hear a hint of jealousy?"

I lick my lips, stalling for time. We're both painfully aware my physical state couldn't handle such a task. Truth be told, I would've been honored to be named Adept, but since I'm barely able to walk, I'm grateful just to be graduating.

"Hey, all I know is I'm smarter than him, even if he won't admit it," I say.

"Just because you're the smartest doesn't mean you need to rub it in," Helena scolds. "As far as magic goes, he's got us both beat anyway."

She's right. I wonder what his magic is like. He has pyro powers, the kind Ignis witches should have. Being the Adept means he not only knows how to access his magic, but he has a decent amount of control over it as well. That's impressive for any witch our age. I envy that. Envy *him*.

Helena and I start our walk home with similar thoughts of magic on our brains. The schoolhouse is positioned at the end of the Grove, giving us a glimpse of each Coven in the Land of Five as we leave the building. Around us, Aens, Mentis, Aquais, and Alchemy witches scatter in various directions. School is the only opportunity we have to co-mingle among the other Covens, but not many witches take the opportunity. Like Helena and I, the other witches tend to stay with witches of their own Coven. Forming friendships outside boundaries only leads to heartache down the road.

Helena and I continue straight, leaving the luxurious green grass and entering the scorching sun-parched path that leads home. A few other Ignis witches head in the same direction. A large ditch, the travel path of something massive, mars the soil to mark the beginning of Ignis. A tilted pole stands nearby with a thin silver whistle hanging from a string on it. Helena scoops it up and blows once. The sound is soft and tinny.

The ground rumbles, and a scaly head pops up from the trench, flinging sand in all directions. A long body follows. Brown and white dappled patterns color its scales, darker toward its tail and lighter the closer they come to its head. The wyrm's head is massive, easily larger than the building we just left. The scaled edges of its face are larger than Helena and I, and one of its eyes are the same size as our head. They could devour us if they wanted.

The wyrm stares at Helena, and she stares back. It dips its head in acceptance and lowers one short wing to the ground. Helena puts the whistle back, and I wait for her as our classmates begin to climb onto its back. Silently, I thank the beast for its service. Wyrms were dragons at one time. Their large, elaborate wings are their last remaining dragon part. Evolution had cost them their legs centuries before.

Maybe that's why I like them so much.

Once everyone is seated, the wyrm easily travels through the sand and harsh heat, speeding for the outlines of houses in the distance. Many Ignis homes lie outside of the heart of the Coven, a ring of evenly spaced buildings. Helena's home is the closest to my parents' and Clio lives about a mile from her. It's why I'm closer to them than any of my other classmates. It also helps that my parents and Helena's parents have been friends for ages.

The orange sun-parched soil changes to light gray stones as we reach the heart of the Coven. This part of Ignis vaguely resembles a spiral with shops and restaurants, along with Ambrossi's home at the very center. Dark stones line the paths to keep them cool in the blistering mid-day heat. The Coven altar sits nearby, the top smoothed by the elements to give it the appearance of a table. When important information needs to be shared, this is where everyone gathers.

The wyrm stops and stretches one of its wings to the ground to help us climb down. Helena hops down first and reaches for me, steadying me when both feet hit the ground. I turn enough to make eye contact with the wyrm.

"Thank you," I tell it.

The creature trills in response and buries itself in the dirt once again.

"I guess I should head home. I need to get in as much time studying as I can," Helena says, gesturing to the Book of Spells held tightly against her chest. The binding is worn and faded in spots from being read at least a hundred times.

I don't have the heart to tell her smarts really have nothing to do with developing powers. That must've been part of the reason none of this week's lectures featured an UnEquipped witch who suddenly developed some sort of ability. Ms. Black probably hadn't wanted to give witches like her false hope.

I watch Helena walk away and consider how I'll prepare myself for the Arcane Ceremony. I need to find out if the telekinetic powers I used were a fluke and whether I can somehow manifest them into pyro powers. I don't have a clue how to begin, so I follow the path out of the heart of Ignis and start the long hobbling trek home. By the time I reach a petrified log that indicates I'm ninety percent of the way there, I'm panting for breath and covered in sweat.

I sit, grateful for the chance to rest. A hawk shrieks overhead, and I watch it readying to dive. A small twitch of my eyes, and it freezes. Its distress is clear as it fights to free itself from its invisible bonds. I mull over the idea that I'm the one holding it—that I, someone who can barely move on the ground, can stop something so beautiful mid-flight.

Always expect the unexpected, Misty's voice rings through my head.

I blink to break the hold on the panicked creature, and the hawk drops a foot before the shock disappears, and it continues on its way. Considering the powers I should have, the bird is lucky. Clio most likely would've charred the poor thing.

* * *

ANGEL PASSES ME a fresh ear of corn, and I pick up my tool to shuck it. I've spent an hour at her side already, and my fingers hurt. I falter a few times trying to get a grip, and I nearly slice my hand. The husk tears away, I set the ear to the side before wiping away the sweat that's gathered on my forehead.

Outside the tiny window in Angel's hut is a perfect view of the buildings at the heart of Ignis. A few of my classmates go by, talking about tomorrow's ceremony. With a sigh, I pick up another ear of corn and pin it in place. I wish time would go a little faster. It doesn't, of course. Coven duties have never been my favorite. They're taxing and mind-numbing, and if nothing else, they're another reminder the UnEquipped will always fall short of the Equipped and will have to scramble to find a way to stay useful to the Coven.

I like Angel though. Spending time with her is easy. She's kind and patient, never scolding but guiding me. Sometimes, I wish she were my mother. Life would be easier if she was.

Angel catches me staring and hands over three more ears of corn. Her long, black hair whacks me as she shuffles across the room to grab a different tool off the wall.

Biting my lip, I cut the husks away slower than I did from the other pieces, and I look up to see Angel staring at me. "Have I done something wrong?" I ask, inspecting the ears for the tiniest error.

"No, you've done a good job," she says and wipes her hands on a towel. "But I think I'll let you be on your way early tonight."

I glance at the large pile of vegetables that have yet to be shucked on the other end of the table. I'd love nothing more than to be done, but I feel guilty leaving her to do so much work alone. "Are you sure? It seems like you need me."

She shakes her head. "I think your time could be better used focusing on your studies for tomorrow."

I want to tell her the same thing that I considered telling Helena. It doesn't matter how often you study. If you're meant to have powers, you're meant to have powers. There is no secret to pushing it along. But Angel is stubborn. So I say, "If you insist."

Angel bobs her head and sets the towel on the table with a soft plop. "Enjoy the rest of your night, kid."

"You too," I say and make my way to the door, knowing my evening will be filled with anything but enjoyment.

Chapter Two
Accident

PROPPED ON A log in the dirt sits a vase. It's a plain, little thing I snatched from the shelf at home. I've always disliked it. The swirling blue patterns seem a bit off-kilter. I stare at it, slowly letting the air filter out of my lungs. The vase flies and shatters against the stones into a hundred little pieces. I stare at the remains, thinking how easy it had been to cause this. These powers may not be the ones I'm supposed to have, nor the ones I want, but they come easily.

"That's incredible!"

I turn and see Helena beaming at me. "I thought you went home to study."

"I did, but then I started thinking that maybe we'd be better off studying together," she says, eyes sparkling. "Apparently, you've taken your studies far more seriously than I gave you credit for."

I scratch the back of my neck, but I fail to find words. Helena seems happy with the discovery, but I can't help wondering if her smile masks emotions beneath it.

"I don't think this has anything to do with studying," I admit, scooping a fragment of porcelain out of the sand. "Yesterday… it just sort of happened. I got into an argument with Mother, and a window shattered. She thought neighborhood kids were throwing rocks."

"You didn't tell her the truth?"

"Of course not," I say. At first, I'd thought she was right, not entirely convinced the magic had come from me. After my parents had gone to sleep, I'd snuck outside and studied the yard and window. Nothing lined up with her version of what had happened.

"She's gonna find out the truth at the Arcane Ceremony anyway."

Everyone will know.

A flutter of nervousness rises through my stomach. The thought of being sorted into Mentis and separated from my friends and family makes me sick.

I hide the reaction by moving over to the remains of the vase. "I couldn't work up the courage to tell *you*, let alone anyone else."

"You were afraid to tell me?"

I look up at her, my lip jutting out in a pout. She sounds shocked, taken aback, and I wonder why I've worried so much about it. "I know how much the ceremony means to you. You've worked so hard to develop powers, and I didn't want to crush that hope."

"That's silly," Helena says, waving a hand as if she were shooting the breeze and not discussing a matter she carries so close to her heart. "If anything, it gives me *more* hope. If you can do it, I can too, right?"

"But these are *Mentis* powers," I remind her, wondering why she skimmed past that part. "I shouldn't be able to do this at all."

"Maybe when they're fully developed, they'll shift to Ignis

abilities. It's happened before."

"Maybe, but maybe not," I say, plopping down on the ground. I gather energy in my mind and use it to piece the destroyed vase back together. "Either way, I'm afraid to tell my parents the truth."

"They'll accept you regardless," Helena says, sitting down next to me. She takes the vase, holds it up, and looks for gaps and misalignments. "Good craftsmanship."

"I know that, but they won't look at me the same way anymore." Just as I can't look at the vase the same when I notice one piece that's slightly off.

Helena's eyes slide half-closed. "Things could always be worse." She passes the vase back. "At least you have parents, unlike Clio, and you have powers… unlike *me*," she says, and I can hear the first real hint of hurt in her tone. This conversation is hard for her.

"You've still had no luck?"

"I thought I heated up my grandmother's soup yesterday, but I'm pretty sure she did it herself. My parents hate that she encourages me, and I'm starting to as well," she says. "Thinking I had done it, only to find out I'd been had? That stung far more than not developing powers at all."

"There's still time," I try to assure her. "It's not over until the Council announces your evaluation tomorrow."

She looks at the Book of Spells still clutched in her arms. Her face goes tight then slackens as if she's putting in effort to keep from breaking down. "I suppose, but what's a day compared to eighteen years? I'm starting to understand my parents. Understand why they want me to focus on Coven duties and skills outside of school." She holds up her book, thumbing through the pages. "Do you know how many times I've read through this thing? I could recite it from memory at this point."

"You can't force it," I remind her, pushing the book down out of eye level. "Never say never and all that."

Helena drops the book with a *thump* and reaches for the vase again. She sets it on the log where it sat earlier and rises to her feet.

"Okay, fine. I want to give it a try," she says.

I struggle to stand, using everything around me to gain momentum, as Helena takes her place. She breathes in deeply and studies the vase the way I had. I watch her movements, hoping for the best. She breathes out, whispering under her breath, but nothing happens.

Her shoulders slump.

"You're doing fine," I say.

In a weak attempt at comfort, I put a hand on her shoulder. A massive gust of force launches the vase into the air. Time slows down, and I count the moments until the crash. A piece flies in my direction, and the force opens an ugly gash down my arm.

"Oh, my Goddess!" Helena gasps, staring at the fresh blood bubbling on the surface as if she might be sick. "Heal it!"

"I'm no shaman!" I screech and clutch my hand to the spot, trying to slow the bleeding. "Get Ambrossi!"

Helena hesitates, glancing between the blood and the broken vase, before taking off toward the Healer's Den. I know what she's thinking. Ambrossi will ask questions. I gather the shattered porcelain remains and attempt to put the vase back together, but some of the pieces are slippery with blood.

Whatever these powers are, I can't control them. If I can't control them, hiding them from my parents—and everyone else—will be impossible. I move my hand to look at the wound underneath. Especially now.

Ambrossi will tell my parents he's seen me today, and I have no idea how I'll explain the visit. I can always make up something about my leg, but I don't like to do that. I've strived to make people forget the thing that makes me stand out. Doing the opposite feels like going against my own cause.

I look up and see Helena running toward me, hand in hand with Ambrossi. He's windblown and panicked by the time they reach me. I can imagine Helena barking out pieces of the story and leaving him to fill in the blanks. His worrywart nature most likely had him envisioning a scene much worse than this.

Ambrossi lets go of Helena and drops to his knees beside me. "How did this happen?" he demands, moving my hand so he can see the cut.

"It was an accident," I blurt out, trying to scoot the damaged vase out of view.

"Lies don't suit you, Lilith."

I keep my mouth shut as he utters a spell, which stitches together the muscles and tendons, leaving a faint, white scar behind.

The smile on Ambrossi's face crinkles the crescent-moon shaped scar on his cheek. "All healed. Now, do I get the truth?" He folds his arms across his chest, and his blue eyes bore into mine, reminding me that he is older than I am and, therefore, has influence.

Nervously, I look at his spiky, red hair to avoid his intense eyes. Helena folds her arms in a gesture that mimics Ambrossi's.

"Is someone developing powers?" he asks, eyes darting between me and Helena.

I try to come up with a lie, but my mind goes blank. I sigh. As Helena had already pointed out, the truth will be revealed at the ceremony anyway. "Yes," I say in defeat, "but… they're not what you'd expect."

"Surely, you didn't burn down a forest?" He chuckles.

"Things would be easier if that was the case," I say, imagining the Grove on fire. All it would take would be a couple good Aquais witches to solve that.

Ambrossi's face grows serious, and he leans a bit closer. "What *is* the case?" He's spent so much of his life worrying about me that the creases that appear from his frowns seem part of his regular appearance.

"I have… telekinetic powers."

"Really?"

"They showed up yesterday," I tell him in a burst of rapid speech. "I thought it was a fluke, but today, they're stronger in a way I can't control. What am I going to do?"

"Nothing, if that's what you choose. The Council will simply give you the choice of where you want to live. Whatever you decide, they must accept."

"Yeah, but my parents don't."

Ambrossi pulls his lips tight. "That's… a trickier situation. Have you consulted your teacher about your options?"

I shake my head. "Of course not. Her focus was, and has always been, on helping Equipped witches become even more

Equipped. I doubt she knows I exist."

"That's that pessimism talking again," he says, disapprovingly. "Whatever the case, the Council will be able to offer you guidance. If all else fails, talk to Tarj tomorrow. Try to catch him before the ceremony if you can. Let him tell you about the actual procedure."

"The Ignis representative?" I ask, trying to picture his face. He's made a few appearances at school this week, but I've never had a one-on-one interaction. "I think he's a bit too busy to worry about my situation."

"All I'm saying is you never know. This is the kind of thing they usually like to know up front."

"I guess," I murmur, glancing toward Helena, unconvinced.

She shrugs in response.

"Seems you've already made up your mind," Ambrossi says. He looks down at my leg. Because of the way I'm sitting, it's sticking straight out at an awkward angle. "Any complaints about your leg?"

"Did you think it would be my excuse for seeing you?"

"I know you well enough," Ambrossi says, his teasing smile back on his face. "Now, answer the question."

"I've been walking every day. No pain."

"You're not wearing your amulet," he notes.

"Don't need it."

He narrows his eyes, clearly not believing me. "Let me see."

I shuffle, revealing the wrinkled patch of pink skin that encircles my calf. Ambrossi runs a finger along it, uttering a spell meant to help with pain. It would have been wonderful if his powers were enough to heal it completely, but no shaman can reduce the damage done by magic.

"Walk for me," he orders.

I use telekinesis more than my own two feet to stand, and I'm grateful I can do it without another witch's help. I walk a few yards across the parched soil and back, and my limp becomes noticeable halfway through.

"All things considered, you're lucky you didn't lose that leg," he marvels as I plop back onto the ground, exhausted.

I smile at him, but it's fake, a mask to hide my bitterness. Telling me I'm lucky to walk is almost like telling Helena she's lucky to be powerless.

Ambrossi's never been good at consoling me, and after so many years of having to deal with me, I feel sorry for him. According to my parents, Ambrossi was first on the scene the day of my accident. I can't remember. Where there should be a traumatic memory, there is an odd blank space. Ambrossi told me that whoever had done this had charred my leg deeply enough to affect the muscles and bone, which would limit my leg's usefulness for the rest of my life.

"I'm lucky for a lot of reasons," I murmur, "but my leg isn't one of them."

He looks at Helena, unwilling to argue the point further. "Will you take her home, or should I?"

"I've got it. After all, it's sort of my fault she got hurt," Helena says, clutching her elbow and somehow looking five years younger.

Ambrossi stands up and stares down at me as if he's

thinking about trying to help me stand. I force myself up without his help, desperate to show him his pity is misplaced.

"Will you tell my parents about this?" I ask, looking at the ruined vase.

Ambrossi follows my gaze. "Not if you don't want me to. It's not as though you've been terribly injured, and it sounds like you need to talk to them. It's not my place to intervene."

"I appreciate it," I say and scoop up the vase. A piece falls off, and I tap my magic to put it back into place.

Ambrossi watches. "That's impressive. Even if you can't control your powers well yet, they're growing. If you insist on keeping a low profile, I suggest you take this." He hands me a clear packet containing green sludge. "And be mindful of any more accidents today."

"What's this?" I ask and squeeze the gift between two fingers. It looks like something Helena's cat would throw up, and I can only imagine it would taste the same.

"It's a poultice to get rid of the scar on your arm."

My eyes shine with gratitude. "I can always count on you." I drop my head, and my gaze drifts to my leg. Through my hair, I notice Ambrossi frown.

"Magical wounds are different. The poultice won't do much for them."

"Fine." I shove the tiny pouch into the pocket I had sewn into the side of my dress.

"It was good seeing you again," Ambrossi says to Helena, then he turns to me. "If you need me, Lilith, don't hesitate to reach out, okay?"

"Sure thing," I say, knowing it's a promise I won't keep.

We watch him walk away, then Helena glances at the white scar. "How's your arm?"

"Better," I say, raising my elbow to see the mark the best I can from the awkward angle.

Helena arches an eyebrow. "Gonna take the easy way out, or do you plan to tell your parents the truth?"

"I don't know yet. I think I need to spend some time alone. Gather my thoughts."

"I get it," she says, bending down to scoop up her book. She brushes the dirt from the cover and stares at it the way a mother looks at her newborn child. "I should get back to studying anyway. Time is short."

I nod, and she walks away, leaving me to study the contrast between her bright orange hair and the green dress she's wearing.

I admire her determination, I think, as I go the opposite direction. I hope it pays off.

Chapter Three
Friendly Animosity

I TELL MYSELF to go home, but, somehow, along the way, I lose steam and head for Fern's oasis instead. It's a beautiful little pond surrounded by a few green plants and a giant tree. It sits at nearly the perfect center between my house, Helena's house, and Clio's house. When we were kids, we used to come out here a lot to play in the water. Now I seem to be the only one who visits it.

By the time I make it there, the moon sits high overhead. The water is almost silver in the moonlight. My breath billows into the chilly air, and I skirt the edge, careful with every step. This is the only body of water in Ignis, and it scares me. My parents told me that long ago, before the Land of Five was formed, humans performed trials on one another. It was a time of darkness when witches were persecuted, bound, and tossed into the largest body of water to see if they'd sink or swim.

I would've never made it, I think, hyperaware that my weak leg would have done nothing but drag me down.

North of the oasis sits the base of the biggest tree in Ignis. At eye level is a tiny hole. I tap my fist beside it and take a step back, waiting for a tiny face to pop out. Shoulder-length green hair curls around Fern's frame as she pulls her small body through, then uncurls her large fern-like wings.

"Lilith! Why so glum?" she asks as she lights down on my

shoulder. Her aura shines in the dark and the minuscule weight of her body brings comfort. "What's this?" She runs a small finger along the ugly white line down my arm.

"I-I had an accident," I say quickly, in almost the same cadence I'd used with Ambrossi. Lying to her is foolish, but I'm uncomfortable with the truth. I pass the pouch of salve from Ambrossi to her with shaking fingers.

"You saw Ambrossi today?" She pauses, and her gaze darts from the scar to the salve.

"In a manner of speaking… I may be developing powers. Thing is, I'm not sure of them or myself."

Fern tears the pack open with her teeth. "You were so curious about magic, I thought you'd be ecstatic to see something manifest, especially in time for the ceremony!"

"I am, kind of, but it's not as simple as that," I say as Fern smears the green pulp on my skin. I shiver from the chill and turn my nose away to keep from inhaling the heavy plant odor.

"Oh?"

I stare into the shadows, not wanting to go into details.

"This is a pretty nasty scar," she says after concluding I won't talk.

"These powers… I can't control them," I say and drop my voice to a whisper. "They're telekinetic."

Fern pauses to look up at me, and her huge, ice blue eyes blink once. "Have you read your entire Book of Spells yet? There should be a page or two pertaining to restraint. Or at the very least getting a feel for your powers. Maybe that'll help."

"I've skimmed over it a hundred times, and the only real information is about controlling powers of your own Coven.

Cross-Coven powers isn't a topic it covers."

"Powers are powers." Fern checks to see how much salve is left in the packet and hands it to me before she flutters into the air. "And the book doesn't discriminate because cross-Coven powers being a permanent thing is very, very rare. I wouldn't worry too much. It's not uncommon to have a surge of powers when they first come to light."

"No, but having powers when both of your parents are UnEquipped is," I remind her. My thumb slides through some of the slime that leaked onto the outside of the package, and I grimace before cramming it into my pocket. "If these powers were going to change or disappear, they would've done that by now, right?"

"Whatever happens with them, your parents will understand," Fern says.

Her tone is soft, comforting, but I'm not convinced. The absence of the white line in the crook of my elbow offers me another possible out from the conversation I dread so much.

"Well, that's one problem solved at least," I say, twirling my arm to observe the patch of blank skin from all angles. "Thanks, Fern."

She dips her head and flaps her wings to carry her to the edge of the pond. A happy tune comes from her as she flutters through the reeds and fireflies, scooping up a small stone.

"Is there any way *you* can help me?" I ask, watching her skip the stone across the water's surface. "Maybe force my magic to be what it's supposed to be?"

"Lilith, I offer wisdom, not miracles," Fern says, glancing at me. "Besides, your magic *is* doing what it's supposed to. You'll see. Sometimes, if it's not meant to be, it's not meant to be."

I push a clump of blue-black hair behind my ear. "I know that, but I figured if anyone knew how to do it, it'd be you."

"And I don't, because I can't," Fern says, picking up another small pebble. "In the end, everything will work out. You have to have faith."

The words resonate in the calm of the early night until a sneering voice breaks the mood and causes us both to jump.

"Aww. Is little Lily developing powers?"

The fairy's attention focuses on something in the dark before returning to me. "I'll leave you to tend to your matters," she says, then she opens her beautiful wings and disappears into the hole she'd emerged from.

I don't blame her for the quick exit. Sometimes, I wish I could do the same in times of extreme stress. I turn to face Clio as he approaches. His glaring, green eyes are his most prominent feature as he detaches from the shadows. He's slim and tall, and the billow of his black cloak and robe make it hard to tell where he ends, and the shadows begin.

How much had he heard?

"I've asked you not to call me that," I mutter and lift my chin with a false confidence to hide how embarrassed I am by facing him of all possible witches right now.

"Well, your name *is* Lilith, and you *are* little so…" he trails off and shrugs, goofy grin on his face.

"I'll get you for that," I tease back. "Because as a matter of fact, I *have* developed powers."

"Look at you!" he gushes with a laugh and holds his hands out in a dramatic gesture. "Last horse to cross the finish line."

"Whatever you say, Mister Adept." I curl my lips into a smirk. "Better late than never." It could be my life motto.

"Care for a little duel?" he offers. I can tell what he's thinking. That this will be an easy win for him.

A training session with the Adept is a high honor for any member of our class. Any member except me. The relationship I have with Clio is different from theirs, and for that reason, I'm not sure if it will hurt or help. I see him as my best friend. One of my closest confidants.

I drop my teasing tone. "I don't think that's such a good idea," I admit and study the blank spot where the scar was ten minutes earlier. Ambrossi had already warned me away from a second accident, and I know not to take his warning lightly.

"Scared?" Clio muses and clicks his tongue. He's still teasing me, not picking up on the fact that my mood has done a complete one-eighty. "Maybe you don't have powers after all. It's interesting because I never took you for a liar."

He's trying to egg me on, and I hate that it works. He has confidence in himself and his abilities. I'd give anything for that ability.

"Forget I said anything," I say, almost tripping over my weak foot as I take pointed paces backward. "A duel sounds perfect."

"Standard rules?" he calls, assuming his position a few feet away.

"You bet." It's hard to see him in the dark, but I don't let it bother me. I take a deep breath and an eerie sense of calm washes over me.

We stare each other down. Clio makes the first move,

sending a blast of fire my way. The spark of orange shines. It's powerful magic, but I knew what to expect, and I'm ready. I copy his gesture and create an invisible shield around me before using my other hand to send a blast of magic his way. The surge knocks him off his feet, ending the battle as quickly as it began.

After a minute, he sits up and stares at me through confused eyes. I can see the gears turning in his head as he tries to figure out what happened.

"Does this mean I win?" I ask in my best innocent voice.

"You didn't say you were *telekinetic*," he replies. He dusts himself off as he rises to his feet.

"You didn't ask," I remind him. "Besides, I thought you heard everything eavesdropping."

"Not enough apparently. You must be nervous as Hell for the ceremony tomorrow," he says. "And here I was thinking I'd have it the worst."

"I'll be fine."

Clio looks up at the sky and judges the time by the moon's position. "If that were true, I can't help but think you'd be home getting ready for bed right now."

"Okay. You got me," I admit. Out of everyone, Clio knows me the best. For that reason alone, I drop my façade and lay it all on the table. "I don't know how the Council will react. How *anyone* will react," I say, waving my hands around to enunciate my words. "What if they tell me I have to go live in Mentis?"

"They'll probably handle it like me. Do you see me freaking out?" he asks, waving a hand in front of his emotionless face.

"No, but I think it's different for you. You *know* me. They don't. When they look at me, all they see is a cripple from UnEquipped parents."

Clio snorts. "So what if they do? You can't care about what other people think. Even if it means switching Covens, you have to do what's best for you. Live in the now because, one day, this will all be a memory. You'll forget about the anxiety and the fear. All you'll remember is your regret."

"If you were in my shoes, you'd pack up everything and go without so much as a goodbye?"

"If that's what I needed to do," he replies, sticking his hands in his pockets.

It isn't uncommon for us not to see eye to eye, but somehow, I'd hoped he would have my back on this one. That he would tell me this fear is normal. "What if I don't want to leave? What if I like my life here?"

"How can you think life without powers is better?" he asks, and it's clear he's genuinely confused by the concept. He grew up with Equipped parents knowing he would one day follow in their path. He doesn't know any other way of life.

"It's not as bad as you think," I say. It's not his fault he has such a low opinion of the UnEquipped. It's something all Equipped witches have in common. "I mean, my parents make it okay. I could too. So far, this gift has been nothing but problematic."

"I don't know how much this means to you, but I'm rooting for you. You'll figure it out," he says.

"Thanks." I take a deep breath. "If only we could switch bodies for the night, things would be a lot better tomorrow."

Clio raises an eyebrow, amused. "How so?"

"I haven't told my parents what I can do yet. If I were you, I'd know how to break it to them. I might even learn how to control my powers, so when we switched back, I could get my life together."

"All these things you're worried about are things you can handle," he assures me, jabbing one long finger into my shoulder with each word. "You don't need me to do it for you."

I don't, but I still wish someone would.

"How's Helena doing?" Clio asks. "I didn't get a chance to talk to her today."

I shrug, imagining her crestfallen expression a few hours before. I can't imagine she's doing much better. If I know her, she's locked away in her room, trying again and again to light a candle that's doomed to remain dark.

"Still nothing, huh?"

I shake my head and keep pace with him as we do a lap around the oasis. "Nope, and she's studied like crazy. I tried to help her a bit earlier, but nothing came from it."

"Is that how you got hurt?"

I tense. "How do you know about that?"

"Eavesdropping, remember?"

I could be mad, instead, I'm glad for the easy segue to my next question. "D-did you have difficulties with your powers at first?"

"If we're being completely honest, then yes, I did. I practiced every single day, every chance I got, and our teacher was more than willing to coach me when I needed it."

Nothing but the best for the Adept.

"Couldn't find anyone to help you?" he guesses.

"Is there anything you don't find out by snooping?" I ask and shove him playfully.

He shoves me back, harder than intended. My foot slides in muck, and I scream as I fall into the water. Cold liquid rushes around my face, up my nose, and into my ears. Clio grabs my hand and pulls me to the surface and onto the ground beside the oasis. Water drips from my head to my feet as I sit there and process what happened.

Clio laughs, and I swat a soaked lock of hair from my eyes to glare at him.

"That was terrible, Li!" he says, gasping for air. "You were so scared, as if you'd drown! It's less than a foot deep!"

"Thanks so much for your help," I say. I rip off my cloak to dab away some of the water that's soaked into my corset. I'm already cold, and my skin is numbing, though it's been barely longer than a minute.

"You're gonna be fine," he says. He rolls his eyes as the last of his laughter fades away.

I stand slowly, purposefully. "We'll see about that."

"Li, don't-don't!" he begs, holding up his hands.

Before he can finish the protest, I tap my abilities and pull a wave of water out of the oasis and over his head. His mouth falls open like a fish's, and I laugh as hard as he had.

He runs a hand through his soaked, black hair to ring out the excess drops. "All right. I deserved that."

"Damn right," I say. I pick uncomfortably at my wet clothes again as I wander toward the line of trees that marks the divide between Fern's oasis and the harsh desert of Ignis soil.

"Heading home?"

"I need a change of clothes in case you haven't noticed." I wring out my hair, making sure I spray as much water on him as possible.

"You and me both. I'll walk with you."

I'm oddly sad with the laughter gone. He peeks at me from the corner of his eye, carefully watching my awkward strides while pretending not to. Despite his tough exterior, he's a gentleman deep down, and that's the part of him that's desperately searching for some way to help.

"You don't have to walk me home," I say quickly. "And you don't have to do that either."

Clio's face scrunches. "Do what?"

"Look at me like that. I'm not helpless."

"I never said you were."

"No, but your eyes do. Just remember who won our duel."

"Hard to forget a beating like that," he says with a crooked smile.

"Good," I say, and the conversation dies.

Without a distraction, the cold takes the brunt of my attention, and I hug myself tight. Somehow, I keep myself warm enough to stop my teeth from chattering. Clio lets out a few irregular breaths, like he's struggling too.

Lights from my parents' house appear, and Clio stops walking. "Good luck tomorrow." When I scoff, he bends closer to me. "I mean it."

"Thank you, Clio. All joking aside, I don't know what I'd do without you." He's the only one who believes in me. I don't even believe in myself.

"Ditto," he says and walks back into the darkness, toward the dunes and his tiny home nestled among them.

I stare at my parents' open window, watching my mother move around inside. If only I had the strength for this. I stay outside for as long as I can before the chill drives me inside. My mother, Raya, hums to herself as she sits at the kitchen table and sews an ornate, faux gemstone to a dress.

"I was wondering when you would show your face," she says when I walk into the room.

"It was a busy day, being my last day of school and all," I say and hobble to the empty chair nearest to the candle. Soaking in its warmth, I push it aside to better see what she's working on "What's that?"

"Your outfit for tomorrow," she replies, and she holds it up with the biggest, proud smile.

I raise my eyebrows. I'm not used to warm expressions on her face.

Her hair is pulled into such a tight ponytail, it exaggerates her frown when her smile disappears. "You don't like it."

"It's beautiful, Mom," I say patiently. I can't stop the sigh that follows. It would be the perfect dress for the version of me that I was twenty-four hours prior.

Her frown deepens. "Something's wrong. What is it?"

"I… it's… tomorrow is…" I struggle for words. Why is this so hard?

"A big day?" she guesses. "It's normal to be nervous."

"It's… it's more than that," I say, wishing she could understand the gravity of the situation. "Is Dad home?"

She shakes her head. "No, he's helping with the

preparations in the Grove."

"Oh." I take a deep breath as the nerve to tell her the truth dwindles away.

"What's the matter?" She sets the dress aside and studies me with fresh concern.

"There's something I need to tell you," I murmur, but it's as if I've left my body. The world goes eerily silent under the exaggerated thump of my heart.

Now or never, I can almost hear Clio encourage me in the back of my mind.

"Something happen between you and Clio?" Mom asks as she resumes her sewing.

I scrunch up my face. It isn't the first time she's been suspicious of my relationship with Clio. "What? No, Mom."

She raises her eyebrow so high, I wonder if it hurts her face.

"I'm Equipped."

She drops the dress to the table where it lands in a colorful pool of fabric. "Lilith, that's great!"

"R-really?" I'm too surprised to think of a coherent response longer than two syllables. I thought she'd be disappointed or upset. It never crossed my mind that she might be *excited* for me.

"How long have you known?"

"Well, since yesterday... the window—" I swallow, and my eyes dart everywhere except at her as I string together my sentence "—was the... was the first time."

"But that would mean..." Her face tightens, and she stares *through* me.

The pounding of my heart grows louder, and sweat makes my hands clammy, as I wait for her to speak. An eternity passes before she lets her breath out and looks at the dress.

"You should get to bed. Tomorrow's a big day."

"Wait, Mom, I—" My heart twists painfully in my chest at the idea that my parents might not accept me after all. "Are you… are you mad at me?"

"I have a lot of work to do to get this done tonight."

The dismissal is clear in her tone. Unable to speak, I go to my room. I want to believe the sudden coldness comes from the possibility of losing me if the Council decides I'm a better fit for Mentis, but she had something else in her eyes—a foreign emotion I can't identify.

I change my clothes, grateful for the dry fabric, then I scan the books on my bookshelf. My Book of Spells is by far the largest, and I struggle under its weight before I drop it on the floor. I sit beside it after giving up on the idea of carrying it to bed and flip through the pages, hoping to find some sort of section on cross-Coven powers.

What if it's not possible to fix this? I think and the weight of my situation begins to sink in. *What if I'm stuck like this?*

I use my telekinesis to pull a book of Coven history from the shelf, and I flip to the section on Mentis. Forcing myself to read the words doesn't help me absorb the information, so I content myself by skimming the pictures. They don't tell me anything I don't already know, and eventually, I slam the book shut. Then, I pull every book off the shelf to join the other two on the floor.

Now, I know how Helena feels. If she can hold her head high at her lowest, I can do the same.

Hours of desperate research pass before my eyelids grow heavy, and I fall asleep on my pile of books, my situation as unresolved as when I'd started.

32

Chapter Four

The Arcane Ceremony

WHEN MOM COMES into my room the next day, I'm still asleep on my mountain of books. She rouses me, and I look up at her, hardly able to remember where I am. My mother helps me to my feet and guides me to the bathroom. Everything hurts more than usual from my odd sleeping position. I clutch the edge of the counter while she runs a brush through my hair, pausing when it catches tangles.

I don't speak as she works. Tension is the only thing I can feel, and it's made more obvious by the lack of conversation. The morning of the day of something this big should be filled with excitement, but it's quiet enough to hear a pin drop. Mom's hair is pulled into her usual tight ponytail, and she's dressed in a gown as nice as the one she made for me. I want to say it's a sign of goodwill, but it could also be for show.

"Are you going to need help getting dressed?" she asks, as she sets the brush on the counter.

I ignore the question and turn to look at her. "Have you told Dad?"

She breathes in deeply, and her eyes narrow to slits. By the gesture, I can tell I won't like what she says. "I did."

"And?"

"He thinks you're confused about your abilities," she starts.

"Wh—" I try to interject but she continues.

"Being Equipped is challenging to get a handle on from what we've heard." She clasps her hands in front of her as if she's trying to keep herself from fidgeting.

"That sounds like a bunch of bullshit." I lift my chin to glare at her. First Mother, now Father too? I never thought *both* my parents would be uncomfortable with the idea of my being Equipped.

"The only thing that's bullshit here is that attitude," Mother says with a frown. "You started fires when you were little. That's how you burned your leg."

I would almost have been convinced that was the truth if she hadn't looked away as she said it. "If I can't pull pyro powers now, I couldn't do it then either. Something doesn't add up here."

"Let me help you get this on," Mom says and reaches for the dress.

"I can do it myself," I snap, and I snag it out of her hands. I almost *wish* my pyro powers worked so I could light it on fire and force her to talk to me.

Mom simpers as if she hasn't heard me. "Come get me when you're done, okay?"

The door closes, and I stare at the dress wondering where it all went wrong. Last night she'd seemed so content with everything. Then I'd told her the truth.

It's odd how defensive she became when I started asking questions.

Then I start to think that switching Covens might not be so bad.

Stripping down to my undergarments, I tap into my powers and slowly lift the dress over my head, pulling it into place.

I admire the way it fits. What my parents lack in magic, they make up for in talent. I smooth the black collar against my neck, then I run the brush through my hair again, watching myself in the mirror. My crystal-blue eyes stare back, full of stress. I'm surprised no one else can see it. Resisting the urge to punch the mirror, I walk out of the bathroom, back into my room. I scoop up the packet containing the remaining bit of salve from my bookshelf and tuck it into my pocket. Never know when it'll come in handy.

Raya waits in the kitchen with my father, Haze. At the sound of my footsteps, he looks up. A receding hairline marks the top of his unhappy face.

"You look beautiful!" Mother gushes as I hobble into the room.

I smile and wonder if they can tell it's forced. "Thanks."

"Nervous?" Father asks and takes a sip of whatever is in his mug. His tone is much lighter than I expected by the look on his face.

"Among other things," I murmur and limp past them.

I try not to focus on the look in their eyes. It was the same odd emotion Mother had shown the night before, and I have the feeling I interrupted a conversation I wasn't meant to hear. I want to ask again about my powers and my accident, but today will be stressful enough without me adding to it.

"Are you ready to go?" I ask, making my way out the door before they can answer.

Footsteps confirm they're following as I step onto the parched soil of our front yard, and that's good enough for me. It's a bit of a walk to the Ceremony Grounds. Riding a wyrm would have made the trip quicker, but it's tradition to walk the path.

Phantom pains curl inside my bad leg, but I'm determined not to show any weaknesses. Instead, I think about the countless number of Ignis witches who have taken this route before and how honored I am to be among them.

I straighten my cloak, staying a few steps ahead of my parents at all times. They try to engage me in conversation, but I shut them down. After last night, I'm in no mood for small talk. Instead, I put my energy into walking. A break in concentration leads to the realization I've been using my powers to manage the trip with seeming ease when I stumble.

Someone grabs me under my arms. I curse and look up into Clio's eyes. As soon as I'm balanced, he lets go and takes his place at my side. His ceremony attire is fancier than mine—a silver suit with red trim and a matching cloak.

"Thought I'd catch you traveling this way. Mind if I tag along?" he asks, tipping his head in the direction of the path ahead.

I shove my hands in my pockets and fidget with Ambrossi's amulet. "I guess not."

Clio glances at my parents out of the corner of his eye and calls a quick greeting to them before leaning toward me to whisper, "Are you okay?"

"I'll be fine," I assure him. I don't want to admit that I'm terrified, that I feel like my life is out of my control.

Something about the look in Clio's eyes tells me he's guessed the talk with my parents didn't go so well. "What are you going to do?"

"I don't know," I admit.

Clio drapes his arm around me and pulls me in for a quick

half-hug. I offer him a reassuring smile, but I don't feel any better. About three-quarters of the way to the Grove, Helena and her parents join us. She wears a beautiful blue gown that complements her green eyes. Her wild orange hair has been carefully groomed into a long braid down her back.

Her parents fall into step with mine, and I watch them, thinking how odd it is that only UnEquipped parents attend the Arcane Ceremony. Equipped witches traditionally don't go. I think about that. The difference of their habits compared to ours.

What's it like to be raised with parents who stoke your powers from the beginning? What would I be like now if I had *one* parent who believed in what I could do?

"I don't think I've ever seen you guys so serious before," Helena says.

"It's a big day," I murmur without looking at her.

Helena knits her brow in concern. Clio shoots her a look that says, *Don't ask.*

"How'd Adept training go?" Helena asks Clio.

He shrugs. "Simple enough. Not really training so much as running through today's list of activities and pairing up for our demonstrations."

"Good luck with that."

"Who needs luck? I have skill."

I remember how easy it was to disarm him with my telekinesis.

"That doesn't count," he says when he catches my eye.

"I disagree," I tease as we close the last of the distance to the Grove.

Half the grounds are covered in shade from the trees

growing along the edge. In the middle of the grassy patch is a rise with a stone-lined path running the length of it. At the top of the hill, the path evens out. Five goblets so large they resemble vases, colored to match the five Covens, rest in a circle. Witches from every Coven are gathered on the shady side of the grounds to keep out of the heat. The crowd is larger this year than in years past, and I wonder if my anxiety is exaggerating it. We join our classmates near the back of the grounds. My parents, along with Helena's, mingle with familiar faces from Ignis. I scan the sea of Mentis students, looking for a friendly face.

"There's a lot of them," Clio mutters. He stands as tall as he can to peer at everyone. He doesn't trust the other Covens much, and I wonder why.

"I'm gonna mingle," I decide and limp toward the group of Mentis. It won't hurt to at least try to make acquaintances before things go down.

Helena follows me, but we don't make it far across the field before her mask crumples, revealing the true emotions underneath. "I'm gonna fail, Li!" she wails. Glossy tears make her eyes seem enormous.

I wish I could give her my powers so my life could return to normal. I don't want to be jealous of her, but I am. She's free to live as she always has, while I must make one of the biggest decisions of my life.

The grass really is always greener.

I bury my feelings deep and pull her into a hug. "It's not failing," I tell her when I pull away. "You're still a valuable part of Ignis."

Clio joins us, giving me a look that says it's probably best for us to stick together for now. With another glance at the Mentis witches, I ditch my mission, and Helena, Clio, and I join the rest of the Ignis group. Several witches call greetings to Clio, and he waves in response but stays at my side.

Time passes, and my anxiety skyrockets. I look up at the sun, trying to determine how much time has passed since we arrived. A tall, lean man, about thirty years old, breaks from the crowd and starts up the rise. His ceremonial cloak glows in the sunlight, silvery hair contrasting his light bronze skin. It's the Council member I've seen around school. Tarj. The Ignis representative.

When he reaches the top, he claps once, twice. The sound cuts through the chatter in the Grove and draws attention to him. The roar of conversation dulls to a quiet that somehow seems just as loud.

"Let me be the first to welcome you to this year's Arcane Ceremony!" he says and stares down at everyone, tawny eyes shining.

A ripple of applause works through the crowd.

"To kick things off, I'd like to introduce this year's Adepts! First, from Ignis, let's have a round of applause for Clio Brawn!"

The applause starts again, and Clio makes his way up the rise. In the sunlight, his skin is pale, so pale it looks as if he never lets the sun touch him. It doesn't take away from his pride as he glares down at the crowd. I may have beaten him in our duel, but I know he's powerful. He knows it too.

"Next, let's welcome Flora Noble from Alchemy!"

A small girl, with short, brown curls, parts from the

crowd. She keeps her head bowed as she travels up the rise and stands beside Clio. With a shaking finger, she pushes a pair of glasses back up the bridge of her nose, but her eyes stay stubbornly focused on the ground.

The Aquais Adept, Grail Rose, is called next. He's a large man with a broad chest and square jaw. Then comes the Aens Adept, Leo, who stares at the crowd with a permanent scowl. So far, none of the Adepts, except Clio, stand out to me. It's the Mentis Adept I'm the most invested in. Whoever they are, they may become a big part of my life if I switch Covens.

"Last, but not least, let's give a shout-out for Dawn Grimoire!"

Dawn's golden hair is the first part of her I see. She walks with a bounce and gazes straight ahead. Her dead, amber eyes seem more serious than her walk. At the top of the rise, her sky-blue robes flow around her, and she turns to the crowd, revealing a birthmark on her cheek.

"Time for a demonstration by the Adepts," Tarj says. His gaze sweeps over the five witches. "First up, Clio and Grail!"

Flora, Dawn, and Leo back away to give the pair room. Clio and Grail take their places a few meters apart and wait for the cue. I reach into my pocket and run my fingers along Ambrossi's amulet. Clio is more than qualified for this fight, but I worry about him anyway.

"Go!" Tarj orders.

Clio shoots a blast of fire toward Grail who dodges and shoots a chunk of ice back. The beam brushes Clio's arm and freezes the sleeve of his robe down to his skin. He shakes the frozen limb, but the ice doesn't dislodge. Frustration causes him to snarl as he rushes forward. Fire blasts from his free hand. It might not be clear to anyone else, but I can see how desperate he is to prove his worth.

Grail tries to rush backward but stumbles over his feet and falls. Fire blooms around his face, and he screams, backing up and out of the circle.

"Clio is the winner!" Tarj declares.

Flora is sent in to demonstrate her healing powers on both Clio and Grail.

A smirk lights up Clio's face as he stares down at Ignis and bows. There's a challenge in his eyes.

"Next up are Dawn and Leo!"

Clio takes his place beside Grail and Flora as Dawn and Leo assume their positions. Tarj gives the cue, and Leo moves first. He sends a blast of wind so powerful, it knocks Dawn back a few feet. She doesn't seem phased. She plants her feet and stares at him until her dead, amber eyes glow. Leo hovers a few inches off the ground and is then thrown a few feet. He lands with a thump and lies there, stunned. When he doesn't get up, Dawn is named the winner, and Flora rushes in to fix Leo's wounds.

"Now, it's time for the final battle—Clio and Dawn!"

"This is bound to be a nail biter," Helena says. She stands on her tiptoes to better see over the crowd.

The fight is too contrived for my liking—a battle between my home Coven and my potentially new Coven. It's as if the universe has heard my fears, my deepest worries, and created the perfect echo to sum it all up.

Clio shoots fire at Dawn, but she's quick to block it. Her eyes shine with the beginning of a spell, but Clio sends a blast of fire that ignites the edge of her sleeve. She panics and pats the flame to put it out, which breaks her focus. Clio sends another surge of fire her way. Dawn generates a shield of energy that blocks the attack, and the resounding wave knocks Clio off his feet as his last attack hits Dawn in the chest.

"Draw!" Tarj announces as Flora runs in for the last time.

I stare up the hill, disappointed. Why do I feel like this? Had I really thought the answer to my problem would come from watching a duel?

"Wasn't that something?" Helena gasps, eyes bright with excitement.

As soon as Clio is healed, he jumps to his feet, smiling at Flora as she heals Dawn. When everyone is back to health, the Adepts stand in a line and take a bow.

"Let's hear it for this year's Adepts!" Tarj cheers. The crowd roars, and the Adepts head back to their covenmates.

Clio looks put out as he approaches us. "I almost had her," he pouts.

"You tied. That's the first time that's happened during an Arcane Ceremony in over twenty years," Helena says with stars in her eyes.

"Definitely an accomplishment," I assure him.

"True," he concedes. "I think I did much better this time against someone with telekinesis."

I tune him out, watching Tarj as he calls the other members of the Council to attention. When they break from their huddle, they begin gathering their designated Covens. Then the ceremony begins. One by one, Tarj calls the crowd forward to take their turn on the rise. This year, there are slightly more

UnEquipped than Equipped, much to my surprise. I glance at Helena out of the corner of my eye, hoping this makes what's about to come a bit easier to digest.

"Helena Gram!"

Helena looks at me, helpless and afraid.

"You've got this," I whisper.

She nods, climbs the hill, and takes her place in the center of the five goblets. Tarj dips his head and backs away. Even from here, I can feel her anxiety. The crowd silences as she strains and tries to force something that doesn't exist. After a full minute, none of the goblets light up. She hangs her head and begins the walk back down the hill.

The look on her face breaks my heart. I want to run to her and tell her everything will be all right, but to her, that would be a lie. Her entire world just came to a halt, and we were all a witness to it. Clio pats her back as she rejoins us, but her gaze doesn't lift from the ground.

A handful of our class are called before Tarj says, "Lilith Lace!"

My heart flutters painfully. Clio stares at me through his wide, green eyes, and Helena offers me an emotionless, "Good luck."

I take a deep breath and begin the trek up the rise, stumbling on my bad leg. Out of the corner of my eye, I notice Clio take a step forward. He pauses when Tarj moves to help me. I don't want help, especially not with everyone watching, and I'm tempted to growl at him to go away, but it's never a good idea to show disrespect to the Council, so I focus on the top of the rise until he lets go.

As I stand at the center of the five goblets, something hums inside me. A pull of magic emits from them. I breathe out slowly and study each one. The white goblet sparks and the *pop* of magic that emits from it gives away all the secrets I'd wanted to keep. I go rigid as I listen to the gasp sweep through the crowd. I can't bring myself to look at them. I can't even make eye contact with Tarj who stands a few feet away.

Now that I have my results, I begin the trek down the hill. Suddenly, the red goblet sparks, then the green, blue, and yellow goblets in close succession.

Chapter Five
Iris White

TARJ EXTINGUISHES THE goblets on the altar and grabs me to pull me out of their range. Shouts of confusion come from the onlookers, and I assume they're because of my results. Then I catch a glimpse of fire from the corner of my eye.

"Get down!" Tarj orders. He pulls his arm off me as another blast of flames flies our way.

My telekinesis blocks it easily, and Tarj stands rigid beside me. He stretches out a hand to return the attack, but it's shaky as if he's unsure who the target is. Witches scatter in all directions. Some run toward the fight and others in the opposite direction, parting to reveal a figure who doesn't fit in—a woman cloaked in black.

She dodges Tarj's attack. There's venom in her eyes as she stares him down, and a stream of obscenities pours from her mouth. A random gust of powers escapes her, and Tarj rushes sideways, doing what he can to counter it.

"You'll all pay for following the ways of the treaty!" she shouts. "You'll all pay for following the lost witches!"

She's lost her mind.

Ranks of Equipped witches stand their ground, using their established powers while the newly Equipped witches try to copy them, using their unpredictable new powers. Hundreds of spells fizzle in the air, and in the middle of it, I stand frozen, unsure what to do. This witch is unfazed by everything sent her way. She puts up a wall of energy to protect herself on all sides.

Pyrokinetic and telekinetic powers. She's like me.

The witch screeches and dashes forward, sending hexes at Tarj, shield still in place. Tarj dodges the first few blows, but a blast of fire catches him and elicits pained screams from the depth of his throat. He collapses to his knees, trying to put the fire out. I rush to his side and cover the flame with my cloak. His burned flesh oozes with a mixture of blood and pus. It's all I can see as I squeeze the extra salve Ambrossi gave me onto his arm.

Without Healer's magic, I'm not sure how well it will work or if it will help at all, but I can't stand by and do nothing. I look up and notice the witch has frozen midway up the rise. Hostile witches surround her, blocking her escape from the grounds, but she doesn't pay attention to them. Her focus is on *me*. I swallow heavily and try to stand, a shield between her and Tarj in case she decides to attack again while he's vulnerable.

"Why are you going along with this?" she asks.

"W-what?"

"You're one of us!"

Tarj rises and takes a protective step in front of me, trying to appear fierce in spite of the pain that's still clear in his eyes. The witch appears to be on the cusp of speaking again when a heavyset girl wearing large, golden bracelets breaks from the crowd and tackles her. They roll over a few times, pummeling each other.

It's odd to see witches with powers locked in a fistfight, but the larger witch eventually wins, pinning the attacker to the ground.

"You are under arrest," she says to her prisoner and ties her arms behind her back. She pulls her to her feet and starts to lead her off the Ceremony Grounds.

I turn to Tarj only to realize he's already staring at me. "Let's get you out of here," he says and guides me toward my parents.

Mother pulls me into a hug, and Father kisses my forehead. They're relieved I'm okay, that the threat has passed, but I'm on edge.

I pull away and stare into Mother's eyes. They're darker than I remember, as if her troubles are seeping out, darkening everything they touch. "What was she talking about, Mother?"

She brushes a lock of black hair from my eyes, and her lips tremble, but no words come out.

"The witch… s-she knew me," I continue.

"That's impossible," Father snarls

Mother breaks eye contact.

I've caught her in a lie, but I don't know how to move forward, to make her admit as such. Helena and Clio appear at my side before I can say another word. Helena hugs me tight, fear on her ashen face.

"That was crazy!" she gasps and pulls back. "I-I can't believe she tried to stop the ceremony."

"Y-yeah," I manage to utter.

"You were so brave rushing to Tarj's side like that. He's the lifeblood of our Coven."

"We can gush about it later," Clio snaps. He grabs the top of my arm with one hand and places the palm of his other on my forehead. "Are you okay?"

I'm unable to speak, unable to think. My mind is miles away, on the results I got before the witch appeared. I didn't light up one or two goblets. They were all glowing. *What does that mean?*

"She's in shock," Clio says to my mother before he lets go of me. "Get her home."

I'm hardly aware that I'm moving. I'm surrounded by loved ones who are fawning over me, and I let them fuss while I think about the witch's words. Before I realize it, my mind leads me into an inescapable pit where thoughts of my accident consume me. Why can't I remember what happened to my leg? If my wound was self-inflicted like my parents want me to believe, shouldn't I remember doing it?

When we arrive home, I'm aware of Helena's hand on me. She talks to me. She's probably saying kind words, but they don't register. A few minutes later, Helena, my mother, and my father try to coax me back from the trance with a fresh meal. I sniff it, but my stomach flops, and I push it away with bleak disinterest. My mother helps me lie down in bed, and I don't protest. I'm not tired, but I'm drained—emotionally and mentally. I want answers, but everything feels a million miles away.

I start to drift off when my brain reminds me there's someone who may be able to shed light on today's events. Someone who's been around for eons and could possibly give me insight into who that witch is—Fern.

But how do I get to her?

My parents, Helena's parents, and Helena are in the house, huddled up in the kitchen and most likely still talking about me. If I try to go out the front door, they're not going to let me leave. Not after everything that happened.

Physically, I'm unable to sneak out. I roll onto my side and stare at the wall. Maybe it's a sign that I'm better off forgetting all of it and going to sleep. I clutch my blanket around me, ready to call it a night, when something knocks on my window. I bolt up and see Clio peering in at me. I gesture for him to open it, and he complies.

"What are you doing here?" I hiss, hoping the people in the other room won't overhear.

"You want answers, right? I do too," he admits. He tucks his elbow under his chest and leans halfway through the window and into the room. "And you know someone who can help."

"If you mean Fern, go ask her and tell me what she says. Getting me out without my parents' noticing will take too much time."

"She won't talk to anyone but you. You know that." His lips press together as if Fern's shyness is a personal insult to him.

"Maybe so, but they're not going to let me leave. They didn't even know what to do with me after the ceremony."

"They'll have to figure it out. Whatever happened today affects you somehow, and you have the right to know why that witch seemed to know who you are. Come on. I'll help you."

I consider my options. I can stay put, go to sleep, and pretend today never happened, pulling the wool over my eyes and never get the truth, or I can choose adventure… *answers*.

Easiest choice ever.

I cast the blanket aside, stand, and struggle to find my balance. Clio watches me. I can hear his unspoken offer to help, but I ignore it and grip my bed post. Confident, I make my way to the window, and Clio helps me through. In the yard beyond, the wind blows through my thin dress and sends chills up my spine. If Clio feels it, he doesn't show it. He loops an arm under mine and helps me walk at a pace that's much faster than I'd be able to manage on my own.

When my house fades into the distance, Clio lets go of me. "So, I have a question, and I need to know the truth."

I wince. I'm used to him sounding serious, but there's a deeper edge to his voice this time as if whatever he's about to say has been on his mind for a long time.

"You really had no idea you have so many powers?" he asks, eyes wide with amazement.

"I really didn't know. M-my parents always told me my accident was my fault, but I never believed them," I say flatly. With the results, I can't help wondering if there is a bit of truth to Mothers's story after all. Great, now I feel guilty. "I've only been able to use telekinesis."

My answer seems to satisfy Clio because he doesn't speak again until the oasis comes into view. Fern is engrossed in skipping pebbles across the water when we spot her. As we approach, she flies toward me, eyes wide with the same fear my parents had shown. "Lilith! I heard what happened! I'm so glad to see you're okay!"

"Thank you, Fern."

"What does having multiple powers mean?" Clio demands. He has no patience for small talk, and with today's tensions still very much alive, I can't say I blame him.

Fern swallows as her relief diminishes. It's clear she's intimidated by Clio. "It's been said there are some who gain multiple powers in the face of a new threat to this land, but it hasn't happened in some time." Fern's eyes dart between me and Clio. "Tell me, were there others like you today at the ceremony?"

No one else had lit two goblets let alone *all* of them. I shake my head. "The only other witch with multiple powers was the crazy woman."

"What did the Council say about your results?" Fern asks, fluttering a little farther away to put distance between her and Clio.

"They didn't say much of anything. Didn't really have the chance to. My turn happened right before she showed up, and afterward, my parents and Helena took me home until my knight in shining armor here broke me out. I don't know what happened at the end of the ceremony." I wish I could've stayed to find out what the Council thinks of me.

"The woman, the one who stopped the ceremony, could she be a danger to the Coven? To Li?" Clio asks. His intense glare doesn't leave Fern, even when she isn't looking back at him.

"I doubt it," Fern says. "It's my understanding she's been arrested. You don't need to worry about her. My main concern, now, is you, Lilith."

"Me? Why? If she's not a threat anymore, what does it matter?"

"You still don't know what your results mean. I can only remember one witch who lit multiple goblets at her Arcane Ceremony. Her name was Willow."

"What happened to her?" Clio asks.

"She was murdered by the Council," Fern replies brusquely.

Clio stares at me as I ask Fern the question we're both thinking, "Why?"

"They saw her as a threat," Fern says simply. "There hasn't been another like her since... well, until you, of course."

I think back to saving Tarj's life and hope my actions will grant me brownie points in the future.

"So, everyone accepted what the Council did? They let them murder a witch and no one questioned it? No one rioted?" Clio barrages Fern with angry questions.

"It's not as if they had much choice," Fern says sadly.

"There are more of us than them. That's the way it's always been," Clio insists. "If they wanted to do something, they could've."

"But fear is a powerful weapon. Willow's death was a warning, a show about what happens to people when they turn their back on their governing Coven," Fern says, meeting Clio's glare.

"They scared them into silence," I say.

"And no one thought about it twice," Fern says, a shadow falling over her eyes. "I don't know why that witch wanted to hurt you, Lilith, or if she was even aiming for you."

"Do they know who she is?"

"Not yet."

"How can they not know where she came from?" Clio asks, incredulous.

"Is it... is it possible there are more witches out in the wilderness? Ones not under the control of the Council?" I ask.

Miles and miles of unnavigated land circle the Land of Five. According to the Council, there's nothing out there but disease and famine and dangers we can't imagine. Once upon a time, it had been populated with millions of humans, but when the Old World crumbled, much of the land died with them. The Land of Five survived by the magic of our ancestors.

Or at least that was what I had always been told. But what if there's more to the wilderness? A secret the Council doesn't want us to find out?

Fern tips her head, considering. "If there are, I've never heard of them before."

I chew my lip. "The woman said I was one of them… whoever they are."

Clio watches me through hooded eyes. "I'd take her words with a grain of salt. She was obviously deranged."

Fern's eyes turn glossy as if she's looking into a memory. "Whatever happened today, I believe we're on the verge of something huge. The winds are shifting. An Arcane Ceremony hasn't been interrupted in centuries. If I know the Council, they won't react well when today's shock wears off. I don't know what the Council will decide about you, Lilith, but what I can say is that all of you need to watch your backs. Dark days are coming, and the Council will come after anyone they deem a threat. Even one of their own."

Chapter Six

Curiosity Killed the Cat

LYING IN BED that night, I can't fall asleep. Fern's words play over and over in my head. For all my worries about my telekinesis and the possibility of switching Covens, I hadn't considered that the Council might see me as a threat. I think of Willow, but I don't recognize the name. None of my books mention her. It's as if she never existed.

Someone knocks on my window, and I sit up, expecting to see Clio again. I catch a glimpse of green instead. It's *Fern*. I've known Fern my entire life, and she's never sought me out. As far as I know, she's never left her oasis either.

I throw myself out of bed, hurry to the window, and pull it open. "What's wrong?" I ask, shivering as the breeze from the chilly night drifts across my face.

"The witch who interrupted the ceremony is named Iris White," she says, and she lands on the windowsill beside me. "They're holding her at the Ceremony Grounds for her trial tomorrow."

"Has she… said anything about me?" The question slips out before I fully decide whether I want to ask it.

Fern licks her teeth. "No. I'm sorry."

I frown. Part of me wishes she'd gathered more information before dangling the little bit of knowledge she does have in front of my face.

She wouldn't be here if it wasn't important, I remind myself.

"Want to talk to her?"

That catches my attention. "Of course, but how?"

"I can get you to her," she offers. "But you're gonna have to be quick."

"I'll try," I promise and shut the window.

I take a breath, hobble to the door, and peer into the hallway. I don't hear any movement in the kitchen, so I assume my parents have retired to their room for the night. I rush out of the house as quickly as I can, but my awkward gait makes my footsteps louder than I want. Fern waits in the shadows at the edge of the yard. She leads me down the path I walked that morning with Clio and Helena. It's odd to think how drastically the tone of the day has changed. I'm on edge again, but this time, it's not from excited jitters.

The trip across Ignis is quiet. Fern's eyes dart in every direction, and her wings flutter nervously as though she fears something will attack her when she's so far from her home, her safety. Her caution lights a fire under my anxiety, and I start to think about the consequences of getting caught out here.

The sandy soil beneath my feet softens into grass as we cross the edge of the Ceremony Grounds. I stay in the shadows by a tiny copse of trees and scan the hill. There's a guard in the distance, standing on top of the altar. I look for Fern, but she's gone.

"Fern?" I ask in a hushed whisper and look left to right.

A glint of light draws my attention back to the guard. Fern. She approaches them, and I realize it's Tarj. Most likely, he volunteered for this duty because of a new, personal vendetta against Iris for the burn she'd tried to inflict. Tarj doesn't notice Fern fluttering around his head. I'm confused until I remember she can become invisible to those who she doesn't wish to see her.

Fern flies a full circle around Tarj before tossing a handful of white powder in his face. He blinks and stares straight at her, but he seems dazed and unresponsive as if he's sleepwalking. Fern shoots me a thumbs up and motions for me to approach.

"What was that?" I ask, glancing between her and Tarj.

"Fairy dust. He'll be okay, but we've got to move quick. It doesn't last long, and we don't want to be here when it wears off."

I let Fern lead the way. Close to the first line of trees is the shadow of a cage. The woman from the ceremony is curled up on the bottom like an animal, and I resist the urge to poke her with a stick. When Fern told me she was here, I wondered why she wasn't in Headquarters with all the Council members able to keep an eye on her. Now I realize that this is another type of punishment. The cage looks uncomfortable, and it's a chilly night. They've given her no blankets or anything for warmth.

"Hey!" I whisper, trying not to feel bad for her. I have no idea if she's friend or foe.

She groans but doesn't wake up.

"Iris!" I hiss, a little bit louder.

Her eyes fly open, and she locks her gaze on mine. She seems confused at first, but she buries it under an amused smirk. "Ah, it's you. The cripple."

I make a face at the insult but push it away as I remind myself she *isn't* my friend. She's a woman who might have tried to kill me today. If I want answers, I'll have to toughen up a bit. "Yes, it's me. You know something about me, don't you?"

"I know many things about you," she says. She narrows her eyes to slits as though she's losing interest in the conversation.

"Why? Who are you?" I ask and clench my hands into fists. Is she toying with me?

"Wouldn't you rather know who *you* are?" she asks and slumps down against the bars, trying against the odds to get comfortable. "I'm sure you've heard plenty about me from your Coven."

Fellow Ignis witches had looked at her the way I had—as a stranger and a threat. "Why would they talk about you?"

"I'm from Ignis, though I suppose the Council keeps that information under wraps after they exiled me," she says and shrugs as if it's the most common information in the world.

I want to laugh, to shrug the comment off as another crazy outburst, but something tells me she isn't joking. "They don't exile witches! That's absurd."

"If you think what I have to say is crazy, then why did you come to see me?" she asks. A wicked smile crosses her face because she knows she has me hook, line, and sinker.

"I came here for answers, not games," I say. "I want to know why you did what you did at the ceremony. Why did you attack me?"

"Oh, my," she says, weathered face drawing tight. "You seem confused. I wasn't attacking *you*. I was after that blasted Council member beside you. And I would've had him except—" she pauses, tilts her head, and stares off into the darkness behind me "—you saved him."

"What do you have against Tarj?" I ask. I wrap my fingers around the bars of her cage, barely resisting the urge to shake it.

Iris leers at me as though the answer is obvious. "We all have many issues with the Council."

"*We?* Now who's the confused one? You're alone."

"Today, maybe, but there are others living in the shadows, ready to claw their way out of the darkness."

"The Council protects us." I point at Tarj. "He's going to stand watch all night to make sure you don't get out and attempt to hurt anyone else."

"If you truly believe that, you have no idea who your real enemies are." She stands and approaches the bars with unbalanced steps. She gets close enough for me to smell her sour breath. "There's a war coming, girlie. Do you know which side you're on?"

"You tried to hurt me today. Not Tarj, not any of them, *you*," I say because I don't want her to know how badly her words are rattling me. "You are the only menace these Covens have seen in a long time."

"You're in denial," Iris says. Her head bobs. "I can't expect anything else from someone who's been brainwashed their entire life. Don't worry. One of these days, your eyes will be opened to the truth of the world. Maybe then, you'll understand why I did what I did."

Beside me, Fern tugs desperately on the edge of my shirt. "We have to go; the spell is wearing off," she announces, but I ignore her.

"The Council keeps the Covens from killing one another," I tell Iris, matter-of-fact. It's the way the Land of Five runs. Each Coven is separated and provides its own asset to the others. Without the Council, there would be fights over land, fights over resources. They keep the Covens in check, balanced.

"They are the ones threatening us harm under the guise of our best interests." She bares her teeth and curls her lip into an expression somewhere between a snarl and a smile.

"Unbelievable," I mutter and begin to walk away.

"You're one of us!" she calls after me, which causes me to freeze. "Deny it all you want, but you wonder about your leg. I know you do. You're too smart to believe their lies."

All traces of anger vanish. "You know about my accident?"

Iris smiles again, but it's not the warped wicked smile she'd worn when I first approached. It looks *haunted*. "Sweetie, it was no accident."

"Time to go," Fern commands.

"I agree. It's time to go," a deeper voice says behind me.

I close my eyes. Busted.

Slowly, I turn to face Tarj, and I'm at a loss for words. I don't know how to explain why I'm here.

"Let's go, Lilith. You know better than to associate with her," he says and leads me away from the cage.

"You want the truth? Ask your parents who you really are!" Iris screams behind me. She punctuates her sentence with a wild cackle.

I watch the shadows swallow her with each step farther we travel. I consider fighting my way back to her, but Tarj tightens his grip and marches me onward.

"What are you doing here?" he grunts and shoots me a dark glare. "And how did you get past me?"

I don't plan to tell him about Fern so I say, "I want

answers about what happened today."

Tarj shakes his head and looks up at the moon as if he can't believe I've said those words. "And you think that crazy old bag of bones is gonna give 'em to you? In case you haven't noticed, she's in a *cage*."

I want to press the matter further, but I remember what Fern told me about the Council and their frank dislike for people like me and decide I might benefit from being quiet. I look for Fern, but I don't see her. That's probably for the best. While fairies aren't under the thumb of the Council, I don't want to draw any negative attention to her.

"You don't have to walk me home. I can make it myself," I tell him when the silence starts to become awkward.

Tarj side-eyes me. "This situation is bigger than you being out after curfew. You're associating with a known criminal."

My heart drops to my stomach. I don't like the sound of that. "You can't tell my parents I was out here," I say in a small voice. Things are already tense enough without them learning I went behind their back because I don't trust them anymore.

"I'm sorry to be the bad guy, but they have to know. Messing with these witches is bad. They have no sense of right or wrong. Their use of black magic is everything that's wrong with our world." His tone is as firm as his expression.

Iris almost said the same about you, I think but I manage to bite back the comment.

We're silent for the rest of the walk, and when Tarj and I arrive at my house, Mother and Father aren't happy to hear about my trespassing at the Grove. Father scowls at me while Tarj explains what I've been up to. They offer him pleasant goodbyes, but as soon as the door closes behind him, I know I'm in for it.

"What did you think you were doing tonight, young lady?" Mother asks, placing her hands on her hips.

"I wanted answers," I say, head held high.

"From a psychotic witch?" Father spits.

"I wasn't going to get them from *you*," I start, rising from the hard kitchen chair I'd been seated in for the last twenty minutes. "At the ceremony, Iris said I'm one of them," I explain, then I trail off, waiting for an interjection. Neither of my parents speak, so I continue. "She said you know the truth about my accident. That you're lying to me because you don't want me to know who I really am."

"She's not right in the head," Father shoots me down quickly.

As expected.

"*Is* she though?" I ask, remembering the wild look in her eyes. It was the same expression as someone who's seen too much, who *knows* too much, and has cracked under the pressure. "You saw what I did at the ceremony. *All* the goblets lit up. Why? Why can I do that when nobody else can? And why can't I remember what happened to my leg? If I did this, why can't I remember?"

Hesitantly, Mother says, "I saw the lights."

"What does it mean?" I whisper. I try to catch her gaze. "I have pyro powers that I can't use, but I'm manifesting telekinesis? Where are the other powers? *What* are the other powers?"

Mother bites her lip and stays silent until Father steps in, pulling her back a step. "That's enough, young lady. Can't you see you're upsetting your Mother?"

I don't see hurt when I look at my mother. I see *fear*. I'm close to something.

"Go to your room," Father adds.

I stare at him, unsurprised. "What really happened to my leg?" I try again, keeping my eyes on my mother. She's the easier parent to break, and I'm determined.

She looks down at the floor. Any progress I made is gone.

"One way or another, I'm gonna find out the truth," I say, moving my gaze from the part of my mother's hair to my father's smoldering eyes.

My leg hurts from the walk with Tarj, but I'm determined not to show any weakness. I tap my telekinetic powers to help me walk out the front door. Pain or no pain, I refuse to stay under the same roof as them right now. Eyes blurry with tears, I sniffle and walk until my parents' home disappears in the distance. I don't have a destination in mind, and I absentmindedly choose the trail that leads to Helena's. Halfway there, Fern appears at my side, eyes wide with emotion.

"Lilith! I am so sorry I vanished on you. You didn't get into too much trouble, did you?"

I shake my head. "A bit, but it's okay. Nothing I can't handle. All things considered, I'm glad you took me to see Iris. For so long, I've thought my parents were keeping something from me, and now, I have proof."

"You believe Iris?"

"I believe her and my parents equally, which is to say not at all," I reply flatly. "All I know for sure is that someone is lying."

"So, where are you going?" she asks, and I can hear the

concern in her voice. As if she thinks I've lost my mind and might wander off into the wilderness and get hurt.

"To Helena's," I say. "Hopefully, she'll let me stay until things blow over." It's been a rough day for her too, and I'm hoping she'll want the company.

"I'm sorry, Lilith," Fern says, wrinkling her brow. She peers up at me uncertainly. "We-we're okay though?"

"Always."

She stays with me for the rest of the walk, hovering nearby and occasionally sending me concerned looks. When Helena's house appears, she says, "Whatever you do next, Lilith, be careful," and she dips her head in farewell before fluttering away into the night.

When I knock on Helena's door, she answers. Inwardly, I'm relieved it wasn't her parents. I don't have it in me to explain why I'm on their doorstep and not at home this late at night. "Li, what's the matter?"

"I-I got in a fight with my parents," I say, hating how close I sound to breaking down.

"About your powers?"

I nod. "Can I crash here tonight?"

Helena waves me inside. "I don't see why not."

I give her a grateful smile as I pass her. In her room, I stare longingly at her bed. I'm far more exhausted than I want to admit. During my rage-fueled walk, the anger and the pain radiating through my leg had been easy to ignore. Now that it's seeped away, there's nothing left but the hollow ache of my day.

"Do you mind if I sit?"

"Not at all."

I gratefully plop down on her bed, and Helena sits in the chair in front of her vanity desk. Lexi, Helena's silver-and-black striped cat, jumps into my lap as I rub my sore leg.

"Tell me what happened," she says.

"I went to see Iris," I say and scratch Lexi between the ears. The cat purrs and looks at me through eyes slitted in satisfaction.

Helena's brow crinkles. "Who's that?"

"The woman who interrupted the ceremony," I reply, and I glance up at her.

Helena's eyes nearly bulge out of their sockets. "Are you insane? Why would you do that? You could've gotten hurt!"

"It's okay. I wasn't alone. Fern was with me," I assure her.

Helena doesn't look any less upset for the additional information. "What could you have possibly gained from that experience?"

"More than I thought I would," I say, staring at the side of Lexi's face. "Iris is the only witch who's ever admitted my parents are lying to me, and I believe her." My lower lip begins to quiver with barely repressed emotion.

"Ah," she says as understanding dawns on her. "That's how the fight began?"

"Well, yeah. After Tarj brought me home, I didn't really have a choice, but to lay it all out on the table. That led to me telling them about what Iris said. So, I asked about my accident, and they pretended I was out of line for wanting to know. So I left."

"What are you going to do?" Helena asks. Lexi jumps from my lap to hers.

"I'm not sure yet, but I think some time away from my parents will do me some good."

"Maybe for a few days," Helena says. "But you can't avoid them forever. Especially if you choose to stay in Ignis. Though I don't blame you if you leave. You can go anywhere you want."

"I know." I haven't given much thought about which Coven I'll choose, but this is definitely a point for Mentis. "I'll see them again, but first, I'm going to give them a chance to cool down and come to terms with all that's happened. In the meantime, I plan to find out exactly what it is that Iris knows about me."

Chapter Seven
Burn the Witch

I WAKE UP to Helena desperately pulling on my arm. "Li! Wake up! Wake up, Li!"

Her voice is slow and wavering as I regain consciousness as if my head is underwater. I sit up, mind bleary with sleep, and try to focus on her. "Wha's wrong?"

"They're burning her. They're burning Iris!"

The words clear my grogginess. "What?"

"My parents were just told they're executing her in the Grove this morning."

I sit bolt upright. "They can't do that! What about her trial?"

"They don't think she deserves one," Helena says. "There were too many witnesses to her attacking Council members to bother with the formality."

"They're doing this because of me," I say, and I'm cold. I don't know why I'm confident that's the reason, but I am. I struggle to stand and murmur, "Because I tried to visit her, t-to get answers."

"What are you talking about, Li? She tried to *hurt* you!" Helena exclaims, watching me with a mix of panic and confusion. "She tried to hurt a lot of witches, don't you remember? She dug her own grave."

I move too quickly, and my foot catches in Helena's

blanket. I lose my footing and slam to the ground. A rough spot in Helena's wooden floor tears a fresh cut in my arm. I think of the ugly wound Ambrossi had stitched up as I rise to my knees.

"Oh, my Goddess, Li. Are you okay?" Helena gasps. She pitches toward me to try to help me to my feet.

"I'm fine," I bark and struggle to stand again.

I get most of the way up before my knees buckle, and I stumble and slam back down on the floor. Helena tries to intervene, and I don't stop her. I let her help me regain my balance. She doesn't let go as I pull my cloak tighter around me and wiggle in her grasp to break free.

"Lilith! Wait!" She tightens her hold. "Whatever you're thinking of doing, don't do it!"

"I have to," I say and pull my arms free.

As Helena stares at the smeared blood on her hand, I rush out of her room. She follows a step behind as we race to the front door. We pass Helena's parents, who are eating breakfast at the kitchen table, but I don't call a greeting. I'm too afraid of breaking my focus.

I'll apologize later, I tell myself.

A few feet from Helena's house, I start to pant and lose focus. Helena digs her fingers into my shoulder to hold me in place.

"Li, you need to slow down. You're going to hurt yourself," she urges. Her breath is a strained huff.

She's right, but I'm not worried about my health. I'm not worried about anything but Iris. If I'm unable to help her, I don't know how I'll get the answers I seek. Or if I can. I can't waste a moment, and yet, my body seems determined to betray me. "No,

I-I have to talk to Iris before it's too late."

"It might *already* be too late," Helena warns me in a low tone.

I whip around to face her. "What if it's *not?*" I demand, waving my hands like a madman. I'm getting tired of everyone trying to hold me back. Of the ostriches wanting to keep their heads firmly planted in the sand. "What if she's the only one who's willing to tell me the truth?"

"You're gonna hurt your feelings doing this."

"So what?" I snap, and I smack her hands away when she tries to grab me again. "If Fern is right about what all this means, my life is in danger anyway, and Iris might know why."

A flash of shock passes through her eyes before she buries it beneath an emotionless mask. I don't think about her feelings nor our friendship. She's an obstacle. Someone in my way. She must sense it because she doesn't argue when I begin to limp forward.

My leg twists awkwardly, and I cry out. I've put a lot of strain on it lately, and it's getting harder to ignore. I try to force away the pain as I think about the distance between me and my goal. If my leg gives out now, I'll never make it. Adrenaline might keep me going for a few more minutes, but not for long. Horrid, ragged breaths tear through my chest and burn my throat, but I'm determined to make it to the wyrm outpost.

"Helena! Lilith!" Clio calls from a distance. "Did you hear the news?"

Helena says nothing, and I have the feeling she's gesturing to him to come stop me. Clio calls to me, then both are at my side.

"Why are you doing this?" Clio asks. A glint in his eyes

tells me he's picking the best moment to grab me, most likely on Helena's instruction.

"Answers. You wanted them as much as I do," I remind him. I clench my teeth as my gait grows more unbalanced.

I take another step, and my leg decides I've gone too far. It buckles under me, and I'm on the ground again. The cut from Helena's throbs angrily when dirt slips into it, but my wounded pride hurts more. Helena drops to her knees beside me and uses her cloak to clean the worst part of the wound. My hair hides my face from them as I sit in my shame.

"Lilith, stop this," Clio pleads. He crouches on the other side of me.

"But we're so close," I whisper. I dig my fingertips into the ground and gaze up at him. Tears blur my vision. "What if she's the only one who has answers?"

Clio takes in a deep breath, and his jaw clenches. I think he's preparing himself to argue with me when his eyes dart between me and the path ahead. "There's still time. Hang on," he mutters and tucks his arms underneath me, lifting me with ease.

I exchange a surprised look with Helena before he repositions me and cradles me to his chest. He hurries in the direction of the Grove, and I hold onto him tightly on the off chance he decides to change his mind and take me home instead.

"Clio, you can't seriously enable this!" Helena yowls from behind him. Her voice is overwrought with disbelief as she jogs by his side.

Clio's focus stays on the path ahead as he says, "She's right, Helena. She deserves to know the truth."

"Iris is a whack job who's being *executed!* You don't want

to give the Council the wrong impression about where your loyalties lie. Do you?" She directs that question to me.

"After last night, it might already be too late," I remind her.

Helena stops and watches as Clio continues onward. Darkness spreads across her face, and I hate the bitter taste the exchange leaves in my mouth. But like the situation with Helena's parents, it's a problem I'll tackle later in the day.

On the edge of the Ceremony Grounds, the crowds are larger than they'd been during the Arcane Ceremony. It seems as if every witch has gathered, Equipped and UnEquipped alike. Chants and angry shouts come from all directions.

"I think all the Covens are here," Clio remarks and lets me out of his arms.

"All the more reason for you not to do this," Helena says. She's out of breath when she catches up to us.

I search the grounds for a sign of Iris. On the altar where the goblets were yesterday is a large chunk of wood surrounded by handfuls of sawdust. Iris stands in the middle, with her hands and feet tied to a stake.

I rush forward, unsure whether Helena and Clio are following me. The crowd of witches is thick, and I use my telekinesis to part them enough to squeeze through.

"Iris White," Tarj's voice bellows from the rise.

My heart sinks. I'm running out of time. Clio and Helena call to me from somewhere in the crowd, but I can't afford to waste a second waiting for them to catch up.

"You're being charged with the crime of treason against your superior Coven. How do you plead?" Tarj asks. He stares into Iris' eyes as he speaks.

The last circle of witches proves to be the thickest and hardest to break. "Please! Let me through!" I wail. A few of them turn to look at me as if I'm insane, but I manage to squeeze through. I hobble past them and cast back a quick, "Thank you!"

"Guilty!" Iris cackles. Her lip curves into her famously wicked smile.

The thought of death doesn't bother her.

I reach the front row, and Iris' eyes lock on me. She begins to cackle louder. Members of the Council form a circle around her as if they're ready to keep me from getting too close, but I take another step forward anyway. The girl with the golden bracelets who arrested Iris the day before holds a hand out.

I peer around her at Iris. "What happened to my leg?" I scream, not caring about the attention I'm drawing to myself.

Mutters ripple through the other witches, and the Council member narrows her eyes at me. "Stay back!" she orders.

Ignoring everything around me, I keep my gaze on Iris. She looks back at me as if she's staring into the depths of my soul.

"Please! You have to tell me the truth!" I plead with her.

"By the law of the treaty, we sentence you, Iris White, to death by burning. An execution reserved for the worst of the worst," Tarj says and rolls up his parchment.

The old witch blinks in acknowledgement and juts her chin toward me. "It's up to you now."

As soon as she utters those words, Tarj uses his pyrokinesis to ignite the wood clumps beneath her. The fire spreads to her gown and burns through the fabric and into her skin. Her face twists, and her agony hurts my heart. I know first-hand the intense pain a burn can cause.

"No!" I scream. I look for someone who can stop this, for someone besides myself who can see this is wrong.

Laughter and cheers come from behind me—the confirmation that I'm truly alone in this. I try to scramble up the hill, but the girl with the golden bracelets holds me back. Iris begins to scream and thrash against her bonds, and all I can do is stare as the last of my hope dwindles. Less than two minutes later, her struggle is over. I can't tear my eyes away from what's left of her. The Council woman lets go of me, and I collapse to my knees, feeling as though I've lost part of myself.

Clio and Helena break through the crowd and kneel on opposite sides of me. They whisper soothing words, but I can't be pacified. The world spins.

Iris was my only chance to figure out the truth of who I am.

Now, she's gone.

Chapter Eight
Decisions

"LILITH, TALK TO me," Clio says, hand on my arm.

"She's gone… my last hope is gone," I whisper and stare at the pile of Iris' ashes. It's almost hard to believe that those tiny pieces of dust had belonged to a living, breathing witch.

"Let's get you home," Helena says.

I ignore her and look at Clio. "What am I supposed to do now?"

"I think you need to get some sleep. It's been a rough couple of days," Clio says, voice unusually soft with concern.

Helena chimes in her agreement.

Tears begin to bubble in my eyes. "Iris knew something about me. You can ask Fern," I say with another glance at the remaining splinters of the stake that stubbornly remain standing. The girl with the golden bracelets blocks my view when she circles the mess, cleaning up the remains.

The softness of Clio's face hardens. "Wait. Fern is connected to this mess?"

"Not connected, just responsible," Helena replies.

"She's not. She just wanted to help me," I say and wipe under my eyes. I tell Clio about the incident last night with Fern and Tarj. His eye twitches as I finish the story, but before he can interrupt me, I say, "Iris was from Ignis. She'd been exiled, but I've never heard of her before the Arcane Ceremony, like I'd never heard of Willow until Fern told me about her." My eyes dart between my friends, and I study both their reactions before I lean toward them and whisper, "The Council is hiding something."

"*Everyone* has secrets," Clio says. "That's hardly a surprise. What I want to know is why they exiled Iris to begin with."

"Um, I think it's pretty clear why," Helena says, motioning to the pile of ashes. "She was crazy."

"I don't know the reason, and now, I never will," I say and tear a few grass blades free to have an excuse not to look at either of my friends.

"If she knew something about the Council that she wasn't supposed to, it explains why they were so quick to put her down, I suppose," Clio says thoughtfully. "But how can you be so sure Fern isn't holding information from you? If she knew this much, who's to say she doesn't know more?"

I'm *not* sure. How can I be after these past few days? "It seems like everyone's hiding something from me."

Helena flares her nostrils, offended.

"Besides you guys." I sigh and struggle to stand.

Clio wraps his arm around my waist to help me balance.

"Let it go," Helena says. "Iris is dead. And what happened is over and done with. Besides, if Fern knows something that could potentially hurt Li, she'd tell her."

"Maybe." Clio considers. "But maybe she wouldn't say a word if she has a stake in the outcome."

My head spins. I can't trust anyone. "So, what are you saying? That she's really an enemy and what... using me for information?"

Hearing the creeping weariness in my voice, Clio holds his palms out. "Calm down. I'm just saying there has to be some reason she's taken so much interest in you."

"She's my *friend*, that's why," I say, and I rise on my tiptoes in what I hope is an intimidating stance. "She doesn't need any reason other than that."

Clio sucks air in through his teeth, clearly not convinced. "Fine."

"You still don't trust her?"

"Not a bit. I think she ties into this somehow."

I chew on the inside of my cheek.

"Lilith, is it?" a voice calls behind me.

Tarj.

I watch him walk the rest of the way down the hill. His windswept, silver hair blows in the breeze the same way his baggy pants do. I'd forgotten he was on the rise, and I realize too late he must've eavesdropped on the entire conversation.

"You clearly know," I reply and narrow my eyes against the sun.

"Can I just ask what your fascination is with Iris?" he prompts. "You've caused quite a scene today."

"Does it matter? She's dead."

Tarj narrows his eyes sympathetically. "True. But we believe Iris is part of something bigger. I don't know exactly why she targeted you, but based on your results from the Arcane Ceremony, you're special."

"Are you going to punish me for my results too?" I ask. "Drag me back to my parents and put me in time out?"

Tarj shakes his head. "Nothing like that. I think this is more serious than you realize."

Fern's warning echoes in the back of my mind. Clio's arm brushes against mine as he steps protectively closer, sensing something looming in his tone as well.

"And how is that?" Clio asks.

"As you know, it's rare for a child of UnEquipped parents to become Equipped, even more so for them to have multiple powers. It's not something that goes unnoticed."

I swallow roughly, unable to tell if his words are a threat.

He continues. "You have a major decision ahead of you."

"Which is?" I ask, wondering if over the past twelve hours they've considered exiling me too.

"Which power is your dominant?" he asks.

"Telekinesis," I reply, unwilling to inform him that I've had no luck with any of the others.

"We, at the Council, recommend you go live in Mentis for a while."

"Shouldn't she have a choice? She lit *all* the goblets," Clio reminds him.

"Why can't she stay here?" Helena adds and grabs my hand.

It's clear she's worried about losing me. The thought of being separated from Helena makes me sad, but the sadness is mixed with the joyous thought of escaping my parents. Tarj stares at me to gauge my reaction, but my expression is blank.

"Usually, we would consider letting the witch choose," Tarj says, "but this is a tricky situation. We have reason to believe the group Iris belonged to is aware of your location in Ignis. If you stay, you will most likely be targeted again."

Clio studies me as I whisper, "You think their attack was against *me?*"

"We can't rule it out as a possibility. If you move to Mentis, we can protect you. You will have the chance to hone your developing powers without drawing attention to yourself. We will set up a place for you to stay and arrange for someone to take care of your Coven duties in Ignis."

I glance down before looking back up at him. "What happens if I decide to stay in Ignis? Stay in my home and pretend these last few days haven't happened?"

"It'll be hard to guarantee your safety."

"You'll do nothing," I say flatly.

Tarj arches an eyebrow. "Not nothing. Just not as much as we can do if you choose to go to Mentis."

Is this about my safety or do you not want them to find me for another reason? I wonder.

"Think carefully about this, Li," Clio warns.

"You don't have to decide now," Tarj says and looks purposefully at my friends as if he wishes they weren't there for this conversation. "I'll let you talk to your parents and get your affairs in order, but tomorrow, I need an answer so we can proceed with next steps."

I press my lips together in a straight line. The idea of a short deadline for such an important decision leaves me sick, but I only have myself to blame. I knew this was coming, but I'd chosen to keep putting it off. "That's fair."

"Whatever you decide will be permanent for the foreseeable future," he warns. He begins walking up the hill. "I'll see you tomorrow."

Clio waits until Tarj is out of sight before he says, "Well, that wasn't a friendly conversation. *Get your affairs in order?* That sounds like a threat."

Helena ignores Clio and turns to me. "You're going to stay, right? You can't up and leave. What about your parents? What about *Fern?*"

"You can't *stay*," Clio interjects. He gives Helena the side-eye as if he can't believe she'd say those words. "You should go to Mentis and hone your powers to the best of your ability."

"Don't encourage her to leave," Helena snaps, face reddening with barely suppressed anger.

"Why do you want her to stay in a place that has nothing left to offer her? A place that's *dangerous* to boot. Seems a little selfish to me! Just because you don't have powers, you don't want anyone else to either, is that it?"

Helena tilts her head back and laughs sarcastically. "At least I'm not telling her to leave because she's complicated. At least I'm trying to help her through this. We've all got problems, Clio, but that doesn't mean we turn our backs on our friends!"

Clio snarls before his expression morphs into a wicked smirk. "You're so lucky you're UnEquipped. If you were in my army, I'd have such fun whipping all of this out of you."

"Stop it, guys," I order and pinch the bridge of my nose. "This petty bickering isn't helping!"

Helena looks at me apologetically, but Clio clenches his jaw, and his irritation seems to increase.

"You're both making great points, but I don't know what I'm going to do yet, okay? I think I should talk to Fern. Get her opinion."

"But she started this!" Clio protests.

Helena glares at him.

I press my palm to my forehead, prepared for them to start bickering again. Fighting like this isn't normal, and that's when I realize the decision before me affects everyone.

"For real, guys, that's enough. Fern didn't *start* anything. She was only trying to help. She knows more about what's going on than any of us. I think it's in my best interest to see if she has any other information to pass my way. *Especially* if I do go to Mentis because I won't be able to visit her anymore."

Clio dips his head in understanding, though I can tell by the look in his eyes that it's a hard thing for him to do. Helena doesn't move. She stares at me with huge, expressionless green eyes. A sudden wave of sadness washes over me as I remember that my biggest problem two days ago was the manifestation of my powers. Now, I have to face the possibility of never seeing my friends and my home again.

"Do you want me to come with you?" Clio asks.

If my time in Ignis really is limited, I want to spend as much time with my friends as I can. If I go to Mentis, we won't get to hang out like this anymore. It's against the Council's rules for people of different Covens to co-exist. Healers, like Ambrossi, are the only ones allowed to break the treaty and move between Covens without consequences.

In the end, I'm better facing this problem alone. Splitting my focus could potentially do more harm than good. Especially if I've got a target on me that could be extended to them as well.

"I need to do this alone," I say at last.

"So, that's it?" Clio snaps. "Goodbye, just like that?"

"It's not forever," I say quickly. "I'll see you guys again before I go anywhere. I-I need some time alone to think."

Helena pulls me into a hug, and I hug her back. A bitter smirk touches Clio's lips, and he tries to hide it by scratching his nose. Helena pulls back and stares at me. There's so much emotion in her eyes that she doesn't need to say anything for me to guess what she's thinking.

"Go, but when you come back, I hope it's with the right decision," Clio says.

What if I don't know what that is? I think, but I begin walking the path to Fern's oasis alone.

Chapter Nine
Home Sweet Home

AS I WALK, puffs of dirt churn into the midday air. The sun beating down on my black hair causes the first trickle of sweat to run down my face. I drag the dead weight of my leg as I force myself onward, focused on the task at hand. I'm confident that if anyone can help me make this decision, Fern can.

In the distance lies her oasis, and I huff. The pain in my leg has grown so intense that I consider dragging myself the rest of the way. As if Fern hears my desperation, she appears. I let out a short laugh of relief, grateful for the chance to rest, and sit down among the bits of grass surrounding the water.

"What happened?" she asks, almost immediately.

"They burned Iris before I could talk to her," I say. The corners of my mouth tremble. "She didn't get a trial. She didn't get *anything*."

"I'm so sorry," Fern says and lights down beside me. "In instances like these, the rules blur and unfortunately, today will pass without consequence. Without question."

I let out a dark chuckle. "*I* question it, but I guess that doesn't matter in the grand scheme of things. Even Clio and Helena think I'm crazy for trying to pursue this."

"They haven't been through what you have. I'm sure if Iris had information *they* were after they would've reacted in much the same way."

"Yeah, maybe." I rest my chin on my knees, not comforted.

"Don't be too mad at them. These are hard times for them as well," Fern points out. "I'm sure that once things have settled, they'll come around to whatever you decide. They're your best friends for a reason."

I glance at her out of the corner of my eye, and I remember all of Clio's doubts. Despite my genuine affection for Fern, I can't help wondering if he's right. Does Fern know more about Iris than she's willing to tell? I want to believe she has the best intentions for me, but as Helena pointed out, everyone has their demons.

What are Fern's? Why was she hellbent on getting me to face Iris?

I clench my hands into fists. If only I could find a witch who can see into the future. That would make this entire debate much easier. "True, but I can't help wishing they wouldn't be so hard on me. I have to decide which Coven to live in by tomorrow, and I don't know what to do. They say it'll be too hard to protect me if I stay in Ignis. I guess, with my telekinesis, they figure Mentis is the safest place because I won't stand out."

Fern presses her lips into a tight line.

"I guess it doesn't matter anyway because I might stay in Ignis. If more of these witches are going to come after me, I kind of *want* them to."

Fern eyes me warily but doesn't protest. "If I may say so, it sounds as though you've already made up your mind."

I smile bitterly at the sky. "Maybe, but it'd be nice to hear someone say I'm not crazy."

"Who thinks that?"

"Clio for sure." I drag my finger through the dirt to avoid meeting her gaze. "And maybe Helena too. She begged me to stay, but I don't think she fully understands the gravity of the situation if I do."

"It seems to me that Clio has issues with *all* your decisions," Fern says. "Sometimes, it's good to hear both sides of a choice before you make up your mind."

That's the beauty of having two good friends with polar opposite opinions on everything. "Clio would never accept my staying."

"Then I guess it's good it's not his decision then," Fern says pointedly. "I understand not wanting to leave your friends and family, but what's your real motivation for staying? Those witches might come in a group next time and it could be bad for your covenmates if that happens. Is that a price you're willing to pay for the *possibility* of learning what Iris knew?"

"They don't have to attack anyone. I'll stand out in the open if it means getting to the bottom of things."

"That still doesn't guarantee anyone's safety."

"Look, I don't know whether Iris was crazy or not, but something in me won't let this go."

Fern flaps her wings. "Then follow that instinct. It's there for a reason."

"So, you don't think it's foolish to stay?"

Fern flaps her wings once, twice, and a third time as she stares across the tiny pool of water. "It doesn't matter what I think. This decision is yours to make."

"You're right." I straighten my back and follow her gaze. "I don't know what I'd do without you, Fern."

"Glad I could help," she says. "But you still have one other problem."

My mind draws a blank.

"Your parents," she continues. "What are you going to do about them? If you're going to stay, you can't avoid them forever."

It's a good question. A problem I don't know how to solve. "You have a point." I struggle to stand and grimace at a fresh streak of pain. I see the frown on Fern's face. "What?"

"You're hurting," she says. "Worse than usual."

As much as I hate to admit it, I can't hide my pain from Fern. "Yeah, it's been a hard couple of days. I haven't had much time to rest."

"I have something that can help with that. Wait here."

She flits away, and I plop back into the dirt. Clio's suspicions play through my mind and fill me with the tiniest surge of rage. No one would be as dedicated as Fern if they didn't truly care.

When Fern returns, she's holding a small, clear pouch with a purple sphere inside. I take it from her and hold it up to get a better look. "What is this?"

"I call it a chew. It's a mixture of herbs and magic used to combat pain from magical damage. Chew on it for a while, and it should help with the walk home. Don't swallow it though, or it'll make you sick."

"Ambrossi gave you this?"

She nods. "With the development of your new powers, he worried you'd have another accident and wouldn't be so keen to report it."

"His anal retentiveness has saved the day once again. Remind me to thank him the next time I see him."

"Will do. Now, get home and sort things out while you can."

I mutter a quick thank you before she disappears through her hole in the tree. I hold the chew up in front of my face. It's ugly, and the pungent smell makes my eyes water, but I've always trusted Ambrossi's judgement. I pop the pod into my mouth and push it around in preparation for the terrible taste I'm sure is coming. To my surprise, there is none.

The radiating pain in my leg changes to a dull ache, and I find it a lot easier to stand. I continue to chew on the thing as I approach my parents' house. I stop before the door. Ambrossi's amulet isn't in my pocket when I reach for it, and I wilt a little when I realize I left it in my room. A shadow passes by the window.

Where is she? Where is she? Where is she? a voice floats through my mind.

I freeze, assuming someone is behind me, but I'm alone. The voice had been loud, as if the words were spoken directly into my ear. I chalk it up to stress and enter the house. Mother stands in the kitchen, twining her fingers as she paces. When she sees me, her face melts with relief, and she rushes across the kitchen to pull me into her arms. I give her a weak hug back and pull away as my father approaches from the other room.

"Lilith, where have you been?" my mother asks. She wipes a lock of hair out of my eyes.

"Helena's."

"Tarj stopped by today. He told us what happened at the trial," Father says in a tone that tells me he's not happy.

Home less than a minute, and an argument is brewing.

"That wasn't a trial," I say pointedly. *Trial* gives the impression of fairness, and what happened to Iris wasn't.

"What were you doing today?" my mother chimes in, any trace of warmth gone from her voice.

"I had to talk to her again."

"Why?"

I stare at my mother, and she stares back. I should love her unconditionally, but I don't feel a thing. It's like there's a barrier keeping us divided. An invisible wall I'd not noticed until this exact moment. "We've already had this talk."

"You're still on that, are you?" I could be hurt that my father has decided to hold onto this level of coldness, but I expect it from him. He thinks the anger will intimidate me, and I'll back off.

"Things don't make sense anymore," I say.

"You've always had a penchant for the dramatic, but you're not a little kid anymore, Lilith. This needs to stop." My father is trying to stay calm, but the anger is creeping into his voice.

I blink my wet eyes. "Tell me the truth, Dad. That's all I want. I can't use pyrokinetic powers. I've tried. I've tried *hard*. That means I didn't burn myself. And if I didn't do it, who did? Who did this to me?

My parents look at each other as if they're communicating through gaze alone. I wish I could read minds.

Mother breaks their strange connection and looks right at

me. "You're right. You didn't start the fire."

My entire body tenses up, ready. This is the moment I've been waiting for. Heart pounding, I ask, "Then who did?"

"We should be discussing the decision you have before you!" Father interjects, angry gaze scorching over my mother before returning to me. "Not rehashing the past."

"How can I think about my future if I don't know my past?" I counter. I look down at my injured leg. My entire life I've lived with the belief that I did this to myself. If someone else was responsible, that changes everything.

"I-I-" My mother looks as if she's going to throw up.

Father sets a hand on her arm and stops her. His face is blank, but rage shines in his eyes. I have the feeling, if he were Equipped, he would've set the kitchen on fire.

"We have taken care of you for eighteen years," Father says. "Put a roof over your head and clothes on your back. That's all that matters."

The air leaves my lungs like I've been punched in the chest. I stumble backward a step and utter, "I can't trust my parents." The dark thought starts to blossom that *they* did this to me, but why?

"You can always trust us," Mom says in a broken whisper.

"Then tell me the truth," I try one more time. My voice is a quivering whisper. "Or I can't stay here."

"You're not going to stay anyway," Father says in a much more commanding tone of voice. "You'll put me and your mother in danger. Your entire Coven. You are going to follow the Council's advice."

I stare at him, cold inside and out. Just when I think my

opinion of him can't go any lower, he opens his mouth and says something else. "Don't worry. I don't want to stay here anyway. I'm going to leave this house, but it's not because you told me to. It's because I want to go. I hope your cowardice keeps you happy. Maybe one day, I'll be able to face you again. For now? Consider this goodbye."

I hobble to my room with the knowledge that I won't be back for a while. Maybe ever. If my parents are so determined to hold their secrets that my father is willing to kick me out over it, then I don't have any reason to return.

Everyone has to leave their home eventually, I tell myself as I cross my room to the bookshelf.

My parents are on my heels as I rifle through my belongings.

"Where are you going to go?" Mother asks as she peers around my father who stands firmly in the doorway.

"I'll see if I can stay with Clio," I say though I'm not sure of anything yet. I pull Ambrossi's amulet out from under my mattress and shove it in my pocket.

"You're making a bad decision if you don't go to Mentis," Father says and shifts his weight in an attempt to catch my eyes.

"Duly noted," I reply. I run a finger along the spines of my books, seeking my Book of Spells. With a flick of my wrist, I pull it from the shelf and cradle it to my chest.

My parents stare at me wide-eyed and open-mouthed as if I've grown another head as I push past them and into the hall.

In the kitchen, I stop to turn my pointed glare on them. "The Equipped… We fight back. I think that's a concept you fail to grasp. You've always hidden from the truth, from a fight, from the *world*, so you might as well stick to it. It's what you're best at."

"We want the best for *you*," Mother tries to protest.

"I wouldn't have guessed it," I say and move through the living room to the door. "But I suppose everything happens for a reason."

"Lilith, please don't go!" Mother calls after me as I cross the threshold into the darkness of the night.

Father says nothing, standing beside Mother as she screams my name over and over, sobbing each time.

I don't look back.

Chapter Ten
Nowhere to Go

WHEN I KNOCK on Clio's door, he answers wearing only a pair of boxers and stares at me as if he doesn't recognize me. "Li, this is a surprise."

"Sorry to drop by like this," I say and lower my gaze, suddenly embarrassed of myself, of the situation I've found myself in. "Is this a bad time?"

"No, not at all. I just wasn't expecting company. And to be honest, I thought you were miffed at me," he admits, scratching the back of his neck.

"It's been such a long day, I've honestly forgotten why I was mad," I say. Inside, I'm hollow and can't feel anything other than my overwhelming exhaustion. "Can I come in?"

"Yeah." He steps aside to open the door. "Let me get decent." He disappears into his house and pulls on a robe that had been hanging on the back of his chair.

I nod absently and stumble to his couch. I place my Book of Spells beside me as I sit down. Clio's house is minimalistic, with only a couch, a chair, a bookshelf, and a fireplace, but it's homey. I've been here a handful of times, and I've always admired how comfortable it makes me feel. A small fire crackles in the fireplace, and it warms the space enough to push away the chill of early nightfall.

"So, what happened with your parents?" he asks, glancing

at me as he ties his robe.

"They kicked me out because I've decided to stay in Ignis," I say and frown at my Book of Spells.

"You're what?" he asks. He stares at me through hooded eyes.

"I'm going to stay," I say, and I hold his look, not intimidated like I could be if I were in another mood. "I'm not afraid of whoever these witches are. I *want* them to find me. It's the only way to get answers."

Exasperated, he shakes his head and plops down into his other armchair. "I was on board for the Iris thing, but don't you think you're going too far now?"

"Maybe, but I don't know what else to do," I admit. "Running away won't solve things. If you were me, you wouldn't run."

Clio doesn't look convinced. "I think some time in Mentis would do you good, but I guess I can see your point."

My mind is far away as I watch the fire destroy one of the logs.

"Well, Helena begged you to stay in Ignis. I'm sure she'll let you crash at her place if you need somewhere to go," Clio says and drums his fingers on the arm of his chair.

My heart drops to my stomach. I'd come here for sanctuary knowing that if I had gone to Helena's, her parents would likely try to convince me to go home. But what if Clio doesn't want me here?

"Yeah, except Helena and her parents don't understand why I'm ruffling the Council's feathers."

"So, you came here?"

"You're not weak, and you're not afraid. I can't think of any better company to keep." From little on, he's always been the one for adventures, even when they got him in trouble. One of our very first stunts together took us to the edge of Ignis, close enough to see the wastelands of the wilderness beyond.

"You're brave. Braver than I gave you credit for," Clio says.

"Is that a compliment?"

"It might be," he replies and takes a sip from a cup on the table beside him.

"So can I... stay?" I ask, tensing up for his answer.

"I don't see why not," he says, then the corners of his lips turn down. "If you don't mind the house being a bit messy, of course. With my training, I haven't exactly had time to play housekeeper."

"I understand. Trust me," I say. "You should've seen my room before I left." I don't mention that I trashed it on purpose.

Clio's face goes serious again. "I still can't believe your parents would do that to you."

"Me and you both." I unclasp my cloak, and it drops, revealing my corset dress beneath.

Clio relaxes in his seat, watching the fire again before he says, "I was making dinner. Do you want some? I'm guessing you haven't stopped and rested today."

As those words leave his lips, a growl erupts in my stomach. I clamp my hands over my abdomen in a pointless attempt to stifle it.

"I'll take that as a yes." He chuckles and rises to go into the kitchen.

I follow him. I've been so distressed, the thought of eating hasn't crossed my mind. In the kitchen, he pulls out a chair as he passes the table and looks at me. I take the seat, and Clio takes the lid off a giant pot, stirring the food inside.

The scent of herbs causes my mouth to water. "Whatever you're cooking smells amazing."

"It's a stew my mother taught me how to make when I was little," he says. There's a bittersweet smile on his face, the kind that always comes from him thinking about his parents. He places a bowl before me, and the steam flowing into my face further ignites the roar in my stomach. "That should help you feel a bit better," he says, and makes one for himself.

"Hopefully."

He slips into the seat beside me. For a few minutes, we're silent as we enjoy the food, the clicking of utensils the only sound.

"Why'd you bring your Book?" he prompts. He stirs the remaining bit of stew around his bowl. "Planning to study enough to beat me again? I won't make it as easy this time."

"I really don't know," I say, looking at the shiny cover. "I gathered up whatever I thought was important because I probably won't go home for a while. I guess part of me thought if I brought my Book, I could read it again and maybe it would help me better control my powers."

"You still think you can change them?"

I clench the spoon a bit tighter. *You didn't start the fire,* Mother's words come back to me. "Ignis powers are in me, or at least the Arcane Ceremony said they were."

"That's your problem. You want to change things instead of letting them come naturally. If you relax and accept them, maybe other powers will form," Clio suggests as if it's the most obvious thing in the world.

I plop another bite of soup in my mouth, letting the flavor sink into my tongue before I swallow it and say, "Or maybe I'm insane."

"You are, but that's beside the point." He smirks.

I bite my lip and stare down at the table, hardly in the mood to joke. Am I insane for wanting to stay?

Clio takes a sip of his drink. "What is it?"

"Do you think I'm making the wrong choice?" I ask softly, hardly able to lift my gaze off my bowl with the fear he would see too many real emotions in my eyes if I did.

"Depends on the perspective you wanna see this from."

I stare at the last bite in my bowl. My stomach is knotting up, and the stew has lost its appeal.

"That wasn't a *yes*," Clio clarifies. "I'm just saying we don't understand everything we're up against. For all we know, the Council is wrong. Maybe Iris *was* a loner."

That thought somehow makes me feel worse. "Right," I mumble. I set down my spoon with a soft *thud*.

Clio stands then picks up his bowl and mine. As he drops them in the sink, he says, "We should get some sleep. We have to get an early start tomorrow."

"That's right. It's the Dedication Ceremony, huh?" I wilt a bit. The last thing I want is to be surrounded by all the witches who watched me have a meltdown in real time. The witches who may see a similar show when I tell Tarj what I've decided.

"You'll do fine," he says.

I don't have the energy to argue so I stand up and gesture

to the couch in the other room. "I guess I should sleep in there."

Clio shakes his head. "You can sleep in my bed."

I blink, unsure if I heard him right.

"Don't look at me like that. I'll sleep there," he says, gesturing to the living room. "I think it's only right that you be comfortable." I give him the stink-eye, and he adds, "Because you're a woman and all that."

"Huh. I never would've taken you for a gentleman," I tease.

"I'm full of mysteries," he says and leads me down a hallway to his bedroom.

The room is small with a desk beneath the window and a bed that takes up most of the space. The air smells of parchment, and I'm oddly comfortable as I approach his bed. I stifle a yawn and sit on the edge of it.

"Do you want a shirt of mine or something? That dress looks like it'd be uncomfortable to sleep in."

"That'd be great," I say. I feel as if I've worn the dress so long it's become part of my skin.

I stand up and strip it off as Clio turns to his dresser. When he hands me the shirt, I kick away my dress and am left only in my bra and underwear. His lips part as he gives me a once-over.

"Is something wrong?" I wonder, glancing down at myself.

"Y-you're—" He pauses to swallow heavily. "You're a lot more... open... than I thought you were," he answers and watches me pull the shirt over my head.

"Does it bother you?" I ask as I fluff the pillows.

"No. Just unexpected," he babbles, and I feel his eyes on me as I work. "You're so buttoned up in public."

"I'm sorry," I say. I glance at him apologetically. "Helena and I change in front of each other all the time. I guess I wasn't thinking."

"You sound like me when I opened the door," he says with a laugh.

I settle into his bed and stare at him, wondering if he can feel how much I adore him. "Why are you so nice to me? I mean, I know why everyone else is, but you've always seen me for me rather than what happened to me."

"I know better than anyone that your past is not who you are."

The reason for his empty house sinks in. I can't imagine what it's like to live with the memory of your parents dying like Clio does. My parents are far from perfect, but the pain of their death would cripple me in an entirely new way.

His assurances helps because I can tell he means it. For a lot of my life, I've had this sensation of taking up too much space. Of *being* too much, and there's a guilt that comes with it. In Clio's presence, I never feel that way. "I can never thank you enough for this."

He smirks. "Nonsense. I expect a detailed thank you letter in my hand before the ceremony tomorrow."

"Yeah, good luck with that." I laugh and tuck my arm under the pillows.

"In all seriousness, know that I plan to help you with this through thick and thin," he says, leaning on the doorframe. "Whatever you need, consider it done."

"Why?"

"It would be wrong of me to abandon you when you need someone more than ever."

My eyes well with tears, and I don't know how I manage to keep myself from crying. After the fight with my parents, I felt so alone. Clio will never know how much his words mean to me.

"Let me know if you need anything during the night, okay? I'm a light sleeper."

I sink deeper into the bed. "Thank you, Clio."

"Anytime."

As I slip away into sleep's embrace, the door clicks closed.

Chapter Eleven
The Dedication Ceremony

WHEN I OPEN my eyes, I'm walking barefoot through Ignis. The sensation of stones beneath my feet is so real, I can hardly tell it's a dream. Thick plumes of smoke darken the sky, and screams echo around me. A group of nearby trees bursts into flames, and I jump away from it.

"What's happening?" I whisper and creep backward. My heart pounds, and it's hard to catch my breath.

"*One of us,*" Iris' voice floats through my head.

I close my eyes and try to block it out, but when I open them again, the yellow eyes of a crouched beast are staring at me. I scream, and the world around me dissolves and is replaced by Clio's panicked face. Concern makes his eyes seem double their normal size.

"What happened?" I slur and sit up.

He backs away, hand to his forehead. "Damn it, Li! You were screaming."

"Was I?" I don't remember. I swallow, still trembling from the dream. I've never had one so vivid before. I push my blue-black hair from my eyes. "Just a bad dream is all."

"You could've warned me you have nightmares," he says. "I didn't know what was happening. I thought one of those bitches had gotten in here."

Bags highlight his eyes and crease marks dent the skin over

his cheekbone. Once again, he's only wearing boxers, and guilt washes over me for waking him up.

"I'm sorry," I mumble. My mouth is dry.

"No harm done. Try to get some more sleep if you can."

I tuck a lock of hair behind my ear, thoroughly done with sleeping for a while. "It's okay. I think I'll start getting ready for the ceremony."

"We've still got a few hours before you have to worry about that," he says and sits on the edge of the bed.

"Then I'll have time to think."

"About changing your decision?" he asks, clearly hoping my nightmares have convinced me I'm a fool.

"Of course not."

"What was your dream about?" he asks. "I've never heard you scream like that."

"I-I don't remember," I say, frustrated that it's slipped away. *It won't do me any good to remember it anyway.*

Clio stands and approaches his dresser, grabbing something off the top. "That's a shame." He hands me a dress. "This is for you. For the ceremony."

"You got me a dress?" I ask, taken aback. I slip the fabric from his fingers. It's not like Clio to get anyone a gift.

He laughs. "No. Helena brought it over shortly after you went to sleep. She had the feeling you'd need it." Clio glances at the top of the dresser at another bundle of clothes. "She actually brought two, but I didn't think you'd appreciate the pink one very much."

"Helena knows I'm here?"

"Apparently," Clio says. "She doesn't need magic. She's

intuitive."

"That she is," I note. I hold up the dress. "Thanks anyway."

"You're welcome," he says. He takes an awkward half step toward the door before he stops and says, "D-do you need help getting dressed?"

I shake my head politely at his nervousness. It's not an emotion he shows often. "I can manage, Clio. Thanks."

"Oh, now you're shy?" He gestures at the patch of my underwear visible through the shuffled blanket.

I blush and pull the comforter up, then wait for the click of the door as he leaves. Once I'm alone, I strip off his shirt, pull the dress on, and lay the discarded clothes on his bed. I walk to the bathroom with the help of my telekinesis. The cold water feels good as I wash the sleep off my face and brush my hair.

"Helena's Equipped with knowledge *and* fashion powers," I mumble and stare at my reflection, unable to help smiling at my own dumb joke.

When I walk into the living room, Clio stands in front of his mirror, adjusting the sleeve of his white dress shirt.

"Look at you dressed all stylish!" I gush, and I hold my palms out.

The corner of his lip turns up as he pats his sleeve into place. "You don't look so bad yourself."

"Thank you," I reply. I eye my Book on the table beside his chair.

"You ready to go?" he asks.

I tilt my head to the side, considering. I'm anxious to get the ceremony over with, but if we leave now, we'll be some of the first ones there. "Can we stop by Helena's on the way? Maybe she'll come with us."

Clio side-eyes me. "She will. You know she will, but…"

"But what?"

"She's not going to be in the best mood," he points out. "After the Arcane Ceremony, and with the Dedication Ceremony today, she's gonna be completely out of sorts."

I hadn't considered what today would mean for her. The Arcane Ceremony had been hard enough, but this would be like the final nail in the coffin. "Guess that means she'll need us more than ever."

"Yep," he says and straightens his collar. "Let's go."

He leads the way outside, and I'm glad he doesn't insist on helping me move. He's probably stressed out about ten other things. I focus on the rhythm of my footsteps. The sleep I'd managed to get—mixed with Fern's chew—makes the walk ninety percent easier than my travels yesterday. I raise my face to the sky and feel the morning sun sink into my skin. Clio glances at me out of the corner of his eye and copies the gesture.

I smile, embracing the odd relationship between us.

When we arrive at Helena's house, Clio knocks, and I stand back a foot, twining my fingers uncertainly. She answers the door with a smile, dressed as beautifully as she'd been at the Arcane Ceremony.

"Hey, guys," she says in a tone of voice that makes it clear her smile was fake.

"How're you feeling today?" I ask Helena.

A shadow hangs over her eyes as she says, "This isn't a *favorite* day of mine."

Clio's face twists in an *I-told-you-so* expression. I ignore him.

"That dress looks good on you," she says, pulling the door closed behind her.

"You have great taste," I reply. I glance down at the dress and grasp handfuls of the soft cloth in both hands and hold it out. If I was physically able, I would've given her a quick twirl to show my appreciation.

"Mmhmm," she says, but she doesn't look at me again.

"Are you okay? You're kind of quiet."

Helena tosses her long, red braid over her shoulder and side-eyes me. "I don't see the point of UnEquipped going to this. I never have. Everyone knows we're not leaving our Covens. We're barely part of them to begin with."

"You're as much a part of things as us," Clio says. "Possibly more important since UnEquipped keep it running with Coven duties. *Everyone* has a place."

Helena's eyebrows scrunch. "It doesn't matter where I live, so why mark me? All UnEquipped are the same. My grandma agrees."

"There's no one like you, Helena," I argue, irritated with her family. It's one thing to be bitter about the circumstances of your birth, but another to drill that bitterness into the head of someone else and bring them down too. "Getting the piercing shows your loyalty to your home, and that's what it's all about. Coven pride."

Helena stays quiet, clearly not feeling better despite our trying to cheer her up. I glance at Clio, and he looks back with a face that says, *You tried.*

"Helena, I didn't formally apologize last night when you dropped off Lilith's dress. I should've, and I'm sorry. For that and for yesterday." He steps into her path and forces her to look at him.

Helena makes eye contact, face stoic. "It's fine, Clio, really. Don't worry about it."

Clio and I exchange a look as Helena pushes past him. The fire in our friend doesn't seem to be kindled by anything. *What she needs now is time*, I remind myself.

Defeated, I fall silent. I count the steps as we travel the path down to the Ceremony Grounds. Like the day before, groups of Equipped and UnEquipped from every Coven have already arrived. The mood is different though. Witches are excited for their piercings and to become official parts of their Coven.

"This is where we part ways," Helena says with a longing stare toward the group of our Equipped classmates.

"See you at the end," I say.

She turns away, but not before I catch a flash of emotion in her eyes—betrayal. The thing that hurts her the most is that I'm not by her side through this. She feels abandoned, and why not? The path we were supposed to tread together has been lost. I'm tempted to follow her when Clio stops me.

"There's nothing you can do for her," he reminds me.

"So why do I feel so guilty?" I tear my gaze away from her. "Things are never going to be the same. She has to go through this alone because... because I'm a freak." A tear drips down my face, and I wipe it away quickly, startled and embarrassed by my reaction.

"Stop it," Clio says. "You had equal chances of developing

powers, and this is just how things turned out. It's no one's fault. That's life."

I'm not so sure. I can't stop the bitter laugh from tumbling out.

"What's so funny?" he asks.

"Did Helena and I really have the same odds?"

Clio folds his arms over his chest, confused. "Am I missing something here?"

"The entire situation with my parents, remember? They won't tell me the truth about my accident, and *that* is what made me who I am." I swallow roughly; my throat is tight and dry.

"That's bullshit," he says. He enunciates each syllable. "Your accident did not shape you into anything. Your choices did. You're a strong person. You're *Lilith*! If you want my honest opinion, I think you need to let things go, if only for five minutes, and tell yourself that everything is going to be okay."

I look away and hear him sigh.

"Come on," he says and grips my hand.

I let him lead me to the group of Equipped Ignis witches. There are only a few in line ahead of me, and they call greetings to Clio. He says a few kind words back, but like at the Arcane Ceremony, he doesn't leave my side.

I scratch my face and risk a glimpse at the Equipped Mentis group. Dawn's at the head of the pack, chin raised to study her classmates and soon-to-be army. I zone out. I'm so lost in my thoughts that I'm aware of nothing until it's Clio's turn.

"Wish me luck," he says.

I squeeze his hand once—it's the best comforting gesture I can think of—and I watch him approach the Council member in charge of Ignis piercings. I'm surprised to see a female rather than Tarj.

Where is Tarj? I wonder before I shrug off the thought. He's the last person I want to see when things are already so chaotic.

The girl holds the gun to Clio's right ear, and he closes his eyes as she inserts the red crystal.

"You're done," she tells him.

He pokes the gem and comes back to my side. "That hurt more than I thought it would."

"You, with the black hair, you're up," the girl calls to me.

An unpleasant smirk crosses my face as I approach. My eyes are on the gun in her hand.

"Wait!" someone calls, which stops me halfway to my target.

Tarj appears from the line of trees separating the Ceremony Grounds from the Grove. He dashes, shouting, "Don't get that piercing!"

His silver hair is windswept, and he's dressed in his Council uniform rather than his ceremony robes. His breathing is rough, and I guess that he's been running for some time to catch me.

This can't be good.

"What? Why?" I ask, oddly defensive.

"You need to come with me to Headquarters."

Chapter Twelve
The Sage

I MANAGE A pitiful, "What?" It's not every day a witch is asked to go to the Council's home. In fact, I don't think it *ever* happens.

Clio must have the same thought because he wraps his fingers around my wrist and pulls me back. He assumes a protective stance between Tarj and me as he says, "Why should she go with you? She's done nothing wrong."

"I'm aware of that, Clio," Tarj replies. "However, I've been ordered to bring her with me. And there are two ways this can go."

I have to go with him. They'll fight if it comes down to it. I try to interrupt the conversation but can think of nothing coherent to say.

This is about Iris, I tell myself. I broke the rules. There's no way they'll let me go without some kind of punishment. *Or maybe they have something else in mind*, I think and remember the story Fern told me about Willow.

"Is this because of Iris?" I finally blurt out.

Clio loosens his grip but doesn't let go as Tarj says, "Partly. But not for the reason you may think. The Sage wants to speak with you."

Clio's green eyes look enormous. "The Sage?" He pulls me the tiniest bit closer to him. "This sounds serious."

"I'm afraid it is," Tarj says. He reaches toward me. "Come on, Lilith. Don't make it harder than it has to be."

I stare at the lines in his palm. Is this how they got Willow to go with them?

Clio lets go and murmurs, "You'll be okay." He tilts his chin down to stare directly into my eyes. His true emotions scream at me from their depths, and I understand the calm words had been for Tarj's benefit. Not mine.

Be careful, that look tells me.

I ignore my instinct to run in the opposite direction and take a few hesitant steps toward our Coven representative. Even if I *had* tried to escape, I wouldn't have gotten far, and it would have given the Council something to arrest me for. Tarj gives me a smile that's likely meant to be comforting, but I ignore the attempt and stare at Clio.

Be safe, he mouths to me.

Tarj guides me away from the Ceremony Grounds and deeper into the Grove. Traveling into new territory seems exciting until I start to wonder what the cost will be. I risk a glance over my shoulder, and I see an unhappy Clio standing ramrod straight, watching me walk away.

That's his silent way of warning Tarj, and the Council in general, that if anything happens, he's watching. If I don't make it back, he'll know.

"Did the Sage say why she wants to meet me?" I finally ask. It should've been my first question, but I'm afraid of the answer.

"Don't you know you're big news?" Tarj says as he carefully picks his way through the thicket.

"I didn't know." I try to follow him. The landscape of the Grove isn't very kind to me, and the phantom ache in my leg begins to throb. "How long will this trip be?"

He stops, looks at my leg, and frowns before he puts two fingers in his mouth and whistles. "Not long at all."

The ground rumbles beneath us, and I hold my hands out to steady myself. The sleek, dark brown head of a wyrm breaks through the soil. It's smaller than the one in Ignis. Its forked tongue tastes the air before it looks at Tarj expectantly. He sets a hand to the side of its head and gestures for me to approach.

It blinks and bows its head. I grasp Tarj's hand and allow him to help me onto the wyrm's back. Its scales are softer than they look, and I wonder how hard it will be to hold on. Tarj climbs up and sits down in front of me. He pats the top of the ground dragon's head, and it starts forward. Convinced I'll be thrown off, I grip Tarj's shoulders, but I don't move much, and I wonder if it's my powers keeping me in place or if the wyrm is so used to passengers that it's learned how to provide a smooth ride.

"You can relax now," Tarj says.

When I realize I'm still holding tight, I let go.

"As I was saying, you're a big deal at Headquarters. We haven't seen powers like yours since well… you know…" He trails off.

"Willow?" I prompt.

He sweeps his silver hair to the side and asks, "You know about her?"

"Somewhat."

Tarj raises an eyebrow. "*What* exactly do you know?"

"That Willow was like me, b-but," I struggle to figure out

the end of the sentence, unsure how much I should say, "…it didn't end well for her."

"Unfortunately."

"Why was she executed?"

Tarj opens his mouth to answer when the wyrm slows down. The large girl who arrested Iris comes through the thicket. Tarj slides down to greet her and encourages me to do the same. As I stand face to face with the woman, I realize she's taller than me. She places both hands on my shoulders and stares into my eyes. Is this it? Am I under arrest?

She has a full, warm face that looks friendly, even though I'm uncomfortable with her proximity. "Lilith. It's nice to meet you. My name is Tricia," she says and takes her hands off me. "I never got the chance to thank you for your help the other day."

I shuffle backward to put some space between us. "It was really no trouble."

"Well, come on. Myrna really wants to see you," she says in a tone that's light and airy.

"That's the Sage's real name," Tarj whispers in my ear. "We're not supposed to say it out loud, but Tricia forgets."

Before I have a chance to say another word, Tricia grasps my hand to pull me through the woods. I glance at Tarj, and he gives me an apologetic look as he watches us go. I make a mental note to bring up the topic of Willow again when a more opportune moment comes.

I hurry to keep up with the witch pulling me along, struggling between the plants, myself, and finding a way to get out of Tricia's grasp without offending her.

A building appears in the distance, crafted of gothic

steeples and glass panes. Shrubs have been perfectly groomed to form beautiful walkways with stone-lined paths bordered with flowers. I strain my ears and pick up a faint burbling, like water in a fountain.

They live like gods. No wonder they have no problems doing the terrible things they do. Everyone has a price. My face twitches, but Tricia doesn't notice.

The path leads us to a grand archway. Through the doors, we step into a living space with six throne-like chairs placed in a circle around a huge, circular, red rug. A bookshelf lines half of one of the walls, and a desk with ritual and alchemy supplies sits near the other.

No one's in the room. I know that's because the rest of the Council are finishing up the Dedication Ceremony. I wonder how many others there are. In my head, I try to run through the faces I saw at both Ceremonies, but the only two who stand out are Tarj and Tricia.

Without conscious thought, I tap my ear and feel the blank skin. Will I still be able to get a piercing or does missing the Dedication Ceremony mean I'll be considered an UnEquipped once again? I'm fine with being put back into Helena's category of Ignis… if I'm allowed to go back, of course. We stop beside a small set of wooden doors.

"The Sage is in there," Tricia says.

I lick my bottom lip and study the patterns in the wood. "What's she like?"

"She's very kind and fair," Tricia assures me. I start to step inside when her fingers grab my upper arm and stop me in place. "But remember, she's the most powerful witch in all our Covens.

You are to address her with the utmost respect."

That depends on what she has to say to me. Respect is a two-way street.

She lets go, and I push open the door. A long, stone-lined corridor separates me from the dim room ahead. I walk the distance, fingers to the wall. It feels like I'm walking into a trap. A dungeon. The room at the end is surprisingly cozy. Books are scattered across the floor, and a scent of herbs mixed with some type of flower—lavender?—fills the air. Piles of alchemy supplies and a candle sit on a small end table in the middle of the room. The candle's tiny flickering flame is oddly capable of lighting the entire place.

"Ah, Lilith, nice to see you, young lady," a voice says.

I jump, and it's then that I notice an elderly woman sitting in a red-cushioned chair beside the window. She's bent over a black cauldron on the table before her, and she's clutching a small, white-handled knife in her hand. As I approach her, the smell of herbs grows stronger.

"Uh… hello, Sage," I reply in my best attempt at politeness.

"Please, call me, Myrna. Take a seat; we have much to discuss," she says as she gestures to the empty chair across the table from her.

I'm quick to obey, finding it odd to be in her presence. She's getting on in years, which is evident from the pile of wispy, white hair on her head and the wrinkles lining her face. She studies me through eyes that carry more wisdom than I'll ever have.

Though the Sage is well-known—and feared—seeing her is rare. From what we learned in class, she never leaves her place in Headquarters so she is always protected. It's an honor to be in the same room as her. The fact she asked for me personally should've been a boost to my ego.

Instead, I'm wary.

I had disobeyed the Council's wishes by speaking to Iris. I'm owed a punishment of some kind, and I wonder if she'll be the one to tell me my fate. She shifts her focus from the potion she had been so intent on to study me.

"How's your leg?" she asks and clasps her hands together on the table.

"You know about my injury?" I inquire. My unease melts. That definitely wasn't something I expected her to talk about.

"As I imagine, many people both inside and outside of Ignis do. Especially after the ceremony," the Sage replies.

A weight crashes down on my shoulders. "Oh."

"I sense your disappointment."

"It's been a hard few days," I admit. I tap my fingers on the arm of my chair to try to bleed off some of my extra energy. "So… uh… what did you want to see me about? You know, Tarj pulled me from my Dedication Ceremony." I move my fingers to my earlobe to show the unpierced skin for emphasis.

"It's all right, my dear," she says. "You're not here for anything bad. You can relax."

I don't feel inclined to believe her.

The Sage picks up her boline and uses the blade to stir the liquid in the cauldron. "I called you here to offer you a better deal than staying in Ignis as an UnEquipped."

"How do you know what I chose?"

A playful smile tugs at the corners of her lips. "Lucky

guess."

Apparently, mysterious is a character trait for her. I'm afraid to speak because I don't know how challenging my tone will be. "What's the offer?"

"I saw the way you protected Tarj and rushed to heal him despite not having the proper know-how. You showed your courage. That's why I would like you to be a member of the Council," she states.

What she's offering is monumental, a once-in-a-lifetime opportunity. The witches of the Council are known for their intelligence and their strength. They have the best powers of all those in their Covens. Handpicked for that exact reason.

"I mean no disrespect, but do you really think I, of all people, can handle this?" I ask.

"I would not offer if I didn't think you were capable," she answers, her tone even as she tosses a handful of chopped up petals into her cauldron.

"I'm sorry to question your judgment," I state, but I do. There must be some mistake.

"Have you met Crowe yet?"

I try to recall all the Council members' faces I've encountered before I wonder why I need to know this one in particular. Finally, I shake my head.

"He's our newest member. He's a shapeshifter and a lot harder to handle than you." When I don't speak, the Sage continues, "You do not need to fear me, little one. I promise your questions will not be considered rude or out of place. I understand things may seem a bit confusing for you right now and that lack of understanding can manifest in many ways."

I manage a ghost of a smile, but I'm still unsure what to say. Everything is happening too fast, and I don't know how to get off this path I've somehow landed on. I can't handle a place in the Council—I can barely regulate my normal witch powers. Whatever those are.

"He'll be your mentor," she says and cuts a leaf in half. "You'll be expected to follow his example until you adjust to your life around here."

"Not Tarj?" I ask. Since he's the Ignis representative and has been the one with whom I've shared the most contact, he seems the logical choice.

"I considered it, but I feel the incident at the ceremony would make the trainer/trainee relationship a bit strained," she explains.

Understandably so, I think and watch as she scoops up the leaf bits to dump into her potion. "When will I meet Crowe?"

"He's still at the Dedication Ceremony," she replies. Her attention is on her cauldron. "I'll have Tricia take you to meet him."

"I have one more question before you dismiss me, if I may." I clench my hands together in my lap in my best attempt at seeming passive.

"Anything, my dear," she says and puts her full attention on me.

My skin tingles when I imagine how much power is behind her eyes. "If I take on this role, are you going to assign me to a Coven, or am I still allowed to make that choice?"

"You'll live here, in the Grove, with the rest of us."

I stare at her without seeing. This is their way of getting

me to leave Ignis. Tarj had already made it clear that the Council wanted me out of there. Now I don't have a choice.

Did I ever?

"I don't want to leave Ignis," I tell her, forcing the words out.

A glaze settles over her eyes. "That's what you *think* you want, but you're young. The problem with youth is that it usually comes paired with stubbornness. Change can be scary, and almost no one welcomes it. That's why it sometimes takes help. A nudge in the right direction."

That's her way of politely saying, *Too bad.*

I'm on the verge of an outburst, and I have to remind myself how dumb that would be in the presence of the Sage. The Council has the final say in *everything.* This will be no different. I can't imagine how I'll break the news of leaving my Coven to those who mean the most to me, but I'll have to figure it out and soon. It sounds like she's already arranged to have me in the Grove for a long time.

In the back of my mind lies the nagging suspicion that their plans for me are like those they had for Willow. I can see how it worked. Lure someone away from everyone who loves them and they're vulnerable. Except I know how Willow's story ended, and I vow not to wind up like her.

Where's your trust? my conscience scolds. The thought is so unexpected I bite harder into my lip. *It went out the window when my parents decided it was okay to lie to me for eighteen years.*

"Right," I mutter finally. I bite down hard enough to accidentally draw a bead of blood. I lick it away before I force myself to add, "Thank you." There's nothing else I can say so I rise, but I have the odd sensation the meeting isn't truly over yet.

"This is for you," she says and hands me a tiny purple flower.

I reach for it with trembling fingers. The scent drifts up my nose and relaxes me a little despite the hurricane of anxiety in my mind.

"It's for luck," the Sage explains.

"Thank you," I say and tuck the flower into my pocket.

I'll need more than luck, but it's a start.

I curtsy and head back down the long, dark corridor, unsure what to do with myself. I look for Tricia. Since hers is the only face I know—other than Tarj's—I have a feeling I'll have to stick to her side until I'm introduced to my soon-to-be mentor, Crowe.

I find her waiting for me in the common area, and she leads me back into the woods. My leg roars at the thought of trekking all the way back to the Ceremony Grounds.

If they want me here, they'll have to fix their landscaping.

Chapter Thirteen
Crowe

TRICIA DOESN'T SUMMON a wyrm, but with her constant chatter, I forget how long the journey is. She tells me details of her life and all about her loved ones. I nod, wondering when she'll finish. I miss the silence of traveling with Tarj.

"That's when I first realized I had mind control powers," she says and waves her arms. "I didn't even mean to make him do it. I got so mad, it just kind of happened, but I tell you, that's what my brother deserved!"

"Your family must've been surprised," I mutter and suppress the sigh I want to add.

Tricia tilts her head. "Eh, I guess so. It's not too far from telekinesis, but it was unexpected. What about you? Multiple powers must be exciting!"

That's not the word I would use. "I think the Arcane Ceremony was wrong. I've only been able to use telekinesis."

"No pyro powers at all?" she asks. She squints to better see me. "But you're from Ignis, right?"

"Right," I say and stare up at the sky.

I think back to the incident a few nights ago, when I'd heard the whispering in my head. I still don't know what that was, but if it was the start of a new power, another one from Mentis, I don't want to acknowledge it.

"The ceremony is never wrong," she informs me.

A sneer crosses my face. "Not even once?"

"As far as I know," Tricia replies, unaffected by my hostility.

For the first time since leaving Headquarters, there's a moment of silence, and I'm thankful. We make it to the Grounds, and I look for Tarj in the crowd. I don't see him. Does the Sage know how close he came to telling me about Willow? Is this her way of keeping me away from the truth?

Tricia's gaze shifts, and she points through a few trees. "That's Crowe up there."

Through a gap in the crowd, I see a slim male a few years older than me. He has shaggy red hair, some of which hangs in his narrow, green eyes. A long scar runs down his left cheek and ends in his cleft chin. He stands by the Aquais Equipped and takes no notice of our approach.

As we weave through the crowd, I take a second to search for Clio. When I see him, he's focused on Helena, and I decide against reaching out. It won't benefit either of us if I do.

Crowe looks from Tricia back to me with a raised orange eyebrow. "Uh, you two need something?"

"Crowe, this is Lilith. Lady Myrna's newest recruit."

"Can't say I'm surprised." He grins and looks me in the eye as he says, "You have quite the reputation."

"Fantastic," I mutter, uncomfortably. I prefer to blend into the shadows, not to stand out. Having a reputation that precedes me is going to take some getting used to.

"Ready for your piercing?" he asks.

I perk up. "Nobody said anything about a piercing. The

Sage said I was coming to meet you. That's all."

Tricia exaggeratedly pushes her lips out. "I had different orders."

I take the smallest step backward, sick to my stomach. Somehow, I would've felt better if they had just slapped me across the face. "*Orders?*"

Tricia nods, bottom lip jutting out in a pout. "She told me to bring you to Crowe for your piercing."

"I didn't agree to this," I say.

"None of us got a choice," Crowe says with an unapologetic shrug. He reaches for my arm, and I shuffle my cloak to dodge him.

Despite risking a burning execution by not following their orders, I can't bite my tongue anymore. "This isn't right. Don't I get time to say goodbye to everyone before I'm permanently bound to a new Coven against my will?"

Tricia shakes her head. "It's better this way."

"For whom? *You?* The *Sage?* It sure as Hell isn't better for me!"

"It'll only make things harder for you, and for them, if you get the chance to say goodbye," Tricia says. There's sadness in her eyes as she explains it, as if she's remembering her own inauguration. "We can't have you showing any weaknesses. You're an authority figure now. It's best you're seen as such as soon as possible. Okay?"

"No! It's *not* okay," I tell them, and I have the urge to run. I wish I was physically capable of complying.

Instead, I stand frozen. My eyes dart between Tricia and Crowe with the feeling that the walls are closing in. Part of me hopes they're pulling a prank on me. It'd be a cruel one, but I'd prefer it to the alternative. The looks on their faces says otherwise.

My heart sinks in horror.

"Don't try to run; it'll just embarrass us," Crowe mutters, low enough that the nearby Aquais witches don't hear him. "Not to mention you."

"But—" I try to protest.

"Relax," he says, taking an exaggerated breath for show. Then he reaches for me again.

"No!" I cry out. I use a gush of power to send him backward. His heels dig into the ground, and he manages to keep himself upright.

I try to push out another attack to make a space big enough to escape through, but my energy is blocked. I turn to Tricia, guessing her to be the cause, before my powers falter and disappear. I gasp for air and stare at Crowe as he grabs my arm and pulls me closer. I'm so rigid with shock that I offer no resistance. It's bad enough that they've practically kidnapped me, but I can't run, and I can't fight, which leaves me no choice but to submit to them.

I'm starting to believe Iris more and more.

"I didn't ask for this," I say. My words are shaky. "And if I go through with it, I don't even get a few more minutes with my loved ones. Why would the Sage do this?"

"We all had to do it," Crowe informs me. He runs his thumb along my elbow as if a comforting gesture could make things better. "It seems unfair now, but you'll come to appreciate it. Now, tilt your head for me, darling."

I shake my head vigorously enough to whip him with my

black locks.

"Please?" he tries. He flashes me a toothy smile.

Don't you think you're fucking adorable?

Tricia's arms are wrapped under my armpits to pin me to her. I struggle in her grip, but her size, coupled with her grip, ensure I can't get away. Her arms crush mine, and I cry out. Desperately, I kick at Crowe to keep him away from me.

Stop it. Tricia's voice fills my mind. My frantic blows halt before I'm able to kick Crowe in his happy place.

Crowe grasps my jaw with one hand, tilts my head to the side, and brushes my hair away from my ear. He lifts the gun. I close my eyes, powerless to fight as he slips the earring into place. It stings like a snakebite. Tricia finally lets go of me, and I lift my fingers to the shining gem. I back away and stare accusingly between Crowe and Tricia.

"You can't force me into my Dedication," I say in a voice so pathetic I wish I hadn't spoken at all.

Tricia watches me with slightly more sympathy than Crowe. Tears bubble in my eyes, and I turn away, desperate for escape, but there is none, and that makes it worse.

Don't cry. Don't show them a weakness.

I squeeze my eyes shut to try and control my emotions. When that doesn't work, I take my chances and push through the nearest group of witches.

"Li… what is—" a familiar voice says.

I open my eyes and see Clio. His gaze is trained on the rainbow gem in my ear. He moves closer. Crowe dashes forward and puts a hand in his path. I try to shove him out of the way with my magic, but I find the phantom hold that stopped me earlier is still there, locking my powers inside me.

"I'm gonna have to ask you to back away," Crowe orders Clio.

Clio, who easily towers a foot over Crowe, smirks down at him. "I think it's okay that I speak to my friend."

"She's too busy today to be your *friend*."

"Why is she crying?" he demands then peers at me around Crowe. "Li! What's going on?"

I try to look him in the eyes, to give him an answer, but Tricia grabs the tops of my arms and drags me through the crowd. I scream and dig my heels into the dirt, trying to break free from her hold. Nearby witches part to make room as soon as they realize members of the Council are in the skirmish.

"Clio! Help!" I cry out.

Tricia picks me up and nearly throws me in the direction of the Grove. I kick backward and aim my blows at any part of her I can contact.

"What are you doing with her?" Clio tries to push Crowe aside to get to me.

Crowe stays stubbornly in place. "This doesn't concern you. This is Council business. Stay back."

"Let me see her!" Clio demands, but the redhead doesn't falter.

Tricia drags me farther away from him and the hope I cling to that I'll be able to return to my old life. I plant my elbow in her gut, which surprises her enough to loosen her grip. I fall on my hands and knees, coughing from the dirt that plumes into the air. I try to get up, to get to Clio, when a warm tickling sensation washes over me. I have the sickening thought that Tricia's finally decided to use her powers to control me. I pick myself up and calmly wipe the dirt and grass stains from my blue dress before I walk toward her.

Inside my head, I scream. Scream for help. I scream for my body to obey me so I can get away while I still have the chance. I scream for a way out. It doesn't work. She guides me toward the Grove and away from Clio, away from my home.

Clio's confused and angry calls continue in the distance, but Tricia's powers prevent me from responding. I can't even turn my head to see if he's okay or if he's gotten into a fight with Crowe. Every time he calls my name, my heart breaks a little more. Finally, we get to a point so deep in the woods that I no longer hear him.

"Well, that was a disaster," Tricia mutters and releases me from her spell.

I round on her. "You think so? You had no right to do that!"

Tricia holds her palms out, deadpan. "I realize tensions are a little high right now, but you need to calm down."

"Don't tell me to calm down," I warn.

Tricia pinches the bridge of her nose as if trying to stem off an oncoming headache. It must've taken a lot out of her to control me as long as she had, and I consider trying to fight some more, to drain the last of her strength away. "Look," she says after a long minute. "He'll hold you back. It's hard to hear, but it's the truth. Our families couldn't keep up with us, so we had to leave them behind. It's part of being chosen. Being a member of the Council requires a lot of sacrifices if you hope to make it work."

"I don't *want* to be a member of the Council," I remind

her. "I *want* to go home." And it's an odd statement considering home is the last place I wanted to be only twelve hours prior.

"If you're always depending on others to make it, you'll never truly succeed," Tricia continues her lesson. "Learn that lesson now."

Based on today, another good lesson would be to never trust my governing Coven.

"Let me explain what's happening to Clio, or I'll join the UnEquipped," I threaten.

Tricia folds her arms across her chest and pins me with her glare. "You think you can threaten me?"

"Why not? You can break the law because you *are* the law, right? If I'm part of the Council, I can do that too."

She stares at me and says nothing, reach for the earring, and search for the stud to remove it. If she won't make the first move, I'm more than happy to do it. I prod the metal again and again, but I find nothing. My heart sinks when I realize there's no way to get it off.

"I can't remove it?" I ask as I continue to tug at my ear.

Tricia shakes her head. "A mark from any of the five Covens, you can, but the Council is special. Once you're brought in, you may not leave. Unless of course you get the okay from the Sage, but she wants you here, Lilith. That means that earring ain't comin' out."

A dry chuckle pours out of me, and I stare up at the bright blue sky, somehow keeping the angry tears from my eyes. "Where's Crowe?"

"Around," Tricia replies. "He had to calm down some folks at the ceremony. Your little show gave them the impression another witch was attacking."

A raven drifts into the clearing and lands on the ground beside Tricia. It *caws* once and cocks its head to the side before the feathers start to melt away. The wings and beak shift and elongate and less than a minute later, Crowe stands naked before us. Tricia pulls a folded set of clothes out of her robes and passes it to him. Crowe thanks her as he dresses.

"Things all good here?"

"If you consider kidnapping all good, then I'd say it's perfecto!" I hiss as I throw my hands into the air.

"Your new apprentice is a handful," Tricia says with an exaggerated breath. She lifts an arm to show bruises dotted along her pale skin. "But you've got this from here, so I'm going to get back to Headquarters."

"See you at dinner," Crowe calls after her then turns to me once she's disappeared through the trees.

"Giving ol' Tricia a hard time already, huh?" Crowe asks with a smirk. "Good for you."

"Don't cheer for me," I say and flare my nostrils. "I'm not on your side, and I'm not on her side. This is wrong, and you know it. Or at least you oughta. Now, if you don't mind, I'm going back to Ignis to talk to Clio and sort things out." I storm past him and use some of my ability to stay off my hurting leg. The last thing I want is for my body to betray me now when I'm already so vulnerable.

"You think you can do that?" Crowe asks, amused. I stop and turn to face him. I think of the earring. *It's enchanted*, I realize, and I wonder what else it can keep me from doing. "They really haven't explained a thing to you, huh? As a member of the

Council, there's a big rule you need to accept."

"What's that?" I ask dryly. Dread creeps through me.

"You may not leave the Grove unless it's been approved by the Sage."

"I thought we were in *charge*," I say mockingly. "Why do we need a babysitter?"

"It's to keep *us* safe," he says. "We may be the most powerful witches these lands have to offer, but there are a lot more of them than us. If we go out there alone, we could get hurt. Look what happened to Tarj."

"I don't believe this." I moan. Then what I've been dreading most happens. I lose grip on my powers, and my weak leg gives out. I topple over but don't try to stand back up. I stay in the dirt, staring at my hands. I haven't felt this low in a while.

"I think I handled this thing about as well as you in the beginning," Crowe admits and offers me a hand. "At the end of the day, I think you'll be okay. You've got fire."

"Is that your idea of a joke?" I snap and glare at him. Ignoring his hand, I stretch out my damaged leg in the grass, showing the wrinkled patch of pink skin on my calf.

"You can take it that way if you want," he says, sounding as if he doesn't care much either way.

I blow a lock of hair from my eyes. "Why, of all the witches at the Arcane Ceremony, would the Sage choose me? Look at what I am. I can't control my powers worth a shit."

"You're so much more than any of that," he says patiently. "When you stepped in and saved Tarj's life without being asked, you showed potential. So many witches ran away, but you risked your life for him. For *us*."

"Yeah, and this is how you repay me," I snort.

"Believe it or not, we're grateful."

"*Grateful*, really? You show your gratitude by ripping me away from my loved ones? My *home*?" I ask. I don't want to cry, but the frustration is making it hard not to.

Crowe holds his palms out. "Don't look at me, darling. Complaints should be filed with the Sage. I'm just the messenger."

I raise my hand to my temple and close my eyes. "Fat lot of good that'll do," I say, peering at him through half-lidded eyes. "Why are you my mentor anyway? You can't help me."

"If the Sage wanted us to know, she would've told us. I want to think she's taken a liking to me. Mentoring you is a huge promotion."

My anger peels away long enough for me to marvel at what he can do. "Shapeshifting—you're the only one in history to pull it off," I say, slightly envious of his abilities. If I could shapeshift, I'd change into someone else and slip away from the Grove before they realized I was gone. They'd never find me again. "The Sage doesn't give you enough praise for that?" When he doesn't answer, I continue. "Which Coven are you from?"

"Aquais." I make a face, and he says, "Everyone reacts the same way." He sits down on the ground beside me. "Feeling a little better?"

"No," I say and pull one blade of grass free.

"Then why the sudden interest in me?"

"What am I supposed to do, wallow for the rest of the day?"

"I'm glad you're trying to make the best of it," he says and looks up at the sky. "What Coven did you expect me to be from?"

"I don't know," I say with a quick look at him before I resume my work on the grass. "If I had to guess, I would've said Mentis. They seem to have the biggest variety of powers."

"The first time I transformed, I was confused, to say the least." He pauses to ruffle his hair. "All my friends could conjure water, and me? Well, I thought there was something wrong with me for not being able to do the same."

That's a feeling I can understand. "What was the first thing you ever changed into?"

"A crow. Hence the name."

"You changed your name?"

"Most of us have. The Sage says a new identity helps us cope with a new title."

"She didn't mention any of that to me."

"To be fair, she didn't mention *any* of what just happened to you," he says. I make a face, and he continues, "But maybe you won't have to. She might figure she's dragged you through enough torture without completely taking the wind from your sails."

I stare into the trees. The stiff breeze causes me to shiver. Things are changing so fast, I don't know how much more I can handle before I snap.

Chapter Fourteen
Advisory Council of Fairies

"SO, ARE YOU ready to get the tour started or do you need to pout for a few more minutes?" Crowe asks with a raised eyebrow.

I pull myself to my feet using my anger as much as my magic. "Don't pretend I have a choice. It's very misleading."

He dips his head, and a crooked smile lights up his face. "Very well," he says and leads the way into the depths of the Grove.

I follow, too exhausted to put up my usual front as we skirt the edge of the magnificent garden surrounding Headquarters. "Where to first?"

"Training grounds."

"Training grounds?" I echo. I wonder if I heard him right.

"You want help bringing out your pyro powers, right?" he asks. "I gotta show you around anyway, might as well make the best of it while we're there."

"Okay," I say. Maybe not all the Council's requests are farfetched.

If possible, he mutters.

"Excuse me?" I scoff and pick up the pace to stare at the side of his face.

He swallows, eyes wide. "I didn't say anything."

"I-I heard you. You doubt I can do it?"

"How do you know that?"

"You said it?"

"No, I didn't."

The look in his eyes tells me he's as confused as I am. I squint, remembering the voice I thought I'd heard outside my house. Could they have been *thoughts*? "A guess then."

"Well…you're right," Crowe admits with a long exhale. "It's not that I *doubt* you. I just know how hard it'll be to manage two different powers. And if you really have five, or one from each Coven, like the ceremony said, then I don't envy you at all."

This is the only time I agree with him.

Beneath our feet, grass fades to sunburned earth that reminds me of Ignis. I breathe in the warm air, feeling more at home on the sand than I did in the woods. Up ahead, the ground dips into a pit. Crowe steps down and looks up at me, eyes shining in the sunlight.

"Since you're from Ignis, this will be the best place for you to train." He holds a hand to his forehead to block out the strongest of the sun's rays.

"There are other spots?"

"Yep. One for each Coven. I think you'd hate Aquais'!"

I shiver at the idea of a cold, soggy marsh, and eye the slope before me. I test it carefully with my good leg before I slide down. I wobble at the end of the rise, keep my balance for a second, then I lose it and fall on my butt with a groan.

"At least you made it," Crowe says with a shrug.

I get up and dust myself off, while trying to salvage as much of my pride as I can. "How does this work?"

"Simple. You're gonna try to set something on fire."

I wrinkle my nose. "I've tried before, and nothing ever came of it."

"Then you didn't try hard enough."

I glance around the barren land, but nothing stands out. "Kind of hard to set the sand on fire, don't you think?"

I return my gaze to him in time to catch the end of his transformation. In crow form, he plucks a feather from his side and tosses it on the ground. There is a look of command in his beady, black eyes.

Try this, he thinks.

I narrow my eyes. Is he testing more than my pyrokinesis? I concentrate on the feather until the veins in my neck bulge. Crowe switches back to his human form and watches me rip the feather to shreds.

"Well, you didn't *quite* do it," he says and studies the black wisps in the dirt.

"I tried." I'm sweating, and I lift my dirty fingers to wipe it from my brow. "I gave it all I had, and nothing happened. Is this when I say I told you so?"

"No," he says. He picks up one of the fluffy bits. "I didn't expect you to get it on your first attempt, but I'm glad you tried so hard. It's the best way to make progress."

"I don't need your approval," I grumble.

"No? Well you got it anyway."

I take a step and lurch forward. My magic reserves are nearly empty, and I can no longer use my telekinesis to keep myself steady. I've never run out of magic before. Before today, I thought it was a myth.

"Are you all right?" Crowe calls.

His voice breaks my reverie. "We're done training today, right?"

"Of course. You're drained," he says, pulling himself up out of the pit. "It'd be cruel to keep going."

"Has this happened to you before?" I ask, staring at the slope of sand rather than him.

"What? Running out of magic?" He purses his lips, considering as he reaches down to pull me out. "It happened quite a bit at first. It's part of why we need to train. You'll gain more stamina as we do. The last thing we want is for you to run out of magic during a battle."

I don't say anything as I follow him away from the Training Ground. It's comforting to know that at least I'm not alone in every problem I experience.

We do a lap around the garden, and into the trees. Water burbles nearby. There must be a river close by. Crowe pushes through some undergrowth, and I see it. The current pulls at the thick reeds on the riverbank, threatening to tear them loose.

"Why are we here?"

He takes a few steps farther downstream and focuses on the water as if he's searching for something in it. "This is a special place—home to the Advisory Council of Fairies."

"The *what?*" I ask. I'd heard of fairies other than Fern in the Land of Five, but I didn't think any of them resided with the Council. Fairies are rebellious, mischievous even, so the thought of proper fairies has me baffled.

"In the same way the Council governs the rest of the Land of Five, the Advisory Council of Fairies keeps track of the fairies," Crowe explains.

"I've never heard of them."

"It's not something we disclose often," he says. "Fairies are delicate. If they wanted attention, they would get it."

"Right." I chew on the inside of my cheek. "So, how do they decide which fairies help the Council?"

"They've got their own criteria, I suppose. All fairies have some form of magic, but these are powerful. Maybe more so than we are."

The idea of a fairy having as much power as a witch is something I never thought I'd hear. Crowe continues his search, and I narrow my eyes to better see through the water plants. I'm eager to see what a fairy of such caliber looks like.

"I guess they're not here right now. You'll meet them later," he says with an apologetic shrug. "Do you have any experience with fairies?"

I think of Fern and idly wonder what her powers are. Based on the stunt she pulled the night I met Iris, the powder she'd used to control Tarj, I'd say trickery is up her alley. She also has a knack for healing. Maybe she's more meant for the Alchemy Coven—it would certainly explain her relationship with Ambrossi.

Somewhere in my reminiscing, I bob my head.

"You should be able to handle them fine then," Crowe says as we travel down the riverbank. "The Sage likes her privacy, so she won't always be on call to answer your questions. At least, she wasn't with me. I might be busy sometimes too, so seek out these fairies. They'll be more than happy to help."

"Crowe, is that you?" a tiny voice calls from the river. The voice is so light and lilting, it's almost musical.

"Oh, you *are* here!" he exclaims.

The fairy has a pixie-cut, blue hair and large, green eyes. Her pink wings are much larger than her body and keep her in the air with ease.

"Callista, this is Lilith. She's new to the Council."

The tiny woman focuses on me and beams. "It's so nice to meet you! What's your power?"

"She's still trying to figure that out," Crowe says. "She's somewhere between pyrokinesis and telekinesis."

Possibly even clairvoyance, who knows?

Callista tilts her head, and I wonder if she heard my thought. If so, she doesn't admit it. Another fairy appears, her black hair matching her black wings. A sour expression crosses her face, and I get the impression she's different from Fern and Callista.

"What's going on?" she asks and takes her place beside Callista. Her black wings are spiky, and their color is solid, not opaque like those of most fairies.

"New recruit," Callista replies with a gesture toward me.

"Who are you?" the new fairy asks. She juts out her chin as she gives me a once over.

Crowe's eyes burn a hole in the side of my head.

"I'm Lilith. Li, for short. You?"

"I'm Thorn."

"As in thorn in my side?" A wide smile spreads across my face before I can stop it. I'm not sure why the idea of a pessimist tickles me, but it does.

"Yes. Mind your manners, *Li*." Her face is pinched and unhappy.

Crowe glares at me, and I clear my throat in a desperate attempt to compose myself. "I-I'm sorry. You remind me a lot of myself. I didn't think it was possible for fairies to be anything other than bright and bubbly. I'm surprised is all. I mean no disrespect."

I'm disappointed in myself. I've always felt closer to fairies than to witches. That I mucked up such an important relationship within the first five minutes shows how out of touch with everyone I've become.

"Differing viewpoints help species survive," she says bluntly. "Not everyone can be bridled with hope and optimism."

"You're right. Again, I'm so sorry." I reach into the folds of my robes to fiddle with Ambrossi's amulet. Though Thorn's a fraction of my size, the strength of her piercing glare makes me more nervous than I'd been during Iris' attack. I know I've messed up and potentially made an enemy of someone who should be my ally. I try to apologize again, but the words stick in my throat. If she really is like me, the apology will only further irritate her.

"You'll have to forgive her. She's under a lot of stress right now," Crowe says. He takes a small, hesitant step toward them. "She was recruited today, and it has *not* been a smooth ride."

"No worries," Callista says with a dazzling smile.

"*Hmmph*," Thorn adds, crossing her arms for good measure.

"Well, we should get going," Crowe says. "Just thought a quick meet-and-greet would help Lilith get settled in."

"I'll see you again soon!" Callista says and disappears back into the reeds.

Thorn follows her friend's lead without a word.

Crowe grasps my arm and pulls me away from the riverbank before I can tell them goodbye. When we're out of Thorn and Callista's earshot, he shoves me ahead of him. Not expecting the force, I topple to the ground. The cut on my elbow cracks open. I get up on my hands and knees and lift it up to show the fresh blood.

"What the hell?" I roar. If my magic reserves weren't so low, I might've thrown him into the river. As a true Aquais, he would have had no problem getting out again.

"Could you have been any ruder?" he snaps. "You're gonna get us *both* on the Sage's shitlist."

"Hey! I *apologized!*" I say and shuffle to a sitting position.

"Doesn't make what you did okay," he says. "You'd think you've never been in public. Honestly, I'm running out of sympathy for you. This isn't a game, and you're not a child. I don't care how badly your day is going, behavior like that will get you sent to see the Sage. If you think how she treated you today was bad, you have no idea what bad really is."

"It won't happen again. Geez," I spit out. I'm embarrassed by the scolding. "Chalk it up to a nervous breakdown. You know, from all the *stress.*" I try to stand, hoping my anger will be enough to keep me steady, but my legs buckle under my weight instead, and once again, I'm on the ground.

Crowe ruffles his shaggy, crimson hair before offering me his hand. "Let me help you, darling."

I smack it away and glare at him. "I don't need your help. I can help myself, thank you."

"I-I smell blood. Is everything okay?" Callista calls. Her eyes drop to my elbow, and her pupils shrink. "Oh, my Goddess!

Hang on!"

She flutters away, and I send a questioning glance to Crowe that he doesn't return. Callista comes back with a packet of green mush that reminds me of the stuff Ambrossi gave me when I cut my arm with the vase. She murmurs a few words and cleans the blood away from the wound before smearing the green stuff over it. She says a few more words then the paste disappears. The wound underneath is sealed shut as though I'd never injured it.

"Thank you, Callista."

She brings her tiny hands together and rests them against her cheek. "You're very welcome! Please do try to be careful!"

I gnaw the inside of my cheek to hold back a sarcastic remark. I've already made an enemy of Thorn; I don't want to do the same with Callista. I again try to climb to my feet, and Callista watches my struggle. She taps her tiny hand against my arm, and I'm able to stand with sudden ease. Shocked, I stare at her. She smiles, waves, and disappears into her home in the reeds.

The fairies really *are* powerful.

"Your arm looks much better, darling," Crowe says in a tone that tells me he's given up on our fight.

I break from my trance and whirl on him. "Stop! That's enough of the *darling* nonsense."

"*Well*, someone's showing her true colors," Crowe mutters.

"I have this entire time. Haven't you noticed?" I brush the dirt off my clothes. "I'm not a ragdoll you can toss around and control."

"I definitely have no right to control you, but the Sage

does," he says and pokes the rainbow earring in his ear for effect.

Frowning, I copy his movement and dig my nails into the skin around the ugly gem. "Because of *you*."

"I had orders! What was I supposed to do?"

I barely repress the urge to lunge and strike him with everything I've got. I can't remember a time I've ever felt so angry. It scares me. "Take me back to the Sage. I want to put in a formal request to go home."

Chapter Fifteen
A New Life

CROWE PROTESTS ALL the way back to Headquarters, but I barely hear him. It's as if I've been submerged under water, and the world is a static haze of sounds and colors. My anger is the only thing that exists. I don't want to be part of the Council. I don't want to carry the weight of the world on my shoulders. I can barely manage my own.

"Please reconsider!" Crowe says behind me.

It's the first coherent thing I've heard, but it doesn't slow me down. I hear a handful of grunts and groans as he shifts, but I don't want to face him. I'm sure he's chosen his favorite bird form to fly to Headquarters and warn them of my approach. I listen for the flapping of raven wings, but an ear-splitting roar comes from behind me instead.

I turn in time to see a grizzly bear charging at me with its jaws parted to show sharp teeth. Lifting a hand, I hope to scrape the bottom of my magic reserves for an ounce of power to help me fight back. I already have one mangled limb; I don't want another one. I try to hoist the massive bear off the ground, to throw him sideways.

Anything to weaken the oncoming attack.

Crowe doesn't slow, and panic sets in. Is he psycho enough to *attack* me?

I glance at my elbow, remembering that he shoved me to

the ground hard enough to cause me to bleed. I can't put anything past him. Pain clouds my mind like the worst migraine I've ever endured as I continue to strain. Tremors rock my body. With Crowe less than two meters away, I close my eyes and prepare myself for what's to come.

A sharp yelp cuts the air, and my eyes fly open. I see a smoldering patch of fur. Crowe drops to the ground and rolls in a patch of mud to put out the flames while I stare at my hand in astonishment.

Did the fire come from *me?*

I scan the riverbank for signs of an ally as Crowe shifts back to his human form. My bewilderment passes when he grins at me.

"You are *insane!*" I screech.

He holds a hand over his singed shoulder. "Maybe, but it worked, didn't it?"

"You had no idea it would! What was your Plan B? Dare I ask?" I demand.

"You only had two options—fight back or jump in the river. Plan B was up to you."

I glance down at my leg, not saying a word, before I drag my eyes back to him.

"I would've saved you, of course," he adds and rolls his eyes.

In retrospect, Tarj doesn't seem so bad compared to the whack job they paired me with. The moods Crowe has shown have all been vastly different—as different as summer and winter, with an occasional fall in between. I don't know what to expect next. "Just get away from me."

"That's not how this works," he informs me. "You're *my* apprentice. You're supposed to listen to *me*."

I laugh and continue trudging down the riverbank, away from the Advisory Council of Fairies and away from Crowe. I don't know how, but I manage to run the rest of the way to Headquarters. Callista's spell most likely has something to do with my sudden physical ability. Whatever the case, when I enter the wide archway at the end of the garden path, it wears off.

My entire body sags with exhaustion, but I push onward, desperate to get to the Sage before my legs give out completely. My lungs ache, but it's only a temporary distraction. When I pass through the common room, I look for signs of Tricia but don't see her. Instead, a pale girl with blonde hair sits in the seat beside the window. She peers over the top of her book through wide violet eyes as I storm through the room.

I swing open the door to the Sage's room and peer down the stone-lined corridor. When I emerge into her space, she's bent over her cauldron. She looks up with calm eyes as if she were expecting this. Expecting me.

"Lilith, dear, what can I do for you?" She dips the blade of her boline in the potion.

"I want to go home." I jab my finger in her direction. "I tried to be one of you. Gave it my best shot, but this isn't right for me."

"Have you checked with Crowe?" she asks and sets her damp knife on her desk.

I shake my head and collapse into the chair I sat in during my last visit, grateful for the chance to rest. "He was my final straw. He's nuts. He changed into a grizzly bear and attacked me when I was almost out of magic. Physically and mentally, I can't handle this. I think you'd better find someone else who better fits this role."

"Who do you propose should take the spot?" the Sage inquires and tips her head.

Under her gaze, my mind goes blank, and I falter. "I-I don't know." I lick my lips in frustration. "But there's got to be someone better adjusted than me."

"I'm sensing a deeper issue than what Crowe's done. Talk to me, Lilith," she says and folds her hands together on her lap.

"I-it's all too much. My powers a-and the forced Dedication." The slight hiccup causes me to pause. *Oh, Goddess, don't start crying.* The Sage's expression doesn't change, and reluctantly, I continue. "I miss my family and friends."

"You don't think the rest of the Council misses their loved ones?"

"I'm sure they do, but they like this job."

"With time, I'm sure you'll come to enjoy the job as well. This is a difficult period in your life. Things are changing, and that takes some adjusting. Even if you hadn't been recruited by the Council, your life would be changing today. Your Coven duties would've changed, and you would've had to move out of your parents' house. Just because this isn't the way you pictured your life going doesn't mean you'd feel any different if you had taken that alternate path."

I shuffle under her stare. My rage dwindles, and hopelessness begins to replace it. "Maybe," I concede. "But never seeing them again? Feels like a punishment."

"It's not forever, dear," she assures me with a throaty

laugh.

I perk up and lean forward to look at the green potion in her cauldron. "Then why does it feel like it?" The questions come easier when I don't look directly at her.

"Change is hard. You'll always have special feelings for your friends and family, but your new covenmates will be the people you come to care about the most."

I compare Helena and Clio to Tarj and Crowe and instantly shoot down any trust in her statement. "Yesterday, things were fine, and now, I'm here, and everything's different."

"You're growing up, Lilith, which means turning a new leaf. There's no changing the past, but you can change the way you think about it. A sour disposition will not solve your problems, but it will make things harder on you and those around you," she says while sorting through a pile of leaves on her desk. "You attract what you think about. If you think about your fear, you will always be afraid."

"That may be true, but I'm not ready. I'm begging you to take this earring out now." I move my hair aside so she can get a good look at it. I'm sure all it would take is one spell uttered from her lips to free me from the curse of a new life. Problem is, I don't know how to get her to say it.

"I can't do that," she says, enunciating each word. "You're not the first witch, nor will you be the last, who does not wish to be part of the Council. This is a hard job loaded with responsibilities and threats. If I let everyone go, there would be no governing Coven. And with no governing Coven, there would be chaos."

I pull my lips tight and stare out the window at the

magnificent garden beyond.

"Let me tell you a little story, Lilith," the Sage says. "When the others were brought here, they were unhappy. They didn't want to do this, didn't think they *could* do this. Because so many of them are unique in their abilities, they didn't have anyone to learn from, anyone to teach them. So, they taught themselves, and the Council was the best way for them to go about it."

Where is she going with this?

"My point," she says, and she leans forward to rest her weathered hands on the edge of her desk, "is to look at them now. You'd have never guessed any of them started out where you are."

Irritation gnaws at my stomach. That wasn't much of a story. "I don't believe this."

"Would you be up for making a deal?"

"What kind of deal?"

The Sage leans closer. "Give the Council a chance. Crowe especially. I know he's a little rough around the edges, but have him teach you everything he knows, and I guarantee you'll be better for the experience."

"Yeah, yeah, I've heard this before," I say, and I roll my eyes. "Say I do go through with it. What do I get out of it?"

"I'll let you go home for a day, talk to your family and friends, do whatever you'd like on Ignis soil. When evening comes, you'll return to the Grove with your priorities straight. The Council will be your number one goal. No more denial, and no more trying to leave. You will focus on developing your powers and adjusting to your new role. Am I clear?"

I stare at her through hooded eyes. On the surface, the deal is perfect, but I wither at the thought of the intense training that'll happen upon my return. If she's okay with Crowe's treatment today, I don't want to think about how bad things will become.

"You promise?" I keep a veil over my true emotions lest she sense them and use them against me.

"If it consoles you, we can write the terms in a Witch's Deal."

A Witch's Deal is the most intense promise witches can make to each other. Considering everything she's already done, I should scoop it up, except it feels too easy. It feels as if there's a catch waiting to smack me upside the head when I least expect it.

The Sage watches me, waiting patiently for an answer I'm not sure of.

"You've lied to me before," I say. My voice is stiff. "You lied about the Dedication. So even though I want to believe you, I don't."

"That's fair," she agrees and scoops a handful of brittle leaves into her palm. "But you must know I did not lie to you because I never offered you the choice of going home. I told you who you are, that you are one of us, and now it's official. Tarj stopped you from getting the piercing of your choice for a reason. I'm sorry if you feel you were misled in anyway."

Anger flares inside me, and it takes effort to hold it back. If I'm rude, she might never make me an offer again. "After this trip, will I be allowed to see my friends and family again, or are you giving me my shot to say my final goodbyes?"

The Sage stares into her cauldron and drops the leaf bits inside one by one. "If you complete your training, I promise you'll be allowed access to them whenever your heart desires, so long as it doesn't create a distraction, of course. Since you'll be representing Ignis, you will be granted free travel between here and there to consort with the Covenheads, as well as the Adept, who I believe this year, is your friend, Clio."

I grip the armrest of the chair a little tighter as I ask, "What are you going to do about Crowe? He could've hurt me today."

The Sage exhales a long breath, and I have the feeling I'm not going to like what she has to say.

"I'm not going to do anything."

I gape at her.

"I'm sure he was doing what he felt was best. I'll certainly have a talk with him about his behavior going forward, but as far as punishment? I don't believe it's necessary."

I lift my arm to show off my new wound, but I stop when I remember Callista healed it. "So, I'm bear meat now? He can hurt me any way he sees fit, and that's considered training?"

"There are boundaries, my dear, but things only seem extreme because you have no threshold to compare them to. Let's face it, Lilith. You need to be toughened up, and Crowe is perfect for that. He's eager to prove his worth, and he's new to having an apprentice, so he's bound to make mistakes. Before you doubt him, keep in mind that he taught himself how to use his powers. That's quite an accomplishment."

"Yeah." The defeat creeps in. I'm trapped between a rock and a hard place. I want to spill my concerns to the Sage, but I don't because I know she'll overlook them.

"Only a few hours together, and he's managed to get you to unlock your pyrokinetic powers. Love him or hate him, you should thank him for that," the Sage points out. "People believe

Crowe was born in the wrong Coven. I think you can appreciate what that feels like."

Much the way you were.

The whispered words float through my mind, but her lips stay shut. Now I'm sure it's a thought. The idea that I'm listening to the Sage's mind makes my palms sweat. Finally, I have a power I can use to my advantage.

It reminds me of Iris' words again: *Deny it all you want, but you wonder about your leg. I know you do. You're too smart to believe their lies.*

If I was indeed born in the wrong Coven, it would explain why my parents tripped over themselves to keep the truth hidden from me.

Chapter Sixteen
Settling In

I ACCEPT THE Sage's deal, as I'm uncertain what other options I have. I can still force the Sage into following through with the Witch's Deal, but I don't see much point in it. With or without it, she'll find a way to get what she wants, I'm sure.

As I rise to take my leave, I feel an odd gratitude for the Sage and her willingness to listen. Even if she did push away my concerns, she has, so far, shown me more kindness than the rest of the Council combined. Thoughts of Tricia, Tarj, and Crowe bring the darkness back. I dread the next interactions we'll share.

I make my way into the common room, so wrapped up in my thoughts, I bump into Crowe. I tense as I wait to see what, if anything, he has to say. He looks at my earring and sighs.

"What did she say?" he asks.

"She said I can go to Ignis." I meet his gaze with the certainty that he'll challenge me and tell me not to go.

His eyes go to my earring again. "You're not done here though?" he inquires. He shifts his weight to his right leg as if he's prepared to stop me if I decide to walk away mid-conversation.

"No. I have to come back and train. That's the deal."

"Well, good," Crowe says with a small, brilliant smile. "I was nervous about losing my first apprentice so soon!"

I don't bother to voice how frustrated I am as I hobble

past him. Something tells me he won't understand anyway.

His voice stops me. "Hey, I'm sorry for earlier."

I round on him. "For which part? Shoving me into the dirt or changing into a monster that could've torn me limb from limb?"

"Both," he says. "The training I endured here was harsh. They tried everything they could to further my magic—burning me, freezing me, leaving me in the elements. I hated it. I cried every day about how unfair life was to give me such magic." He pauses to take a breath. "Then I realized it wasn't the extreme conditions that would help me, it was my own tenacity. I wanted you to learn that right away, but it was too soon, and again, I'm so sorry for it."

Doesn't explain his fit after meeting the Council fairies, I think, tempted to remind him of that before I reconsider. Maybe that one was my fault.

Compared to when I met him earlier in the day, he looks like a deflated version of himself. Defeated. This is his way of trying to make peace. I should jump at the opportunity. But part of me isn't so easily convinced. He's unstable and hard to read.

That's why you should apologize. A voice floats through my head that's not my own.

I scrunch my face as I search for the source. Crowe and I are the only ones in the common room, so I push it away.

I lift my hand to stop him from rambling. "At least some good came out of today," I say in a tone colder than intended. "Just… nothing super crazy in the future, please."

"Those are terms I can agree to," Crowe says, visibly relieved.

"So, what comes next?"

Crowe glances at the clock behind him. "It's close to dinner time."

My stomach grumbles at the mention of food. As Crowe leads me to the hallway perpendicular to the grand archway, the scents of a dozen different dishes reach me at once.

"You're gonna love the meals," Crowe assures me. "They're my favorite thing about this place."

I only half-acknowledge him as I make my way into the enormous dining room. A long buffet table in the center stretches the length of the room. It's piled high with silver dishes and food. Blankets with each coven color hang on the walls, one for each, except for Aquais which shares a space with Aens. The two blankets cover a large portion of the windows that make up one of the walls. A few members of the Council, including Tricia and the blonde girl I saw in the common room, are already seated. I've yet to see the representative from Alchemy, and I wonder who it is.

Tarj is missing from the meal as well. Is he still in Ignis, trying to smooth things over after my sudden disappearance. To avoid introductions, I sit at the least crowded end of the table. As I reach for a small roll, Crowe slides into the seat beside me.

"You'll want to eat more than that." He spears a steak with his fork and drags it onto his plate.

"Don't you worry, I will," I say and bite into the soft piece of bread.

Crowe begins to wolf down his steak like an animal, and I wonder if he's aware of how many traits his animal and human forms share. Halfway through my roll, I make the mistake of glancing up and meeting another Council member's eyes. I shoot my gaze back down to my plate, embarrassed. I'm sure the Sage insisted I come to this meal to meet the others and make friends, but being friendly is the last thing on my mind. I'm focused on me and on meeting the biological requirements necessary to keep me alive.

A bite of food sticks in my throat, and I cough loudly to dislodge it before it chokes me. Crowe hands me a goblet of punch as he swallows the last bite of his steak. I down the entire cup, then take a few rough breaths once the liquid's gone.

"Thank you," I say and hide my embarrassment behind my veil of my hair.

"Don't mention it," he says.

I'm reaching for a steak when I realize there's another witch missing from the table. "Where's the Sage?"

"She doesn't eat with us," Crowe replies. He drops another hunk of meat on his plate. "She takes her meals in her room. Basically, the only time you'll see her is if she requests to see you. Otherwise, she's a ghost."

"Oh."

I'm not sure why the information is such a surprise to me. I hide my emotions by scooping a variety of vegetables and other dishes onto my plate, then I sample each one. The more I eat, the more the pains in my stomach lessen, and I start to relax.

Tricia wipes her mouth with an embroidered napkin, then gets up. My heart pounds. Somehow, I already know she's going to approach me. I close my eyes, waiting. She stops at my side.

"How was the tour?" she asks.

I resume eating, determined to ignore her. The way she

held me down at the Dedication Ceremony hasn't left my mind.

Crowe frowns, grabs her arm, and pulls her toward him. "Lay off, Tricia, she's had a rough day. Give her some time to decompress."

"Fine," she says and gives me a fake smile. "Sweet dreams, Lilith. I'll speak with you tomorrow."

"Whatever," I grumble and sip the last of the liquid in my goblet. I have a new concern, but I wait for Tricia to walk away before I share it with Crowe. "Where am I going to sleep?"

"For now, you'll share a room with Tarj while we ready something for you," he says. "It's not the most comfortable arrangement, but it'll only be for a day, two tops."

I can't put into words how much I hate the idea. I almost suggest sleeping in the Common Room, but I won't win the argument. "I guess that'll work."

"I'll show you where it is," Crowe says, and we rise from the table.

A couple of the other members' eyes fall on me, but I pretend not to notice as Crowe and I head toward the Common Room.

"If things are too weird between you and Tarj, you're more than welcome to crash with me tonight. Or even Tricia, though I know she's not your favorite person."

"I'll try to make this work," I say, remembering the contingencies of the Sage's deal. No matter what's thrown my way, I have to try.

Crowe leads the way through the garden, to a path that winds through a strip of trees and toward a group of buildings hidden among the vast foliage of the Grove. Compared to the simple homes of Ignis witches, it's eye opening.

But then, so has been this entire experience.

A cobblestone path connects each building. They're virtually the same with the exception of a stripe of color on each door. Crowe knocks on the red one.

"Come in!" Tarj calls from inside.

Crowe opens it, and Tarj dips his head in greeting from the chair he's seated in.

"Lilith was wondering about sleeping arrangements," Crowe explains.

"Ah. Well, I can handle it from here," Tarj says with a dismissive wave of his hand.

Crowe takes two steps toward the door before turning back to me. "See you tomorrow, Lilith. Good luck in Ignis."

The door clicks shut. "What's happening in Ignis tomorrow?"

"The Sage is letting me go back to say goodbye because I didn't get the chance before I was marked," I say as I flick the ugly earring.

"If tying up loose ends is what it takes to get you under control, I'm all for it."

"You're from Ignis. Don't you miss it? Everything's so different here. Too different."

"Of course, I miss it, but I also accept that that part of my life is over. I've made this my home. The same way you need to."

I gnaw the inside of my cheek. Is everyone going to feed me the party anthem when I try to explain my feelings?

I go so long without speaking, Tarj continues, "As you can see, there's not much room here, but it's comfortable."

I take it all in. Red blankets hang on the wall like they do in the dining hall. On the wall by the bed are shelves covered in various knickknacks from Ignis. There's a desk and chair, and on the opposite side of the room, a tiny nook with blankets and pillows. The room is warmer than the entirety of the Grove.

"You can sleep here," he says, gesturing to his bed. "I'll take the cot."

I don't argue. I limp over to the bed and sit down on the sheets, relieved. I've been on my feet too long, and the muscles in my damaged limb throb in desperate need of rest.

Tarj pulls a night shirt out of his dresser and tosses it to me. "Here. The Sage had it custom made for you."

"Thank you."

He nods and opens the door. "I'll step out and give you some privacy."

As soon as the door closes, I let my cloak drop and struggle out of my dress. I want to change quickly, but exhaustion makes it hard. Night clothes in place, I sink into the softness of Tarj's mattress.

"Are you good?" he calls through the door.

"Yes!"

Tarj comes back in and adjusts the sheets on his cot. "Comfortable?"

"I am, thank you."

"You're welcome." He plops down on the mess of blankets, sets his head on the pillows, and stares through the window at the moonlight streaming in. "I hope this goes to show we're not all monsters here."

It's such an unexpected statement that it shatters the peace

I've managed to cultivate. "But some of you are?"

Tarj stays quiet.

I seize the opportunity to pick up the conversation we dropped. "Are we gonna talk about Willow again, or are you going to pretend you weren't about to tell me her story?"

Tarj tenses and pulls his blanket up to his chin. He's silent.

I stare hopelessly at the dark ceiling. I've never been good at making friends, but here, I seem to swing and miss every time.

Just when I start to drift off to sleep, Tarj sighs. "It's not that I don't *want* to tell you, it's more like I shouldn't."

"Why?"

"She's been forgotten, and that's what the Sage wants. The last thing we need to do is pry open the wound. Some things are better left buried."

Chapter Seventeen
Reaching Out

IN THE MORNING, I'm woken by Tarj prodding me in the ribs with much more force than necessary. I gather the blankets around me, sit up, and stare at him.

"Is something the matter?" I ask, as I rub my eyes.

"It's morning," Tarj announces with a gesture to the window. Early morning rays pour into the room. "And you had nightmares the entire night."

I drop my hands and look at him, spotting the creases and bags. He looks as if he hasn't slept a wink.

"I did?" I ask, sucking in air through my teeth. When I try to remember anything, nothing comes to mind. "I'm sorry."

"I'm going to get breakfast," he replies. "You should join us before you leave."

The door clicks closed behind him, and I toss the blanket off. Yawning, I test my weak leg and stand, then head for the door on the other side of the room. Inside the bathroom, I spot a pile of clothes on the sink along with a note.

Lilith,

This outfit comes from the Sage. Please don't disrespect her by choosing something else.

Tarj

The shirt is made of a thin material more common in Ignis than in any other Coven. I pull it on before picking up the black capris made of almost the same material. Now that I'm dressed, I try to straighten my knotted hair with my fingers. Despite a night of nightmares I don't remember having, I feel better today.

My stomach growls, and I'm excited for breakfast. I cross through the garden and grand archway in high spirits. In the dining room, I take my place beside Tarj. I'm glad to see Tricia is nowhere around. An unfamiliar Council member is seated beside the blonde girl with the violet eyes, and like the day before, I avoid eye contact while scarfing down a few bites of food. By the time Crowe arrives, I'm already full and itching to be on my way. I pass him on my way out of the dining hall.

"Where are you off to in such a rush?" he asks.

"Home," I say. I don't wait for his reply before I slip out of the building.

I cross the garden and walk through the trees, trying to pinpoint the place where Tarj had summoned the wyrm. It's early in the day, but it's already hot, and I'm glad for the clothing the Sage lent me. I'm sure it's twice as warm in Ignis.

I see the glint of the silver whistle, and I snag it and blow it as hard as I can. The wyrm emerges from the dirt and stares down at me with such an intense expression, I'm worried it won't help me. A soft coo erupts from its chest, and it sets its wing down to encourage me to climb on.

"Thank you," I tell it as I settle on a spot near the back of its head.

It makes another soft noise and slithers through the grass and trees. The green fades to brown, and the pent up tension from the last twenty-four hours melts away. The wyrm stops short of Ignis, and I'm tempted to ask what's wrong before I realize it's probably uncomfortable in the heat. It's accustomed to the forest of the Grove, and it's done me a favor by carrying me this far.

I slide down its back, look into its eyes, and give it a soft smile before it dives underground to head home. It's not too far of a walk to the center of Ignis, and I'm in such good spirits, I don't mind the trip. When I make it to Angel's home, I hear footsteps behind me. I'm pulled into someone's arms. The air leaks from my lungs with a squeak.

"Thank the Goddess, Lilith. I thought, for sure, they were going to kill you!" Clio says and somehow hugs me tighter.

I look up at him and press my cheek to his chest in an awkward attempt to hug him back, but my arms are still pinned at my sides. He lets go, pulls back, and swipes a lock of hair from my face.

"They didn't hurt you, did they?" Helena, who has appeared at Clio's side, asks.

"No, I'm okay," I reply, unable to tell if I'm lying or telling the truth as I force the words out.

"What happened yesterday?" Clio asks. "I waited, but you didn't come back. I even reached out to Fern, but she wasn't much help."

"They marked me." I show them my despised earring.

Clio reaches out with shaking fingers to stroke the gem. His green eyes harden. "Did you consent to this?"

I shake my head. "The Sage ordered it. I didn't know, and well, you saw them drag me out of there."

Clio presses his lips together in a straight line.

"The Sage?" Helena gasps. Her voice is full of wonder.

I consider what to tell them about the past day, knowing the truth may destroy their sense of wonder. All the interactions I've had with her so far have been odd, uncomfortably so, and I don't foresee that changing anytime soon.

"Yeah. Apparently, I caught her attention by saving Tarj at the Arcane Ceremony."

"Did she mention Iris?" Clio asks.

I shake my head, though I know he suspects that's the true motive behind the Sage's actions. "I almost got Tarj to talk about Willow though."

"Who's Willow?" Helena asks. Her face is scrunched up as if she's eaten something foul.

Clio's face goes tight as he says, "A witch who was like Lilith. She was executed by the Council."

"Why would they do that?" Helena asks, baffled.

"Who really knows? There's theories, but no one can say for sure." Clio stares into the distance, then adds, "What did he say about her?"

"He seemed surprised I knew who she was," I admit. "When I tried to bring the subject up again last night, he shut me down. Said the Sage wanted her story buried."

Clio grunts. "Of course, he'd say that."

"You think it's odd too?"

"If you ask me, someone got a little punishment between those two conversations."

"That doesn't make me feel better," I say and look at Helena. She's been silent, her eyes darting between us.

"What's she like... in person?" Helena asks. She's

completely disconnected from the conversation, still focused on the Sage.

"Reserved," I reply, carefully choosing my words. *Also, a manipulative liar.*

"She requested you personally," Helena murmurs and takes a step backward as if she can't comprehend that.

Clio and I watch her like she's a dangerous animal. She's as unpredictable as one. A flash of emotion goes through her eyes before she turns and bolts, long orange hair streaming behind her.

"Helena, wait!" I'm intent on following her, but Clio grabs my wrist and brings me back to focus.

"Let her go."

Wistfully, I stare after her. I want to follow her, to comfort her like old times, and be there for my best friend. But I can't afford the time that would cost me. I go slack in Clio's grip. "Everything's changing," I say with a hint of despair. I stare at the red gem in his ear.

"They promoted me today," he says, tapping it. "I'm going to be helping train the others." Clio doesn't seem to notice my tone because his is light and airy. In contrast to the previous conversation, it's almost haunting.

I smile. The expression feels odd after the day of frowning I've endured. "That's great news!"

His eyes gleam. "Considering I'll have access to HQ, it means we don't have to lose touch."

Remembering the Sage using Clio as a bargaining chip to get her way the previous day causes me to grit my teeth. "I wish things were going as well for Helena," I say and cast another glance in the direction she disappeared.

"She'll be okay," he says.

"I know." And I do. But I worry about how long that process will take, and how much harder it will be for her to have to do it without me.

"What have you got planned for the rest of the day?" Clio asks.

"I need to visit Fern."

"What about your parents?"

I close my eyes and shake my head. *Much the way you were,* the Sage's words bounce around inside my head. Forcing it all down, I say, "I burned that bridge, remember?"

Clio doesn't look convinced. "I'm sure if you go back, they'd be happy to see you. They should at least hear from you what's happened."

"I don't want to take the risk," I tell him. I feel certain they'll remember the fight as well as I do. And I don't want to spend my limited time reliving the same day I've already weathered.

Clio says, "Fair enough, I suppose. When do you think you'll come back to Ignis?"

I dig my nails into my palm. "Wish I knew. I've been told I'm not allowed to leave the Grove without the Sage's permission, and she wants me to focus on my training when I return. Today's kind of a one-time thing."

"Really?" he asks and runs a finger along his chin as if he's deep in thought.

"Yeah," I reply. I watch as he takes a step closer.

His gaze is strong and unrelenting as he stares at me. My heart flutters when he reaches out and touches my chin with his fingertips. I can't move, can't even breath, as I wonder what will come next.

"I guess this is the last chance for me to do this then," he whispers. His face is an inch from mine, and he kisses me.

He pulls me in. His other hand rests on my hip, and I go limp. When the shock wears off, I lean into the kiss and wrap my arms around his neck. He pulls away first and buries his face in the crook of my neck before setting his forehead against mine. Clio closes his eyes, and I can tell he's reveling in this.

I try to do the same, but when I open my eyes, he's gone. I touch my lips, the feeling of him still there before I smile and bow my head. I hope I'll get to see him again before I'm sent back to my prison at the Grove, but even if I don't, I have the sudden feeling everything is going to be okay.

Gauging the sun's position in the sky, I estimate that I have only a handful of hours before it starts to get dark. I try to not let the hope drain from me as I make my way to Fern's oasis, carefully organizing my thoughts. When I arrive, she's out and about, fluttering above the water as if she hasn't a care in the world.

She flaps her wings in greeting. "Lilith! Clio told me about the ceremony! Nice earring," she says. I try to determine if she's being serious or sarcastic, but I can't tell.

I collapse beside the water and curl my knees to my chest. I've always felt safe in Fern's oasis, but that comfort isn't enough this time.

"I don't want this," I say in a hoarse whisper.

Fern's face wrinkles. "But it's such an honor."

"That's not how you made it sound last time I was here,"

I point out. "I'm not a good fit." I stretch out my leg, and with a grimace, I poke the ugly, scarred skin on my calf.

"You know better than anyone that you're not limited by your injury," Fern says. She lands next to my leg, sets her fingertips on the devastated flesh, and traces a patch of it.

Thoughts of the bear incident with Crowe remind me of how helpless I felt. I'd never been so desperate. "I'm not so sure. The Council… they're strong."

"Of course they are. They're handpicked for a reason. The best of the best from each Coven," she says and tilts her head. "That includes *you*."

"But why me? That's what I can't figure out. I'm not the best. And I'm not special."

"You're stronger than you give yourself credit for."

"You sound like the Sage."

Fern's eyes go wide. "I'm sorry, I didn't mean to offend you."

I shake my head and feel guilty for giving her even an ounce of anxiety as I pluck a clover free from the dirt. "No, don't apologize. You're only trying to be supportive." I pause and watch her flap her wings. "Have you ever heard of the Advisory Council of Fairies?"

She stiffens. "Yes. Yes, I have." She fidgets with her collar and glances toward her home in the tree as if she's thinking about leaving me to drown in my questions. "If you must know, I served them for a short while a long, long time ago."

"What happened?"

"They dismissed me. Said I was too much of a troublemaker."

"You?" I ask. My mouth hangs open before I remember the incident with Tarj on the night Fern took me to speak with Iris. Maybe I don't know Fern as well as I thought I did.

"That's how I heard about Willow for the first time."

Now she's got my attention. "So, you know what happened?"

Fern chews her lip. "I-I don't. I wasn't told everything, just as you probably haven't been. The Council purposefully strings you along by deciding what information they'll feed you. Trust me."

Oh, I do.

"You feel as if the decision is unfair, don't you?"

"Of course. Didn't you?"

Fern drops her chin. "I was proud until I realized how hard it could be to fit in. The other fairies were so different. I wanted to help the humans, to blend in, but they wanted power and control. They sit on their perches and look down their noses at the rest of us, and I couldn't do that."

I nod in complete understanding.

"Can I say something that may help change your mind?" she inquires.

I glance at her, silently urging her to continue.

"The Sage is the most powerful witch in the Covens. If anyone has the answers to your questions about your accident, and the incidents with Iris and Willow, it'll be her."

Much the way you were, the Sage's words come back again, and I think I have more motivation to go back to the Grove after all.

THE COUNCIL

＊ ＊ ＊

HOURS LATER, AFTER I've left Fern's oasis behind, I step into the cool circle of stones around the altar at the center of Ignis. I take in the beauty of my second favorite spot and gaze at the strip of purple sky far above me. Taking in a breath of air heavy with humidity, I lean against the smooth stone and enjoy the breeze that blows through my hair.

Arms snake around my waist, and I turn my head slightly as Clio's scent engulfs me. "Almost time for you to go, huh?"

"Yeah." I lean into him. "I have to say goodbye to Ambrossi and Angel, and then it'll be time."

"Still against seeing your parents?" he asks. He turns me around to face him.

"I don't want to have bad memories. After I leave, just… tell them I love them. Please?"

"Of course," he says and hugs me tight. "Though I wish you didn't have to go."

"Yeah, me either," I reply. I can't imagine what horrors await me in the Grove.

"I expect you to check in as soon as your training's through," Clio says, as he touches me under the chin. "And whatever you do, please come back to me in one piece."

"Tell that to Crowe."

Clio stiffens. "What did he do?"

"He's a shapeshifter, and he went full grizzly on me when my magic reserves were almost empty."

"He *what?*" Clio demands. His nostrils flare as if he's ready to fight Crowe here and now.

165

"He wanted to see what I could do under pressure. It made me mad at the time, but I admit, it was a good tactic. I used pyrokinesis, Clio."

The struggle of emotions running through him is clear. "I'm proud of you, Li," he says with a forced smile, "but if I hear about them pulling any more stunts like that, I'm not going to be quite so calm."

"You don't need to fight for my honor. As soon as I figure out what I'm capable of, I'll fight back myself," I say. I smile at him, then my focus shifts past him to Ambrossi's house. Candlelight flares in one of the front rooms, and I have the feeling he's sitting nearby, listening in.

Clio notices my shift in focus. "I don't want you to be late, so I'll see you later, okay?"

He bends down to kiss me as deeply as he had the first time before he disappears into the twilight. I watch him until the shadows swallow him, then make my way to Ambrossi's hut. I knock twice on the door, and he calls for me to come in. The inside of his house smells of herbs and flowers, like the Sage's area. A huge circular table sits in the middle of the room, covered in a variety of plants.

Ambrossi peers up at me from his seat beside the table. His dark blue eyes are glazed over with exhaustion. Beside him, Angel holds a boline and slices a stem of lavender.

"Lilith! So nice to see you," Ambrossi greets me. "What can I do for you?"

At the sound of my name, Angel glances up.

"I want to say goodbye before I go back," I say and shuffle my feet awkwardly. "And Angel, I want you to know I'm sorry for missing my Coven duties. The last few days have… gotten away from me."

Angel sets down her knife and wipes her hands together to get rid of any clinging traces of plants. "It's okay, Lilith. I've heard the good news. I'm so proud of you!"

"T-thank you," I mumble, but I think about how misplaced that pride is.

"I always knew you were capable of great things," Ambrossi adds.

For a second, I'm unsure how to respond. I'm not used to be complimented for anything.

Angel senses my tension and says, "The Council picked out a new apprentice to cover your Coven duties, so don't you worry about a thing."

"Glad to hear it," I say. Then as an afterthought, "Who's the apprentice?"

"Your friend, Helena," she replies, as she resumes her work on a new stalk of lavender.

"Oh." What happened to Helena's last apprenticeship? Did she act out and get fired or did she just stop showing up?

"She's been helpful."

"What do your parents think of your new position?" Ambrossi asks. He pulls a flower I don't recognize out of a cubbyhole on the wall.

"I haven't exactly told them. Things are complicated," I say, for lack of a better explanation.

"Ah, I see," Ambrossi says, but there's a look in his eyes that says he understands exactly what's happened. "When I was chosen as Ignis' Healer, my parents had a difficult time adjusting.

Remember, things won't always be this hard."

Why does everyone keep telling me that?

"Do you have your amulet?" Ambrossi asks.

I dig in my pocket, pull it out, and hold it up.

He shoots me a thumbs up. "Good. If your pain gets out of hand, don't hesitate to get a pass from the Sage to visit me. I can't stress that point enough. I know the Council has their own Healer, but I've been taking care of you since I was an apprentice, so I'm the best person to treat you."

Something about the tone of his voice reminds me of Tarj. The tiniest waiver makes me think Ambrossi doesn't trust the Council to take care of me.

Why? I can't help but wonder.

The Council are revered as the best, brightest, and strongest in the land. What has Ambrossi seen that's taken away his complete trust in them?

Chapter Eighteen
Crossing Over

"*THE SAGE IS the most powerful witch in the Covens. If anyone has the answers to your questions about your accident, and the incident with Iris and Willow, it'll be her.*" Fern's words stick with me. They play over and over in my mind as I summon the wyrm and ride it to the border of the Grove. She's right. That much I know, but I'm unsure what I can do about it. What I *should* do about it. If I confront the Sage, will she answer me?

"So, did you get done all you wanted to do?" a voice calls from the woods as I climb down from the wyrm.

I jump and curse under my breath when I spot Crowe emerging from the tree line. "Were you following me?"

He nods, unfazed by my anger. "I wanted to make sure you were okay off grounds. It's vicious out there."

It's no better in here.

"Did the Sage tell you to do that?" I grumble. The deal had gone too smoothly. Of course, there were catches.

"No, she didn't," Crowe says and sticks his hands in his pockets, strolling to my side as if he doesn't have a care in the world. "I thought I'd take on an extra assignment and keep an eye on my apprentice. Make sure you made it back safe"

Had he tracked me since this morning? "That's uh, sweet and all, but I can look out for myself. Remember? That's how I landed in this mess in the first place."

He shrugs. "I meant no offense."

Right.

I stare at him for so long, I don't realize how much energy I'm pouring into the look, until I blink. A blast of telekinesis sends him flying across the clearing.

"T-that's for yesterday," I stutter, trying to seem as if I'm in control. As if I meant to do that.

Crowe groans, stands, and brushes himself off. "That's fair, I suppose."

"No hard feelings," I say in the same tone he'd said *I meant no offense* in. "I didn't expect to be ambushed. Though, really, I should expect anything from you people now, huh?"

Crowe rolls his eyes. "I'm glad you're back."

I can't muster up the energy to argue. I'm tired, and now, I have to readjust to the Grove. Permanently. Silence keeps us company on the way back to Headquarters. Crowe tries to keep pace with me so I exaggerate my limp to fall a few paces behind him. Despite the truce we called before I left, I have a feeling everything won't be rainbows and sunshine for the foreseeable future.

"There are two more people in the Grove you should meet before you call it a night," he says and glances at me. When he sees how far behind I am, he slows his pace to match mine.

"Members of the Council?"

"Of course. You have yet to meet the Aens and Alchemy representatives, though I'm sure you've seen them around."

"I have. What are their powers?"

"Hyacinth is a clairvoyant. She reads minds. She can

probably read our thoughts right now," he says and stares at the path ahead. "While clairvoyance isn't the rarest of gifts, the range at which she can hear is pretty remarkable."

The voice I'd heard in my mind the day before had no doubt been her trying to get an idea of who I am and what I'm about. Introductions aren't required for her to snoop around my life. All my fears and worries have been exposed, laid out on a silver platter, because I hadn't known to hide them.

There's no safety anywhere.

I now understand why the Sage wasn't surprised by anything I had to say. Hyacinth had most likely already told her all the dirty little secrets in every crevice of my mind. "And the other?"

"His name is Lynx. He's a healer," Crowe says.

"No surprise there," I murmur. "How does being a Healer get you into the Council?"

If any Healer should've been given the spot of Council Healer, it should have been Ambrossi. His legendary skills should've secured him the position years ago.

"Well, he's not very good at it yet, because—"

"New powers are hard to control. Got it."

"Don't tell anyone I said this, but he's been able to do something no other Healer has ever been capable of," Crowe says. He dips his face close to mine as if he's afraid of being overheard.

His statement catches my interest, and I walk closer to him. "What can he do?"

"He was able to heal an injury caused by magic. One that would've otherwise been fatal."

"Magical damage? As in, a wound caused by a witch? No

Healer is capable of that!"

I think of all the years Ambrossi has tried to heal my leg, the complex books he's studied, and the potions he's brewed, all in vain.

"Apparently he is," Crowe says. "I wish I could've seen it. I heard it caused quite an uproar in Alchemy. As you can imagine, it drew the Sage's attention and is why she brought him to the Grove."

"How long ago was this?"

"It's been a few years," he says, scratching the back of his neck as if he's trying to remember the exact day. "Before I joined the Council. The only one who can tell you much about it is Lynx, but you'll have to meet him first."

I stare into the distance as I try to get my emotions under control. Part of me is afraid that I might not be able to rein them in. My lungs ache on the verge of a panic attack, and I reach out, presumably for balance, but my telekinesis keeps me from collapsing.

I look up at him, face blanched. "I-D-do you think he—"

Crowe's face softens. "He might be able to help you, but I don't know how good that chance is. He's been in training for a while but his situation is the most complicated. He'd probably hurt more than help you at this point, and I don't think any of us want to take that risk."

I can't imagine my leg in worse condition, but I blink to try to hide my disappointment. "Right."

"Maybe one day," Crowe says, voice hopeful. Then brighter he says, "Come on. I think you'll enjoy meeting him."

I follow Crowe, steeling my nerves for whatever comes

next. Inside the building, Tricia is the first person I see. She is sitting in the seat farthest from the door, knitting a sweater. When Crowe and I enter the Common Room, she barely glances up at us. The blonde girl is seated in the corner. Her gaze is on me. A small smile graces her lips. A burly man sits in the seat beside her. He's older. If I had to guess, I'd say he's around Ambrossi's age. His shaggy, dirty-blonde hair conceals his aquamarine eyes as he stares down at the floor, hands clasped together in his lap as if he's deep in thought.

"Lilith, this is Lynx," Crowe says, gesturing to him.

I'm so tired, the words nearly escape me. My thoughts were on dropping to the carpet and sleeping, but at the sound of his voice, I remember the experience of meeting the Advisory Council of Fairies, and I cringe.

I'll make a better impression with these two, I tell myself. I limp toward the man Crowe had pointed out, hand extended, in my best attempt at civility.

When Lynx looks at me, it's my leg he sees first. He returns the handshake but doesn't speak.

"Over there, that's Hyacinth." Crowe gestures to the blonde.

She dips her head. *It's nice to meet you.* Her lips don't move with her words. Crowe stills beside me as if he's waiting for my greeting. *I know you can hear me. You did yesterday.* Her tiny voice floats through my mind again.

A-are you in my head? I ask, scrunching my face. I risk a glance at Crowe and wonder if he can hear the conversation too, but his face remains passive. *Why are you in my head?*

Congratulations, Lilith, it seems as if we both have the same power.

"Lilith! Are you okay?" Crowe asks. He waves his hand in front of my face. "Why are you staring at Hyacinth like that?"

I snap out of my trance. "Huh? Y-yeah. I'm fine," I manage, and I tear my eyes away from her.

"Are you gonna say hi or stand silently in the middle of the room the rest of the night?" he inquires.

I clear my throat, unsure how to explain what just transpired.

Chuckling, Hyacinth looks at the floor. *We'll talk soon*, she promises.

Of all the people I've met in the Grove, she's the only one I believe could be a friend. I'm weirdly glad she can read my mind. Otherwise, I never would've let her in to find out.

"The Sage will want to know you're back," Crowe says and looks at Hyacinth. There's a knowing gleam in his eyes as if he can guess there's something between us that's deeper than what he can see.

I almost expect him to ask about it as he leads the way to the Sage's door, but he doesn't. He knocks, eyes shining with an unknown emotion before he sends me inside. I trace the stones as I walk, dreading the conversation before me. Part of me fears the Sage might force me into the Witch's Deal she promised earlier to ensure I keep up my end of the agreement.

"Lilith, my dear, feeling better?" she prompts as soon as I emerge from the walkway.

She's seated in her usual place by the window, with a book open on the table. The scent of herbs fills the air.

"Yes, thank you," I say politely.

"Have you had a chance to meet the rest of your

covenmates?" she asks, closing her book.

I awkwardly slip into the seat across from her. "I think so."

"Good, good. Now that your mind is clear you can properly focus on the work at hand."

"May I ask you a question?" I start. I consider adding *ma'am* to end of the sentence to really push my attempt at civility, but it sticks in my throat. I doubt she's the type to enjoy the title much anyway.

She arches a thin eyebrow. "Only if I may ask you one first."

"Anything." I wring my hands and wonder what the *Sage* could possibly want to ask. Judging by the look on her face, I won't like it.

"How long have you been able to read minds?" she asks and takes a sip from her mug.

I stiffen, caught off guard by the question. My nails dig into the soft material on the chair. Should I answer her honestly? "Who says I can do that?"

"I caught it during our last talk. There's not much I don't notice around here."

"Right." I scratch the back of my neck with the disheartening realization that between her and Hyacinth, I'll be incapable of keeping anything to myself from now on. "Like the rest of my powers, I'm not very good at it yet."

"I don't expect you to be. Part of your struggle in coming to terms with your role seems to be the belief that we expect immediate perfection. We don't. All we ask is that you do your best. We will find a way to bring out any power for which you show a slight inclination. Guaranteed."

I bob my head and train my eyes on the edge of her desk.

"On a side note, I think Hyacinth is thrilled to see what you can do."

It seems like it. I remember how the pretty girl's eyes had lit up when I responded.

You're so sweet, Lilith!

Hyacinth? Get out of my head.

"I wonder if you would benefit from training with *all* members of the Council at some point," the Sage says. A coy smile crosses her weathered face as if she's already got my entire future mapped out for me.

"All of them?" I ask. I run a list of their powers through my mind. "Tricia and Lynx can't possibly teach me a thing. I really don't think Crowe has much to offer either, besides teaching me the ropes. Hyacinth might, but I doubt the others can help."

"That's where you're wrong, my dear! You'd be surprised what a lot of focus and determination can do."

"Wait… are you saying…" I pause and stare at her, remembering my Arcane results. It's hard to see the true intention behind the Sage's actions, but I think I can guess. "Do you think I'll develop their powers?"

"Anything is possible."

Besides living a normal life.

"Don't sell yourself short. You've come a long way. Remember, a little over a week ago, people thought you were UnEquipped."

What a simple time that was. Half my life has been lived in only a handful of days. I feel the same as I did when my powers first reared their ugly head, but I'm not who I used to be. I can't be.

The thought sits in my gut like a rock.

"Can I ask my question now?" My voice is weak, and it's hard to hear to my own ears.

"Of course," the Sage says, grinning as though she's eager to hear it.

Everything about her expression and demeanor is pleasant, friendly, but I don't know how to get the words out of my mouth. "Do you know… the *truth* about me?"

The Sage clasps her hands and leans back in her seat, thoughtful. "I wondered how long it would be before you asked me."

"Is that a yes?" My heart pounds with a surge of adrenaline, and I can't tell if I'm excited or ready to throw up.

"Knowledge can be a burden as well as a blessing."

"What does that mean?" I demand. My shoulders slump with an overwhelming feeling of defeat that seems cruel after the hope I'd felt first.

"There are some things in this life that you must face alone. Birth is one of them. Death another. Sometimes, things won't be clear to you until it's the right time for you to know," she says.

That's the biggest line of crap they've tried to feed me so far.

I flare my nostrils. A surge of telekinesis picks her book up off her desk and flings it across the room. "I hear you perfectly. You know, but you won't tell me. Times like this make me wonder if the fiasco of bringing me here is some sort of twisted joke that everyone is in on except me."

The Sage quietly watches my fit. Her mouth is twisted in an odd expression as she waits for me to finish.

Something about it makes me angrier, and I sit up, holding the edge of her desk. "What do you have to lose by telling me?" I ask, my words harder and harder to hear. I want to scream, to shout, but my body doesn't cooperate. An overwhelming wave of sadness puts the fire out.

The Council purposefully strings you along by deciding what information they'll feed you. Fern's words float through my head.

"I mean no ill will toward you and have no bad intentions." She scoops up the book from where it landed by her feet and puts it back on her desk. "I simply believe it is not my place to tell you."

The corners of my eyes burn with unshed tears. Normally, I would be able to control them, but this conversation on top of my exhaustion equals all self-control out the window.

I'm ready to curse at the Sage when Hyacinth's voice floats through my head. *I may be able to tell you the things she is unwilling to.*

Chapter Nineteen
The Poisoning

HYACINTH'S EYES ARE on me when I stumble into the Common Room. She giggles when I trip over my foot, but I ignore it and approach her, almost giddy. It feels as if victory is in my grasp. After the trials of the past few days, part of me doubts the answers can come so easily. What if this turns out to be a set up? Some sort of test orchestrated by the Sage that I'm failing by approaching her?

Hyacinth reads the chaotic stream of my thoughts and offers a gentle smile. I don't hide behind a filter. She's been in my head for days and knows my demons as well as I do. I use the opportunity to prod her mind, but it seems empty. Too empty, as if she's purposefully keeping it clean.

Hyacinth's violet eyes shine when I slip into the seat beside her. *It's nice to be able to communicate like this. I prefer it. Anyone can eavesdrop when you talk out loud. But this? It's peaceful.*

I don't see Crowe, and I wonder where he went in such a hurry. Through the glass panes on the far wall, I study the night outside. Tricia is still content with her knitting, but Lynx has moved to sit by the door. His elbows rest on his knees, and his unfocused eyes stare into space. I can't help wondering what he's thinking about so intently.

Hyacinth sets her hand on mine, and I jump at the contact. *A-am I the only one other than you who can do this?* I ask. I scratch my cheek nervously.

She nods. *I've been on the Council a long time, and I've seen members come and go. Each of them has unique gifts. Never have I had a conversation of this caliber in this room. Clairvoyance is a rare gift.*

What do you know about me? I ask, afraid of what she'll say.

Hyacinth goes rigid. *Bits and pieces; what I know of everyone, really. The biggest misconception people have about mind readers is that we see everything. We don't. Some people are more open than others, and the same is true of their thoughts.*

Her words make me feel slightly better. I don't know if the Sage asked her to pry into my thoughts, but it's reassuring to know I'm not the open book I assumed I was.

Have you ever met someone whose mind you couldn't read?

No.

Even UnEquipped minds?

She prods my mind and draws me back to the memory of when I'd read my mother's thoughts in Ignis. *But you already knew that. Are you testing me, Lilith?*

I prefer to be called Li.

Let's cut to the chase. The Sage is the only one with all the answers. I'll try to help you anyway I can, but it's best you learn that now to avoid any misunderstandings.

I utter a string of expletives in my head but carefully conceal them in the depths of my brain. The serene expression on Hyacinth's face lets me know my cloaking is working. Maybe she's not really trying to be my friend. Maybe this is her version of the bear incident with Crowe or the mind control faux pas with Tricia at the Dedication Ceremony.

Hazing for the new witch.

You gave me false hope, I tell her and make it clear how unimpressed I am.

I'm sorry. I want to tell you, really I do, but there's only so much I know.

I look at Tricia and Lynx. Tricia doesn't so much as glance at me. Her interest in forging a friendship seems to be over. The novelty of my newness is already wearing off. As far as friends go, maybe Hyacinth is my best bet.

They'll warm up to you eventually, Hyacinth reassures me. She tucks a strand of flowing blonde hair behind her ear.

I flinch. I hadn't cloaked that thought. Rather than be embarrassed, I ask, *How is it you can only know half the story?*

You've been in the Sage's presence. Tell me, have you been able to read her mind?

I'm sure the Sage thought plenty of things during our talks, but none of them had reached me. *Much the way you were.* One line made it through, and I'm still certain that's because she wanted it to. Slowly, I shake my head.

That's because she puts up barriers. It's a lock and key system, if you will, that keeps us out if she doesn't want to be heard. Anyone can put up a barrier if they really want to, but compared to the Sage, everyone else's are like paper.

Why am I able to hear thoughts? I ask.

You've already figured out you're not who they say you are.

"Yeah, yeah," I mutter out loud.

Lynx looks at me. "You say something?" he asks and raises an eyebrow.

Hyacinth jumps out of her seat, horror in her violet eyes. Her lips part as if she's about to speak, but she says nothing.

She's reading a thought. I strain to pick up whatever it is.

Silence. I remember what Crowe said about the range of her ability.

She rushes over to Lynx, her petite footsteps barely making a sound on the rug and sets her hands on his knees. He looks up at her through uncertain, aquamarine eyes.

"Callista's in trouble!" she says. Her voice quivers as if it had been a fight to utter those three words.

Lynx jumps up and rushes out the door, leaving Hyacinth behind. I shake off my shock and start to follow Lynx, but Hyacinth stops me.

"Where are you going?" she demands. She looks at me as if she thinks I'm the craziest person she's ever seen.

"To help," I say and race off though I don't know if I possibly can.

I don't see Lynx as I travel across the Grove. I open my mind and listen for voices to help me pinpoint Callista and Thorn's home among the reeds. I'm confident other emergencies will happen in my time on the Council, but this is the first one I'm part of, and I want to be on top of it… even if I'm not entirely sure what I'm doing or if I can help.

Despite the rising pain in my legs and lungs, I don't stop as I approach the riverbank. Commotion rattles the still night air as I break through the foliage. Lynx is already there. He's crouched on his knees in the mud. Callista lies on the ground in front of him. Her tiny eyes are closed, and her body is limp. Her radiant, pink wings are faded, almost see through, beneath her.

"I-is she—" I begin. I hold my hand over my mouth.

"Dead?" Thorn guesses. She's hovering a foot above

Callista. Her midnight black wings blend into the night as she looks between me, Lynx, and Callista. Although her face is empty of emotions, there's a sparkle akin to grief in her eyes. "No."

"What happened to her?"

"The water… someone poisoned it." Crowe's voice drifts out of the foliage a few feet away.

"Did she drink it?" I ask.

"No. She's connected to nature. The river especially. When the temperature changes or the water becomes polluted, it affects her," Thorn says.

"Will she be okay?"

Lynx looks up at me. His faced is creased with the onset of tears. I interpret the look. It doesn't look good for Callista.

"Why would someone do this?" I ball my hands into fists. "She hasn't hurt anyone."

"If I had to guess, I'd say it's the witches who worked with Iris," Crowe says. "She threatened that others would come. And if that's the case, it makes sense why they would target our river."

My heart pounds. If they came this close, were they searching for me? Did they do this because I'm here instead of in Ignis?

"Callista collapsed about ten minutes ago," Thorn says in answer to Lynx's question that I completely blocked out.

"Then the culprit is still close," I say.

Compared to Lynx, Callista seems so tiny, so precious, and my guilt for not keeping her safe bubbles to the surface. All I want is to hurt the person responsible for hurting her. I rush down the riverbank before deciding what I'll do if I find someone.

"Wait! Don't go out there alone," Crowe calls from

behind me. "You could be headed for a trap!"

The sound of his footsteps trailing me is insignificant compared to the thoughts coursing through his head. He's torn between stopping me and letting me unleash my rage on whoever's responsible.

The bushes up ahead rustle, and I tense, ready to pounce. A woman emerges. She's maybe a year or two older than I am, with short, brown hair that curves around her triangular face. Her expression softens when she sees me, and it doesn't matter how angry I was, how ready for combat, the malice in me drains away. The attack I'd been ready to send dissipates into energy. I can't remember the reason for my rage.

Something's not right.

I try to break the spell, but I can't move. I use the only powers I can and try to pick through her thoughts to find out how to achieve my freedom.

"You'll thank me later," she whispers. She pulls her hood over her hair and disappears into the night.

I stay rooted to the spot, not compelled to chase her. I watch the shadows swallow her before I turn to make my way back down the river. Not five yards away, I bump into Crowe. His eyes glitter with the rage of betrayal.

Chapter Twenty

Repercussions

"YOU LET HER go?" the Sage asks with raised eyebrows. She leans her elbows on her mahogany desk, watching me fidget. There's no surprise or disappointment in her voice. Curiosity, maybe.

Crowe stands rigidly beside me, face stoic. He's in the same mood he was in after introducing me to the Advisory Council of Fairies—the mood that led to him morphing into a bear. He barely spoke the entire walk back to Headquarters, even after I tried desperately to explain myself. The anger nearly radiates from him, and I know I've messed up.

"Yes, but I don't know what came over me. I-I—"

The Sage lifts a weathered hand. "The Elemental Coven is a powerful group."

I look to Crowe for some sort of explanation. The Elemental Coven? My entire life I've been taught of five covens: Ignis, Aens, Alchemy, Aquais, and Mentis. Crowe's expression remains the same as if he's heard the name a dozen times before.

"You should be familiar with them by now. Iris White was one of them," the Sage continues, and lowers her hand to her desk. "The Elemental Coven has hidden in the shadows for a long time. So long, I assumed they were no more."

I blink rapidly, trying to process the information. An entire Coven of witches outside of the Land of Five? How is it possible? "These witches… where did they come from?"

"They are rogues. Witches who left the guidance of the Council for whatever reason," the Sage explains. "Some have been banished. Others are a mystery. We are not sure who all of them are, but a few, like Iris, we have tabs on."

I furrow my brow. There could be hundreds, even *thousands*, and the Council is made up of us five and the Sage. Why don't they attack us and get it over with? Flashes of Iris' pyrokinetic and telekinetic powers blow through my head. Are they all capable of using multiple powers? What does it mean that I can do the same?

I try to mask my thoughts before the Sage can pick up on them. "If you know who even a few of them are, you must know what they want."

"I do," she says, lips pressed into a tight line. "They want the treaty dissolved."

"The one governing the division between Covens?"

"The very same," the Sage replies. She folds her hands in her lap. "The Elemental Coven believe the treaty hurts us more than helps."

"But that's… that's foolish. If the treaty didn't exist, the Covens would go to war for land, for food, for resources, like in the old days. We're not… meant to blend." I think about all I'd learned in class about the treaty's background. Before it was formed, witches murdered each other on a daily basis.

"That's why we have to stop them," Crowe says.

If the Sage is right, it makes sense the Elemental Coven would target the Arcane ceremony which was created to separate us.

"So, why poison the river? Thorn and Callista aren't witches, they're not bound by the treaty. It makes no sense to harm them."

"If I had to guess, I would say they want us gone and think this would be the easiest way to go about it. Maybe they don't know about the fairies and intended for us to drink the water. Without us to enforce the treaty, it can be destroyed much easier," the Sage ponders.

"And you let her go," Crowe sneers. He curls his lip at me. "Now, she'll be able to plot the next thing against us. Way to go."

"I-I couldn't control myself," I stutter. I try to explain what I'm sure the Sage sees as a traitorous act, but I can't find the words to describe what happened. Instead, I pull up the memory of the sensation that swept through me. The utter peace and calm that took away all worries and fears. I make the image as clear as I can and push it into the Sage's mind. Part of me wishes I could do the same to Crowe.

The Sage lifts a hand. "Don't feel as if you must justify yourself to me. I understand your actions."

"You do?" I ask, just as Crowe says, "What?"

"Your ability to read minds leaves you as exposed to them as they are to you." Her face softens. "I should've warned you about the downside of your gift."

"Wait? Read minds?" Crowe asks, craning his neck to look at me. "When did this happen?"

"Her powers are developing well," the Sage murmurs with a pleased smile.

Crowe's jaw hangs open. *She can't access the powers from her own Coven.* His thought drips with venom. *Why is it that nothing she does makes sense?*

He knows I can hear him. I bite my lip to keep from responding. When the immediate rage washes away, I find myself agreeing with him. Why do I have such an influx of powers from Mentis? I've only been able to access Ignis powers under duress, and there's been no signs of anything else.

"Why are my best powers from Mentis?" I blurt out.

The Sage tilts her head, considering. "Because your accident was of a magical nature, it may have sealed some of your abilities."

"That doesn't make sense!" I say.

"It's very simple when you break it down," the Sage says, tapping a long bony finger to her desk. "You were born with the ability to use a variety of powers. When you were hurt, your body tried to protect itself from further harm by sealing your wound with powers most fitting the damage. It might've worked too well, however, and may have completely sealed some of your powers away, at least for the time being."

"Can something like that be broken?" Crowe asks. "When I was training her, she hit me with fire."

"That was the only time I've ever used it," I remind him, "and that was only because my telekinetic powers were gone."

"Seems to me my hypothesis is correct," the Sage murmurs. She looks slowly from me to Crowe as if she either can't sense the tension in the room or doesn't care. "It may take some intense training, but I think that seal over your pyrokinesis can eventually be removed to allow better access to your powers."

Crowe stares at me, eyes glazed. He's imagining how much work it'll take for me to accomplish that, and he's responsible for seeing it through to the end. "That might be beyond my skill set."

"I have faith in you, Crowe," she says. "Otherwise, I would not have assigned you to her."

"If you value me so much, tell me she'll be punished for her hand in what happened tonight," Crowe demands.

I snort to myself and think about the irony. Only a day ago, I was in his position, saying the exact same words to the same person. *What goes around, comes around, Crowe,* I think, and I see the Sage smile from out of the corner of my eye.

"We have no idea where that witch has gone or if there are more hiding in the Grove. If Lilith would've acted and arrested her, we could've gotten some information," he continues, oblivious to our exchange.

"On the contrary, I have a mission for the two of you," the Sage says.

"A mission?" Crowe asks. His face is empty of emotion as if the conversation has completely exhausted him.

"I want you to do a little flushing for me."

"Flushing?" I ask.

"Visit each Coven and see if you can find any members of the Elemental Coven hiding among them," the Sage clarifies. "I believe there are spies who are passing information from the Land of Five to these rogue witches. I want them brought in for questioning."

"Will the entire Council be on this job?" Crowe asks, and it's pretty clear that assignment has spiked his anxiety because all traces of his previous anger are gone.

The Sage shakes her head, and her withered face turns

serious. "Just the two of you. I don't want to draw suspicion."

"How will we know who's working for them?" I ask. The thought that any of the people I've grown up with could be an Elemental makes my skin crawl. How many of them are here? How long have they been watching us?

How long have they been watching *me*?

The Sage leans forward on her elbows. "You'll know because they'll show an unusual interest in you, like Iris did. I don't know what their plans are, but I think it's safe to say what happened tonight wasn't by accident. They knew you were here. And most likely have other schemes waiting on the back burner."

I stare down at the floor. The Sage's entire plan consists of putting me in each Coven as bait to draw out wild criminals who are cloaking themselves as innocents.

How could it get any worse?

Chapter Twenty-One
Stuck Together, Torn Apart

CROWE IS ICILY quiet as we travel down the corridor between the Sage's room and the Common Room. I pry into his mind, but as I had feared, it's hazy as he attempts to keep everyone out. Outside Headquarters, he turns to me with a sudden lack of emotions that I'm sure is hard to pull with the storm raging in his mind.

"We have some long days ahead of us, especially with your leg," he says.

"Guess that means we need a good night's sleep." My body droops with exhaustion, and I think about how comfortable Tarj's bed was despite the awkward tension between us. "Am I sharing with Tarj again?"

"Not tonight. He'll likely be in and out most of the night, so you'll bunk with me," Crowe says. "That way we can get an early start in the morning. It's gonna take a while to get to the heart of Aens."

I'm unsure which point to bring up first—the fact that he's making me share a room with him or the fact that he picked the farthest Coven from the Council to travel to first. I also can't help but wonder what Tarj could possibly have to do that would require leaving multiple times during the night. "We're going to Aens first?"

Crowe stares into the distance as we walk through the

Council's garden. "I know what you're thinking, but I figure that after we get that one done, we can slowly make our way back through the other Covens, and if another Elemental attack happens while we're out, we'll be closer to the Grove."

"Right," I murmur as we approach a building with a door decorated with a blue stripe. It's not a terrible plan, but my leg already hurts in anticipation.

Crowe starts to push the door open, but he pauses. "It's a mess, so keep your comments to yourself, please and thank you."

I roll my eyes and follow him. My thoughts are of Clio. From what I've seen, *every* boy's house is a mess.

Mud and algae, the smells of marshland, fill my nose. When Crowe turns on the light, I see a thin layer of water on the floor. He splashes through it as if he hasn't noticed it's there.

"There's water on the floor," I point out, hovering by the door.

He adjusts the blankets on his bed. "Yeah?"

"You… like it this way?" I ask, dreading the thought of treading through it.

"I love it," he says wistfully. "It reminds me of home. The Sage specifically designed it with Aquais in mind."

I can understand that in a way. Most people aren't fans of the arid heat of the desert, but I can't imagine a place more comfortable.

Unlike Tarj's room, with the nook by the window, Crowe has a hammock-like bed hanging between two bookcases. "I guess that's where I'll be sleeping," I say and step into the water. It's cold, sinking into my feet within ten seconds. Uncomfortably, I slosh toward the hammock.

Crowe plops down on his bed. "Yeah. It's a lot more comfortable than it looks, I promise."

I poke one of the pillows. It's plush, and the blanket is just as soft. Problem is my clothes are soaked with sweat and now water. Once again, I'm faced with the dilemma of not having any personal belongings.

"Did the Sage send me anything to wear? I can't sleep like this," I say and stare down at the outfit I'd been so proud of that morning. The only thing I have left to connect me to Ignis.

"She didn't, but I'm sure I've got plenty to spare," Crowe says and crosses to his dresser.

The water moves around him in gentle waves as if he's gliding through it rather than walking. He pulls out a matching set of blue cotton pajamas and hands them to me.

"Bathroom is that way," he says and points to a door beside his window.

I bob my head gratefully and enter it. Water covers the floor here too, and with the blue paint on the walls, I almost feel as if I'm underwater. I do my best to change while keeping the new clothes dry.

By the time I leave the bathroom, Crowe is already lying down. His back faces me, but I have the feeling he's listening intently for signs I'm thinking of sneaking away during the night. I hold up my pantlegs to keep them out of the water and wrestle my way into the hammock. I'm glad Crowe isn't watching to see how much I struggle.

When I'm finally situated, I lie down, tuck my arm under the pillow, and stare across the room at Crowe's messy red hair. Somehow, it reminds me of my conversation with the Sage and all she said about my powers. Most of the witches in Aquais can manipulate water into any form of their choosing. I shift focus to the water on the floor and imagine turning it to ice. I stare and stare, but it doesn't freeze. The most I can do is splash it around with my telekinesis.

Maybe the Sage made a mistake.

I push the thought away almost as soon as it springs up. Throughout the history of the Land of Five, one thing has always been true—the Sage is never wrong. Our entire way of life functions on that one eventuality.

So, why did she look so uncertain? I think, as I recall the Sage's expression when she spoke about the poisoning.

The switch in memories isn't mine, and I have a feeling Hyacinth is behind it. I tense as I realize what she's trying to say. During that conversation, the Sage wasn't sure of herself, and if she wasn't sure, there's a possibility she could be wrong.

You're not who they say you are. Hyacinth's words move to the front of my brain again. If I'm not who I believe I am, then who am I?

"Something wrong, Li?" Crowe mumbles into the covers.

I snort at the irony of the nickname. My whole life is a lie.

Somehow, I manage to clear away the worst of my doubts and say, "No, I'm fine."

Tomorrow is going to be a long day.

* * *

THE MORNING COMES like a slap to the face. I'm awakened by Crowe, who is wide awake and excited at the first sign of dawn.

I groan and pick up the nearest pillow, using it to shield my face from the weak light. It feels as if I've only slept ten minutes, and I'm ready to claw the faces off anyone willing to tell me otherwise.

"Come on, Lilith! Rise and shine!" Crowe says in an annoyingly cheerful voice and rips the blanket away. I move the pillow to glare at him and notice he's already dressed.

He's been up for a while, Hyacinth informs me.

"Gift from the Sage," Crowe says and dumps a handful of clothes onto my chest.

"Thanks," I say and sit up.

I stretch as well as I can without making it awkward, and half slide, half tumble out of the hammock. The water on the floor makes it hard for me to gain traction, and I strain to keep from falling. I don't. I make it to the bathroom before I look at the clothes I was given. It's a t-shirt and shorts, but the material is much thicker than that of the outfit I'd worn the previous day. The yellow color is different as well.

Yellow is Aens Coven's pride color. It makes sense to wear the outfit. The Sage probably hopes it will keep me from standing out when we arrive. A shiver passes through me at the considerable amount of danger I'm trekking into.

And I'm not even sure it's worth it, I think. Goosebumps break out down my arms, and I rub my hand over them to get them to disappear.

Back in Crowe's room, he leans against his doorframe, arms folded across his chest as he stares out into the open garden beyond. When I emerge from the bathroom, he gives me an approving nod.

"Let's go get breakfast," Crowe says and holds the door

open for me.

Outside, the morning air is crisp and warm, and I take it as a good omen. In Headquarters, we take our seats at the dining table and start to eat. Hyacinth is the only one who looks up at our appearance. My mind and Crowe's are filled with thoughts of Aens. The second his stomach is full, he's going to be ready to get on the road.

I eat what I can, but my nerves ensure it's not much. Content, I push my plate away. Across the table, Tricia stands, and I wince as she approaches me. Gently, she grabs my hand and pulls me to my feet. Crowe doesn't look up from his meal, and I have the feeling Tricia told him in advance she had this planned.

She leads me toward the mouth of the hall. In the shadows of the pillars, she stops to look at me. "I heard you and Crowe are going on a pretty important mission." Her eyes go to Hyacinth who watches us from a distance.

I dip my head but hold my tongue. How much does the Sage want me to tell the others? With Hyacinth around, it's a wonder she thought the secret would be contained. "Yeah, we'll be away from the Grove for a few days."

"The Elemental Coven are a crazy bunch," she says. There's a warning in her eyes. "My mother used to tell me horror stories about them. It's that insanity that makes them what they are."

"Okay. Um, not to sound rude," I say, honestly not caring how I sound, "but why are you telling me this?"

"Hyacinth told me the Sage fears they're after you. If what I've heard about them is right, you'll need more than Crowe to watch your back while you're out in the fray."

"Thanks for your concern, but I can take care of myself," I state curtly and raise my chin, wondering what else she expects me to do. Does she want me to invite her along? The Sage had been specific about her orders for me and Crowe to travel alone.

Tricia sets a hand on top of my arm, and her hazel eyes bore into mine. The seriousness in them unsettles me. "Be careful out there, Lilith."

Chapter Twenty-Two
Papra

T HAT I AM potentially at risk at all times is the last thought on my mind as Crowe and I leave the Grove. Our stomachs are full, and the ride on the wyrm is oddly soothing, as long as I don't think about the journey ahead.

I've never set foot on Aens land before, and the prospect of meeting new people sets me on edge. What are they like? Will they welcome me with open arms or see me as a threat? Other than Hyacinth, I've never met anyone from there. I had classmates from this Coven, but they weren't anyone I associated with.

Now, I have no choice but to interact with them. Out of the corner of my eye, I catch the dark expression on Crowe's face. I prod his mind and find he's reliving the conversation in the Sage's room—her parting words that if anything happens to me, it's Crowe's responsibility.

I open my mouth. I want to tell him to relax, that things will be okay, but I don't know how to convince him. For all I know, he's justified in in his fear. We could be ambushed at any time. The river poisoning could've been the Elementals' way of flushing *us* out and we're walking right into their trap.

Crowe notices the twist of my face and raises an eyebrow. He studies our surroundings in detail and part of me wonders why he hasn't changed into some kind of ferocious animal if he's worried about someone sneaking up on us from the tall grass.

The plains have miles of open ground. Farms take up about ninety percent of that. The lack of civilization for miles is eerie, and I understand Crowe's uneasiness. I long for the stones in the middle of Ignis territory and the shelter they provide.

How do they get water out here? I strain my ears for the sound of a river or creek.

A chilly breeze blows through the early hours of the night. It shuffles our clothes and sends chills across the bits of skin that are exposed.

"Guess this is as good a place as any to make camp," Crowe says.

A long howl rings out in the distance. I'm not convinced, but I put faith in his judgement. He gets the wyrm to slow so we can dismount. My legs feel like noodles when I touch the ground from sitting for so long. Though we've traveled miles through Aens, the area looks no different than it did when we crossed the border.

"It's sort of peaceful here," I say and stare up at the moon. Aens has a breathtaking view of the stars.

"It's a lot more open than I care for," Crowe counters, staring into the darkest cluster of shadows.

"Still think we're being watched?" I ask as he surveys the miles of fields around us.

"Can never rule out the possibility."

He's got a point.

Crowe slips his bag off his shoulder, pulling out a variety of supplies. The first of which is a tent we work together to assemble. Crowe uses a handful of matches to light a fire. The wind twists the flames and threatens to blow them out every time they start to grow. Crowe uses his body to shield it, and eventually, it grows large enough to give us warmth.

We sit side by side and warm our hands. Watching the firelight lick the shadows away from the edges of Crowe's face, I ask, "So, tomorrow… do we have a plan, or are we going to barge into the heart of the Coven, drag people out of their homes, and demand to know if they're working for the Elementals?"

Crowe snorts and pulls a wrapped sandwich from his bag. He takes a bite before he says, "Of course not. That would be reckless and unnecessary. Not only would it be unprofessional, but it would frighten a shitload of Aens witches for no good reason. No, we'll properly survey the group and take it from there."

"Okay." I don't know what else to say.

He's been here before, met these witches. He has an idea of what to expect. Meanwhile, I'm clueless.

"Hungry?" he asks and hands me a sandwich.

Until that moment, I hadn't thought about food. I'd been so inundated with my worries that everything else didn't seem important. As soon as I take one bite, I want more. I devour it. Beside me, Crowe takes his time with his. He stares into the fire, and I can see the thoughts flying around inside his head. I finish my sandwich. Not wanting to disturb Crowe, I slip into the tent, ready to call it a night.

* * *

CROWE WAKES ME up before the sun rises. He throws breakfast and a change of clothes my way before I can protest. As

I get myself ready, Crowe summons one of the Aens wyrms. Unlike the others I've seen, this one is a deep, forest green, and its scales are more prominent. Its eyes are also green, rather than the yellow I'm used to.

Crowe climbs up and hoists our bags to the wyrm's back before helping me up. The wyrm starts to move, but it doesn't feel like it. The creature moves with an eerie, gliding precision the others don't.

It's like it's used to moving through the grass and making no sound, I marvel.

I flinch as a sudden thought occurs to me. If something this big can navigate without being noticed, what horrors could be hiding in the Aens moors?

"Cold?" Crowe asks.

"Uh, yeah," I say. I don't want to add to his already sky-high paranoia. "So, who's the first person we're going to see once we find the actual witches who live here?"

"Papra," Crowe says. "Hyacinth's mother. She's a lovely woman."

My eye twitches involuntarily. I don't want to tell her my thoughts about her daughter. "Why her?"

"Her home's a guaranteed safe place until we're done with business," he says.

"Makes sense."

"And she doesn't share Hyacinth's ability if that's what you're thinking."

"What's her power?" I find it difficult to hide my disappointment. If Papra could read minds, she would be an asset to us. We'd be in and out of Aens in no time.

"She manipulates wind. Most members of Aens control some aspect of the weather." He pauses and gazes across the field. "It's why they feel so comfortable with these damn open spaces."

They're friends with the wind. Imagine being able to control the weather. "Powerful group."

"Which makes me more inclined to believe the Elementals will have some kind of following here," he comments and narrows his eyes to slits. "Plenty of places to hide."

"If they're as strong as the Sage says, they'll have members everywhere, right?"

"Yep," Crowe murmurs. "But with this Coven being so large, I have a bad feeling about it."

Now I do too.

The conversation fizzles and is replaced by the smooth sound of the wyrm slithering through the grass. When the sun reaches its highest point in the sky and starts to descend again, Crowe encourages the creature to stop and let us off. We're still very much in the middle of nowhere but stopping gives us the opportunity to eat.

"Are we close yet?" I ask.

"Yeah," he says with an annoyed huff. "You're so impatient."

"Perhaps," I say, "but maybe we could've ridden the wyrm a little longer."

Crowe stays silent, and I take that as a victory. We walk for an hour before a house appears in the distance. It's the first sign of life, other than the wyrm, we've seen since crossing the borders into Aens, and I'm not sure how to feel. The house is dark brown, and the door is so dark it blends in with the siding. It looks like it's made of a straw-like material. How does it hold up against the impossible winds of the Aens moors?

They're friends with the wind, remember? They probably use it to help hold their houses together.

Crowe barely stops walking before he begins pounding on the door. It's clear he's been here before, and I wonder what happened in the past to cause him to travel this far from Headquarters.

I hear footsteps, and a moment later, the door opens to reveal a woman who shares Hyacinth's white-blonde hair and hooded violet eyes.

Are violet eyes something all the people of Aens share? I can't remember.

"Crowe!" the woman exclaims and throws her arms around him. The white dishtowel in her hand catches the breeze as she does so. "This is a surprise!"

"Good to see you, Papra, though I'm sad to say. We're here on business," he says when they pull apart. He drags me a bit closer. Papra looks at me and her excitement dims a bit as if she's just noticed my presence.

"I haven't seen this one before," she says.

After the chaos of the Arcane Ceremony, I'm surprised. The Sage made it sound as though I were the talk of every Coven in the Land of Five. I probe her thoughts and realize she's being polite. She knows exactly who I am.

"I'm new to the Council. Name's Lilith," I state, holding out my hand to her. "But people usually call me Li."

She returns the handshake and leads us inside. Her house is nicer inside than out. It's small, but the scent reminds me of flowers in a meadow. An open window draws my attention. I'm sure she has plants outside I didn't see on the way in.

"I'm Papra," she introduces herself. "I don't have much to offer, but you're welcome to stay as long as you need to."

"Thank you. We need some rest after that trip." Crowe runs his hand through his messy red locks.

Though we spent most of the day riding the wyrm, the portion we walked took longer than necessary thanks to the long grass. I'm exhausted. Judging by the look on Crowe's face, he feels the same.

"How's Hyacinth?" Papra asks and sets her dishtowel on the edge of a tiny coffee table.

"She's doing well, but she's concerned for Callista as we all are," I reply.

Crowe gives me a weird look, and at first, I think I'm in trouble. I have no idea how much people know about the Advisory Council of Fairies. Did I accidentally spill too much of the Council's information?

I didn't know you talked to Hyacinth, Crowe tells me in thought.

I resist the urge to smile. It's good to know that the Council has no way of knowing *everything*.

"Did something happen to her?" Papra asks, pinching her eyebrows together in an expression similar to Hyacinth's.

"No. Nothing like that. She's okay, but the number of incidents throughout the Land of Five has increased. The Elemental Coven's responsible," Crowe says and makes a face that tells me they've had a similar conversation before.

How out of the loop am I when it comes to Land of Five

matters?

Papra sighs. "I've heard more and more about them over the past few days. It's such a shame they ruined your Arcane Ceremony. You must've been so disappointed."

"Actually, I was fine with it." Thoughts of that day bring to mind Helena's devastated face and a sudden desire to see her again. I shove the longing into the darkness at the back of my mind. I'll see her when we visit Ignis.

It's then I notice the silence. I'm outside of Hyacinth's hearing range. It's eerie having my thoughts to myself again. I'd almost forgotten what it was like. Papra's had to deal with Hyacinth's tricks so long, I'm not surprised to find her thoughts open and free without any attempt to cloak them.

"The Sage thinks we'll find Elementals scattered around, waiting for commands for whatever they have planned next," Crowe says.

"I wouldn't say you're wrong, but you may be too late," Papra says and sits on a small loveseat by the door. Her long, white-blonde hair falls limply over her thin form. "Half the Coven seems to have disappeared overnight. Entire families, gone."

"Think it's related?" Crowe asks.

"If not, the timing is pretty coincidental," I point out.

"Let's get to it then," Crowe says.

Papra raises a pale eyebrow. "It'll be dark soon. The last thing you want to do is scare those of us who are left."

Time isn't something we have a lot of, but Papra has a point.

"Fine," he says. "We'll ask around in the morning to see if anyone knows anything."

Does he really think the answers will come so easily? If they're affiliated with the Elemental Coven, they have no reason to be honest with us. "Even if they do know, it doesn't mean they'll tell us."

He smirks. "That's where your mind reading will come in handy. A witch from Ignis? They won't expect it. When we brought Hyacinth, they knew to cloak their thoughts, but with you? They'll be confused, and that will make it easier for us to extract what we need."

That's a lot of responsibility to put on my shoulders.

"Well, make yourselves at home," Papra says as if she senses my tension and rises from her seat. "There's a bathroom down the hall you can use to freshen up, and you can share Hyacinth's room for the night."

"Thank you," I say, surprised to hear Crowe shriek in protest.

After all the time we've spent together, and sharing his room the night before, I'm confused. When I prob his mind, his overwhelming exhaustion is the first thing that surfaces, followed by his concerns. He's upset about our sleeping at the same time. We'll be vulnerable.

Crowe narrows his eyes. He's aggravated that I read his thoughts, but he doesn't voice his complaints. He disappears down the hall in the direction of the shower, and I say my goodbyes to Papra before finding Hyacinth's room.

The room is simple, with light yellow bedding, a small bookshelf, and a bucket of knitting supplies in the corner. The inside of her room reminds me of her mind—both of them are so carefully tidied. Her Book of Spells is on her bookshelf. I make sure I'm alone before I pick it up and riffle through the pages. I look for anything on clairvoyance and whether it's possible to extend my range like Hyacinth's, but all I find is information I've already discovered.

I slam the Book shut and put it back. I focus on the rest of the room and am faced with a new dilemma—unlike the rooms at Headquarters which have additional sleeping nooks, Hyacinth's room has no such provision. That means the sleeping options are either the bed or the floor. I decide on the floor after realizing, with horror, if I choose the bed, Crowe might try to find a way to make us both fit.

I take off my stiff, yellow shirt and straighten the thin, red tank top I had on underneath. The shirt hits the floor as Crowe steps into the room. Without the dirt and grime from our travels, his ivory skin sparkles. A towel hangs around his neck. His usually spiky, red hair is still wet, and the long tendrils fall flat against his forehead and neck.

"You can have the bed," I tell him before he's had a chance to fully scan the room. I drop to my knees and arrange my discarded clothes in a comfortable pile.

"You're the woman here. It's more right for you to take it," he says, as he watches me curl up on the floor like Helena's cat.

I tuck my face into the crook of my arm, already in the beginning stages of sleep. "It's okay, really. I'm fine right here."

"You're shutting me out."

My mind is already too far gone to come up with a decent response.

"If it's about earlier, I'm sorry," he says. "I'm worried

about being here is all."

He thinks he's hurt my feelings, I realize. I hold out a hand without opening my eyes. "It's fine. I'm fine. Everything's fine."

Crowe mutters something about "inadequate provisions" and stomps over to the bed.

I'm asleep before he blows out the candle.

Chapter Twenty-Three
Aens

CONSIDERING I'D BEEN the first to go to sleep, I'm not surprised I'm also the first to wake in the morning. I glance at Crowe who is spread across Hyacinth's bed. Despite his worries, he couldn't resist a good night's sleep. I sit up, groan at the stiffness in my joints, and briefly regret my decision. Then I think about how I would've fit next to Crowe and know that would've been the worse choice. Crowe's arm hangs off the bed, his fingers nearly touching me.

I stretch out my bad leg and massage the muscles to ease some of the pain before I force myself to my feet. I'm craving a bath, so I go to the bathroom. Water fills the tub a quarter of the way before I get in. The warmth soothes my aches and puts me into a state of relaxation I haven't felt in quite some time. Scrubbing away the dirt from the past few days takes effort.

When I'm clean, I feel a bit better. I have one outfit left in the bottom of my bag, and I pull it on. I unknot my hair with my fingers and wander out to the kitchen where Papra is making breakfast.

"Need some help?" I offer. "One of my Coven duties in Ignis was working in a restaurant."

"No, I don't. You sit right there," she says and gestures to the dining room table.

I oblige. Stifling a yawn, I push a few wet locks of hair

from my face. Papra deposits two fluffy pancakes on a plate and sets it before me. "I hope you slept well," she says and passes me a fork. "Crowe didn't complain too much last night, did he?"

I reach for the syrup. I'm surprised by how upbeat she sounds. If someone complained about *my* home, I don't know if I'd be able to do the same. "He tried, but I fell asleep before I heard too much."

"That's good," Papra says.

I offer her a gentle smile. "It's okay. Didn't bother me a bit. My parents' house in Ignis is a bit smaller than this one; it's cozy." I pause and pop a bite of food in my mouth.

"Crowe comes from money." Papra sits at the table with her own plate. "They practically run Aquais. It's part of the reason he got the position. The Council is hard for him sometimes. He never really got to be a kid, you know? His entire life, he's been responsible for looking out for others. Always had an image to maintain."

"I can understand that," I say. I think about the way my parents never wanted me to talk about my accident and wanted to play happy family.

"Though really, I can't imagine it's easy for any of you to transition. You must miss your family like crazy," Papra takes a sip of orange juice. "It was hard for Hyacinth in the beginning."

"It's not so bad once you get used to things." I push around a bite of food with my fork. "Things weren't exactly great with my family before Tarj recruited me, so I don't miss them as much as I probably should. My friends, however? I miss them so much it hurts."

"You'll see them when we check Ignis," Crowe's voice

drifts in from the doorway.

I glance up as he steps into the room. His hair and clothes are disheveled from sleep.

"Good morning," Papra calls to him and stands to grab him a plate.

He nods gratefully and sits beside me. "You're up early."

"I'm ready to get today started," I say and eat the bite of food I'd been playing with. I don't mention that I'm also ready for it to be over. The idea of being faced with hostile witches for a majority of the day leaves me unsettled.

Papra passes Crowe his breakfast. He eats so quickly, I wonder if he tastes anything. A particularly hot bite gives him pause, but he doesn't stop long before he continues to shove it down his throat.

"Shouldn't you shift into a snake before you try to swallow your food whole?" I ask.

Papra pours him a glass of juice. She's concerned, and she's resisting the urge to cut his food for him like a toddler. My lips twitch in amusement at the picture the thought conjures.

Crowe doesn't notice the emotion on our faces. "Good one," he says and takes a swig from his full glass. "Get ready to head out soon."

"Already done." I place my fork on my empty plate for emphasis, swallow my last mouthful of juice, and set my elbows on the table to watch him.

"I never would've taken you for an early riser," he murmurs thoughtfully and wolfs down two more bites.

I never would've taken you for a crybaby, I think, as I remember his tantrum.

Crowe finishes eating while I gather our bags. He slings his over his shoulder, and I take mine. We call our goodbyes to Papra and step outside her little home. I'm blinded by the morning sun and surprised to find that, even in the daytime, Aens is as strange as it was in the dead of night. Down the hill from Papra's lies a handful of shacks.

None of their lights are on, and I think about Papra's earlier words. Exactly how much of the Coven is missing?

A short patch of grass leads to a cobblestone path that winds past houses and ends at a boulder in the middle of the Coven, it rests on a rise, much like the one on the Ceremony Grounds. The breeze feels stronger, more focused. Delicate yellow lines are painted across its surface in symbols important to Aens history. Crowe runs his fingers along the top, and an eerie yellow light shines underneath his hand.

I hear murmuring nearby as thirty to forty people, Papra included, fill the ground at the base of the hill. They were summoned by the stone, and now, they watch us cautiously. Some share Hyacinth and Papra's violet eyes, while the rest seem to be amber.

None of the witches look thrilled to see us.

Leo breaks from the crowd and storms past his people. His massive form reminds me of a charging bull as he gets closer.

"What's going on?" he demands and scowls. He looks from me to Crowe. "You guys don't do house calls."

"We're sorry we didn't tell you we were coming, but our plans were last minute," Crowe says. He sets his hand on Leo's shoulder even though the Aens Adept stands at least a half a foot taller than he does.

"What's this about?" he demands and pushes Crowe's hand away. He looks and sounds angry, but there's a hint of confusion swimming in his eyes that gives away his true feelings.

I know all too well what it feels like to be left out of the loop.

Crowe focuses on the crowd. "Hello there, Aens witches. Lovely morning we're having."

Unamused grumbles come from them, and Leo turns his confused gaze to me. I respond with a shrug.

Crowe claps his hands to seem as upbeat as he can. "I know things have been a little intense in the Land of Five lately."

"Is this about the Arcane Ceremony?" a boy asks.

"Yes, it is," Crowe says. "Though Iris White was punished for her crimes, we have not yet reached the end of this battle. We have information that's led us to believe she was not working alone. We think she had accomplices who know of her plans. So, we're here to search for people who may have had a reason to help her."

Someone scoffs, and I trace the sound to a middle-aged woman wearing overalls. Her skin is sunburned as if she's spent long days in the fields. "Look around! Half our Coven is gone. Left without a word, and you're worried about testing *us*?"

The crowd roars. Dozens of similar questions fly at Crowe.

"How is it you have no idea who these witches are?"

"How could you let this happen?"

"This isn't going well," Crowe whispers to me and Leo.

"I'll handle it," Leo says. He holds his hands an inch apart. Clear green strands form between them, which grow steadily darker before losing their transparent charm. They twist and morph into a ball. Leo tosses it into the sky, and it explodes with an ear-shattering *bang* that forces the witches to duck and clamp their hands over their ears.

"Did anyone speak with any of the witches who disappeared?" Crowe asks.

"We all did at some point," Papra says as she makes her way to the front of the group. I'm relieved for her decision to speak up. Considering the hostility of the rest of the witches, she's our best bet of getting to the bottom of things. "None of them acted unusual or said anything."

"At least we know none of them are hiding out here," I point out and glance between Leo and Crowe. "They all left."

"Maybe that's what they want us to think," Crowe says and turns to Leo. "How long have they been missing?"

"I can't say for sure. It seems as if everyday we wake up and someone else is gone. At first, it was only a handful of witches, and we thought maybe they were sick and just staying bedridden. Then entire families disappeared."

"And they didn't leave a note or tell anyone where they were going?" Crowe asked.

"If that was the case, don't you think we would've let you know?" Leo asked sarcastically. "They're gone. What do you think happened?"

I'm glad his question is directed at Crowe rather than me because I have no answer. My focus is drawn to the Aens witches gathered at the base of the rise. Even from here, I can see the exhaustion as if they're feeling the absences of the missing witches and have been for some time.

Seems like they've been gone longer than a few nights, I note to myself. But why wouldn't they report the witches for leaving?

I open my mind and try to read their thoughts. A hundred voices fill the air. I try to close the connection, but it doesn't work. Desperate, I clamp my hands over my ears, shake my head, and stumble to the ground.

"What's wrong with her?" Leo asks and grasps my arm to pull me to my feet. His strong grip allows no room for protest.

Crowe doesn't look concerned. He lifts an eyebrow as soon as I'm balanced. "Don't try that again until you've had some training."

"I wanted to help," I mutter, though I'm glad I won't have to subject myself to that degree of agony again.

A few witches in the crowd watch me, but none of them ask questions. I rub my forehead and look at them, but they look away.

How many of them know what happened to me?

Crowe's scowl returns to the crowd. "Thank you for your time," he says and dismisses them with a wave of his hand before he says to me, "Into Aquais we go."

Chapter Twenty-Four
Aquais

THE BUFFETING WINDS are the only sound we hear as we travel. At first, the silence was welcome. Now, though, it feels as if it's screaming. Desperate for some interaction, I pry into Crowe's mind, but he's getting better at cloaking his thoughts.

That could be bad news.

"Where do you think the Aens witches went?" I ask when I'm unable to find any thoughts of them on his mind.

Crowe frowns. "I don't know, but they better hope we don't find out."

"They all looked so tired, way more tired than they should if the witches left a night or two ago," I point out. "Like they're having to take on extra coven duties to cover for them. I wonder if they left all at once, or if they've been gradually disappearing, and no one's bothered to report it."

"There's no way to tell at this point," Crowe says with a wistful sigh. "Unless of course more happen to disappear."

"If we were smart, we would've brought Hyacinth. She could've handled this."

"We've been over that. Besides, we didn't need her to see how suspicious they were," Crowe says. "You could *feel* their hostility. It's never been like that in Aens."

I'll have to take his word for it.

I peer at him from the corner of my eye not wanting to ask the question I'm sure I must. "Do you think the entire Coven could be involved with the Elementals?"

"We can't rule out the possibility," he says. "It's either that or something driving them out by making them feel as if their homes are no longer safe."

"Do you think they started leaving before Iris' attack?"

"Maybe, but if that's the case that would mean they knew about it and said nothing," Crowe says. His face is twisted in thought. "Papra said nothing you found odd? Or have any thoughts she forgot to keep cloaked?"

I peer up at him. "No. She seemed… *normal*. Everything I picked up were the same things she told you."

Crowe huffs. "Well, this makes no sense. Were you able to pick up anything from anyone else?"

Remembering the pain of the swarm of voices makes me flinch. "No. Just a lot of anger."

Crowe scratches the back of his neck. "Yeah, we didn't leave the best impression on them."

I think of the dozens of hostile eyes and though we're miles away now, my skin still breaks out into goosebumps. "Will all the Covens react to us like that?"

"Probably," Crowe admits. "Tensions have been high since the Arcane Ceremony, but even without Iris, they've never been too thrilled to see us outside of the Ceremony Grounds because these kinds of visits usually mean bad news. Now, it's worse. The Land of Five is still reeling, and fear tends to show itself as anger."

"Why hasn't the Sage put more work into calming

everyone down?" I ask. Maybe then we could've gotten to the bottom of what's really going on in Aens. "When people are scared, they riot. In this case, it means driving them into the arms of the witches we want to save them from."

"It's not as easy as that," Crowe replies. "There's no magic spell to take away everyone's worries. And she's doing what she can to make some changes that would hopefully smooth things over. That's part of why she's been so preoccupied with getting you sworn into the Council."

"What about Lynx, Tricia, and Hyacinth? Couldn't they have done something? At least made some rounds to talk to their covenmates?" I can't be the only one who's considered this.

"I don't know what the Sage has them working on, if anything. The only thing I can say for sure is that Lynx is forbidden to leave the Grove, and Hyacinth's job includes watching over him."

The information doesn't surprise me. As bitter as I am about my start with the Council, I'm glad the Sage worked out a deal with me that allowed me to go home for a little while. "She's holding him prisoner?"

"I guess you could say that," Crowe says. He adjusts the straps of his backpack. "But the way I see it, it's keeping him safe. Given his gift, we can't afford the possibility of losing him."

I glance down at my bad leg. I'm as guilty as they are. If he really has the potential to heal magical wounds, I can find a way to convince myself that his current restrictions are necessary. "Yeah."

Crowe looks at the sky to gauge the distance the sun's moved since we started our trek. The houses on the plains are far behind us, but it seems no matter how long we walk, they aren't any farther away. In the distance, I spot the gleam of a wyrm outpost. Crowe sees it at the same time and starts to run toward it.

"Excited about going home?" I call after him. Papra's words from this morning replay through my head.

"Of course," he says and pulls the silver whistle off its holder. "It'll be good to see Mother again."

"When's the last time you saw her?" I ask, as a sharp blast sounds.

He stares across the field and waits for the wyrm to appear. "I'm not sure. I don't think I've really had a chance to go home since I was recruited." The shadow across his eyes tells me I've asked more than I should.

I twine my thumbs in the silence, but the wyrm doesn't appear. "I don't think it's coming."

Crowe surveys the tall grass and blows the whistle again, but the creature doesn't appear. "Guess you're right. Seems we'll have to walk the rest of the way to the Aquais border."

My leg aches at the idea, and I flick the whistle as I pass it, wondering why the wyrm decided to turn us down. He takes the lead, and I adjust my bag before following him. "Think the witches who left took it with them?"

Crowe purses his lips as if he hadn't considered that. "Most likely. We'll summon one in Aquais."

Miles of tall grass plains stand between us and the border, and I try not to think about it too much.

"I know you hate water, but Aquais is beautiful. A lot more so than Ignis," Crowe says with a hint of a challenge.

"Is that right? I heard it's a swamp," I shoot back. "That's probably why the wyrm didn't respond. It didn't want anything to do with your marshes."

Crowe smirks. "Marshlands and swamps aren't the same thing."

"It's all the same to me," I say and shudder at the idea of cold, murky liquid.

He rolls his eyes. "You Ignis people always complain about water. You might as well be cats!" After a brief chuckle, he continues, "Seriously though, Aquais is a lot smaller than the other Covens, so this should be an easy one."

"Papra says your family runs it."

"Correct!" he says, with a pleasant smile I've only seen once in the few days I've known him. "I come from a long line of good people. My ancestors noticed a trend of witches with water-based gifts and recruited those who were denied entry into the other Covens. They made a safe haven for them. Didn't matter what they could do, my ancestors took them in, built homes for them, and trained them."

"Sounds like your family cares for the people more than the Council does," I note, then I clamp my hand over my mouth when I realize I said it out loud.

Crowe scrunches his eyebrows. "You don't think the Council does a good job of keeping its people content?"

"I think it's hard for six people to manage five Covens, each of which is home to hundreds of witches," I point out.

"There's a lot more to the Council than you know."

I gnaw on my nail, wondering if I should question him or move the conversation forward. "The story—about your ancestors in Aquais—almost feels like history repeating itself with the Elementals. Except this time, no one is taking them in."

"You don't know that. There's enough of them and if they're still around, that means they've got a home somewhere. Besides, there's a difference between them and the witches in Aquais." He pauses and turns his hawk-like gaze on me. "Elementals are out for blood, while we are not."

I haven't met that many witches from Aquais so I can't really say. "So, what is it the Aquais people do? Make it rain?"

"Some of them. Some of them do other things. I mean what do Ignis people do? Make it warm?"

We grin at each other.

"In all seriousness though, I'm not sure what happens in a normal household," Crowe says. "Like you, I came from UnEquipped parents."

I stop walking, and a pain blossoms at the base of my neck when I turn my head to look at him. "Really?"

"Yeah, what did you think?"

"I thought—"

"Thought they had to be Equipped to be in charge?" He chuckles. "Nope. Perseverance works well too. I would have thought you'd know that." In the brief pause between sentences, I think of Helena. "Even though they didn't have powers, they gave those people a home, and the witches repaid their kindness with protection and respect. They never needed magic."

"That's certainly impressive," I say. My UnEquipped parents aren't anything like his. "So, what kind of powers did your friends have? Assuming you *had* friends, of course."

"Some made ice, others could make tidal waves. I think

the most impressive one was a witch who could make you feel as if you were drowning on dry land just by looking at you.”

I raise my eyebrows, surprised the Council didn't pick his friend. I'd hate to face them in battle. “Why didn't the Council recruit them?”

“I think they considered it, but they liked my gift better. Typically, the Sage tries to keep only one member from each Coven on the Council at any given time.”

What does that mean for Tarj now that I'm here? I haven't seen him in a while, and I deflate slightly. *Most likely he'll be in and out all night.* Had he been moving out?

I file Tarj's disappearance in the part of my mind where I'll be sure to remember and ask about it later on. “Are all your friends still in Aquais?”

Crowe pushes his bangs from his eyes. “I assume so, but I can't say for sure. We fell out of touch when I got deep into training. Last I heard, they were all fine.”

“Ah,” I murmur, and I think of Clio and Helena. Falling out of touch with them is one of my biggest fears. As much as I don't want our relationships to atrophy, I'm not sure how I can stop it from happening.

The second we step into Aquais territory, I become aware of it. Wet grass squishes beneath my feet, and I shudder when a bit of water seeps through the holes in my shoes. I stare up at Crowe, already disenchanted with his home Coven.

Crowe's smile is superior. “Get used to it. It only gets worse from here.”

Chapter Twenty-Five
Crowe's Origins

223

B Y THE TIME the sun reaches its zenith, Crowe and I have trekked to another wyrm outpost. My legs are soaked up to my thighs when the beast arrives, and I can't imagine anyone enjoying life here. The smell of muddy water sticks in my nose, and I grimace as the wyrm navigates the deepest parts of the water. Unlike wyrms in other Covens, this one has a set of fins that help it push through the muck and grime.

I pick at my wet clothes, wincing at the way they peel off my skin. Crowe laughs. I consider dunking him under the water, when the wyrm stops, to see if he still enjoys it. After a few hours of travel, the swamps give way to dry land. The wyrm comes to rest beside it, and I step down, gratefully. Crowe climbs down a moment later and thanks the creature before we start to walk up the slope.

Crowe points to a shape on the distance. "We're almost there."

I squint, trying to see it better. A mansion sits at the top of the rise—a Victorian beast with black siding and a rounded Gothic archway that marks the entrance. A spire on the left side of the building juts into the sky.

I gasp. "It's beautiful! Is this really where you grew up?"

Crowe smiles, but it seems haunted, as if he's deep in his memories. I don't ask him to explain as he leads the way to the front door. We stand under the archway, and I study every detail while he knocks. The door opens and reveals a male with traits similar to Crowe's. The only difference is his size.

"Little brother! What are you doing here?" He wraps his arm around Crowe's neck and presses his knuckles to Crowe's messy, red hair.

Crowe growls in frustration, and I raise my eyebrows as I watch him struggle for freedom. "Yes, well, good to see you too, I suppose. Is Mother home?"

"She is," he says, then he catches sight of me. "Well, well. Hello, Doll! Name's Kieran. Who might you be?" He grasps my hand and places a kiss on the skin just below my knuckles.

I chuckle awkwardly and jerk my hand back, uncertain how to respond.

"Show some respect! That's Lilith, the newest member of the Council," Crowe scolds and pushes past Kieran to enter the house.

The second I step inside, the water soaking my legs and feet disappears. I guess there's some type of spell at work that keeps witches from trekking muddy water onto the floors.

Even their spell casting is rich, I think, and I barely suppress the snort that would otherwise accompany the thought.

A beautiful chandelier hangs from the ceiling above a wide staircase. Expensive rugs stretch across white tile floors, and paintings decorate the walls between expensive, silver moldings.

I gesture to the nearest painting and, with a wide grin, say, "Watercolor?"

Crowe blinks, unamused. He glances down the lengthy corridor that leads out of the room. "Mother!" he calls and starts to walk away.

Kieran and I follow.

"Council, huh? Impressive feat," Kieran says to me.

"Not as if I had much of a choice," I mutter and side-eye Crowe.

Crowe returns a bitter look. "This is hardly the place to discuss that."

"Alexander! Is that you?" a voice calls before I can respond.

A tiny woman adorned in a blue corset dress appears and pulls Crowe into a tight hug. Her chin rests in his red hair.

"*Alexander?*" I ask slowly. I try to repress my laughter at the look of embarrassment on Crowe's face.

"Yeah. It's, uh, my birth name," he says. He peers around the grip of his mother's arm before he pulls away. "It's certainly good to see you again."

"It's been too long!" she says, hands on her hips. "You need to make your family a higher priority."

"Mother, we've discussed this."

She presses her lips into a tight line before she diverts her attention to me. "I don't believe I've met this one," she says before offering me her hand. "I'm Breanne."

"Lilith," I introduce myself with a polite dip of my head and return the handshake. Her grip is firm and strong, surprising for such a petite woman. "It's nice to meet you."

"Business or pleasure?" Breanne asks Crowe as she lets go of me.

A blush spreads across his cheeks before I realize the meaning of the question.

"Business," he says quickly.

"I see." She appears a bit crestfallen as she reaches up to fiddle with her silver necklace. "I suppose this means a short visit then."

Crowe cuts me a sideways glance. "We were hoping for some lunch, then we have to talk to some Aquains so we can be on our way to Alchemy by nightfall."

"Well, you're in luck, I suppose. Lunch is ready." She leads the way to the kitchen, and Crowe walks beside her.

"Great! What are we havin'?"

I limp along a foot behind them, dreading what Crowe said. Why wouldn't he want to spend a night at home in his own Coven?

Why the rush?

"What happened to you?" Kieran asks, breaking me out of my thoughts.

"Kieran!" Crowe snaps. "Could you be any more rude?"

"It's okay." I clear my throat before adding, "I was in an accident as a kid. A fire that permanently damaged the muscles in my leg." *Or something like that*, I add silently when I remember the secret my parents, *and* the Sage, are keeping from me.

"I'm sorry to hear that," he says. He's oblivious to the whirlwind of emotions sweeping through me. "You're still beautiful though!"

I'm not the least bit cheered by his compliment. "I'd be in a better mood if I hadn't had to slosh through swamps for hours to get here. How do you people do it?"

"From one of the dry Covens?" he guesses. He has a sly smirk on his face, as though he assumes he's got me all figured out. "Here, this will help." He pulls a polished stone from his pocket and places it in my palm. "Keep this close to you, and the charms on it will keep you dry."

"Thank you," I say and brighten. "This is the best gift I've gotten in a while."

He laughs. We step into a large dining room, and I try to keep the amazement off my face, but I know I'm failing. This room is bigger than the dining hall at Headquarters, and I wonder how much money Crowe's family has. This room is about the same size as my childhood home. Maybe even larger.

"Sit wherever," Crowe says. He gestures at the red, padded chairs around the grand dining table.

Grail is seated at the end of the table. He holds a goblet to his lips and has a newspaper spread across the table before him. He nods to me and sets his cup down. I offer an uncertain smile back before sliding into the chair closest to me. Kieran sits beside me, while Crowe and Breanne sit on the other side of the table.

"What's Grail doing here?" I ask.

"Don't you know the Aquais Adept practically lives here?" Kieran replies with a roll of his eyes.

Grail picks up a roll and chews on it absently, pretending not to hear us talking about him.

How much of the Coven lives here to protect Crowe's family?

A butler comes in and places goblets in front of Breanne, Crowe, Kieran, and me before using his powers to fill them with water. I give him a sympathetic smile which he ignores. Carefully, he places fancy bowls full of a creamy, white soup in front of us, then leaves without a word.

"So, how has life been treating you?" Breanne asks Crowe as she dips her spoon into her soup.

I take a bite and don't hear his response. The flavor sings on my tongue, the memory of Papra's meal long gone. I eat quickly before I stop, overtly conscious of the company around me. These are upper class witches, and I don't want to seem rude or uncivilized. I clank my spoon against the side of the bowl as I adjust my grip, and some of my hair comes close to dipping into the liquid.

Grail peeks up at me. He has the smallest hint of a smirk on his face.

Is it that obvious I don't belong here?

Beside me, Kieran takes a big gulp of liquid from his goblet and smacks his lips. "So, what is your power?" he asks me and wipes his mouth with a fancy blue napkin. "Must be pretty special to be scooped up into my brother's ranks."

I'm uncertain how much I want to tell him. How much I *should* tell him. "I have telekinetic powers."

"But you're not from Mentis?"

I shake my head. "I'm from Ignis. My powers are pretty average. I think the Council is fussing over me because of the way I helped Tarj during Iris' attack."

"That's not the only reason," Crowe interjects.

"What you did was brave," Kieran says.

Breanne and Grail agree, and heat rushes to my face. I hate being the center of attention, but it seems it's something I'm going to have to get used to.

Kieran chuckles and runs his hand through his medium locks of red hair before leaning back in his seat. "Want to hear about average powers? My brother can shapeshift, and all I can do is cause it to rain for five minutes."

I blink at him, surprised. Crowe had made it sound as though his entire family was UnEquipped. "Would you rather be UnEquipped?"

"I don't see much difference if we're being honest."

"There have to be some advantages to your gift." I lean my elbows on the table and think about the Aens farms. I bet they would be grateful for some rain.

"Well, if you figure something out, let me know because, so far, I haven't seen it," he says.

I take another bite as I digest what he said. Maybe he's right. Aquais witches can't grow their own food like the other Covens, thanks to the wetlands. They depend on the Council to send them the supplies they need to survive. It's part of the reason they remain the smallest Coven.

"So, nothing too suspicious then?" A snippet of the conversation between Crowe and Grail floats to me.

I probe their minds to catch up. Things seem normal in Aquais as far as either of them is concerned.

"No, you know as well as anyone we're close. Closer than the other Covens anyway. Everyone's still here, and as far as I know, no one plans on leaving anytime soon," Grail replies.

"Aens was practically deserted," Crowe tells him.

"What'd Leo have to say about it?"

"Not much. It seems as though none of them really want to talk," I add to the conversation.

"It's the weirdest thing I've ever seen," Crowe agrees and sets his spoon down on his napkin. "Mother, you're sure there's been nothing odd around here?"

"Things have been as they always have, Alexander, dear."

Crowe doesn't seem convinced. His eyes glaze over as if he's seeing a memory. I open my mouth to ask, but he snaps out of it as suddenly as it began. "You about finished?" he asks and stands so fast, his chair screeches across the fancy floor. "I want to get to Alchemy before nightfall."

My leg twitches in painful protest. I want to argue, but there's a look in his eyes that tells me there's more to this than I'm aware of.

"Yeah, let's go," I say and stand. I bow to Breanne and stumble over the leg of the chair. "Thank you for lunch."

"I insist you two get a change of clothes before you go!" Breanne calls. "If I know my son, he didn't give you time to pack proper provisions."

She couldn't be more right. We'd brought enough supplies for the first two days of the trip and not a moment longer. "Fresh clothes sound great. Thank you."

Crowe flashes me a look that says *Really?* but he starts to walk down the hall anyway. I do my best to keep pace with him and Kieran who walk on either side of me. The butler appears from one of the adjoining rooms with a fresh change of clothes for each of us. Crowe and I depart for different rooms and pull on the blue clothing. We arrive back at the main room at almost the same time.

"When will you be back?" Kieran asks his brother.

Crowe stares at him, lips pulled into an intense frown. "I don't know. I really wish this could've been longer, a *real* visit, but things are bad, worse than we've seen in a while."

"Whatever you do, stay safe and good luck," Kieran says. He pulls Crowe into a one-armed hug. "And good luck to you for having to put up with him."

"You can say that again," I murmur, with a hint of a smile.

Kieran leaves us beneath the grand archway and closes the door behind us.

"They seem nice," I remark as we make our way down the hill.

"If nice equals obnoxious," Crowe scoffs. "I apologize for my brother's behavior."

"He's not so bad," I say. I'm grateful for Kieran's stone when I realize my legs and feet are still dry in spite of the water around us.

"If you say so," he murmurs, but his voice is sharp with sudden bitterness.

I flinch. What did I miss? At the table, Crowe had seemed excited to be home with his family again.

I'm tempted to probe his mind, but I think better of it. I don't want to get into the habit, or he might start veiling his thoughts. So, I let him lead the way while I think about the next Coven on our tour. Alchemy. Home of the Healers. Logical witches. Witches connected to nature on a level the rest of us will never be, not to mention Ambrossi's place of origin.

When I assume we're about to slosh down into the water around Crowe's home, he skirts to the left and we walk the edge of it. Behind the sprawling grounds of the mansion, a strip of land goes over the moat, leading away. Either side is lined with reeds and water plants.

As we step onto the strip, I stare at the surface of the

water, wondering what creatures live in it. To distract myself, I ask Crowe, "Where are we going?"

"I want to say hello to some people," he says but avoids looking at me as he speaks.

He's hiding something, my gut tells me.

I don't say anything. The path eventually opens into a patch of land that's ringed with several bungalows. The dark wooden sides make them nearly blend into the vegetation.

"This is the heart of Aquais," he says.

"Oh," I say and it's the only thing I can manage. I understand why Grail likes to live and operate out of Breanne's mansion.

"It's not much, I know," Crowe says, deciphering exactly what my tone means.

"Does your Coven have an altar?" I ask, not spotting anything out of the norm.

Crowe nods and jerks a thumb over his shoulder. "Of course. It's up the hill."

"Do most of your covenmates live with your family?"

Crowe shrugs. "It doesn't make sense to have a large house if you're not going to share it. There's never been that many of us anyway."

"Fair enough."

Crowe leads the way to the nearest house. In the water next to where the land ends, a fish swims by, moving a lily pad.

An older witch answers. "Crowe? Is that you?" she asks and pulls him into a hug. "How are you?"

"I'm doing good, Marnie," he says. "I just wanted to see how you were doing."

"I'm good, sweetie. Do you want to come in? I'm about to start dinner," she says and looks at me as if she's just noticed Crowe isn't alone.

Crowe doesn't try to introduce me. "Oh, no. I've eaten at home. Just wanted to say hello while I'm here."

"Well, it was good to see you," she says and closes the door.

The cheer on Crowe's face goes out, and I realize that it was fake. "Onto the next house," he says.

I watch him curiously but don't speak as he goes through the same series of steps with the next house. Part of me had expected him to ask some questions about if they've noticed anything strange, but he doesn't. He smiles and gives the same conversation to every witch who opens the door.

When he approaches the fifth house, he knocks and knocks, but no one answers. This one is smaller than the others with one large window in front and a sloping roof. It looks more like a tool shed than a home. Crowe clenches his hands into fists and raises his hand as if he's going to knock again, but I stop him.

"No one's home," I tell him.

His nostrils flare as he looks at the door then me. "Yeah," he says finally and moves onto the next house.

The rest of the time we spend in Aquais, he periodically looks toward that door, but it never opens.

Chapter Twenty-Six
Alchemy

I DON'T ASK Crowe whose house that was, or why he seemed so focused on it. All thoughts stay to myself as he bangs on every door in Aquais. At first, I think his motivation comes from his duty to serve the Council, but midway through the quest, I realize he's driven by his genuine care for his friends and family.

Leaving Aquais, he says very little, and I don't feel it's the appropriate time to ask. If he wanted to tell me what was wrong, he would. The sun slips beneath the horizon as we reach the edge of a clearing. The forests of Alchemy remind me of the Grove with towering oaks that block so much light it's unusually dark long before nighttime. We stand outside a house that looks like my parent's home in Ignis. Even the wyrm who brought us here looked like those I'm used to seeing in the Grove with dappled patterns that help camouflage them in the woods.

Crowe knocks, and we wait patiently for the occupant to answer. Crowe hadn't mentioned who we'd be staying with tonight, and the longer we stare at the door, the more I wonder who they are. Do they know Ambrossi or Lynx personally?

I wrap my arms around myself to block out the chill that's swept in with the early hours of the night. I'm thankful again for Kieran's magic stone that kept me dry during the last few hours in Aquais. I can't imagine how cold I'd be right now if I were soaked.

Crowe's sour expression has softened, but his frown is still there. I don't like it. Our entire day had been ruled by it. Now that we're out of Aquais, his mood doesn't seem much better. I wonder if I should *ask* him what's on his mind.

A thought from Crowe's mind echoes loudly and prominently in my head, as if he senses I'm thinking about him. *The man you're about to meet is the oldest witch in Alchemy. He's trained most of the Healers and knows more about herbs than anyone. He trained Lynx before the Council recruited him. Treat him with the utmost respect, please.*

As if on cue, the door opens to reveal an aged man cloaked in long blue robes. His tiny, blue eyes watch us from a face framed in a gray-white beard.

"Ah! Is that Crowe I see?" he asks.

"Indeed, Lazarus. We're here on Council business," Crowe says and smiles despite his concerns. "I've brought company this time."

Lazarus turns to me, and like the Sage's, his ancient eyes seem to bore into my soul. "Are you with the Council as well, little lady?"

"I'm Lilith." It's a simple statement that doesn't suffice for all that I want to say. The questions I want to ask. His eyes tell me he's a gentle soul.

I try to probe his mind to see what I can find out about him. Almost immediately, I pick up images of a much younger version of Ambrossi—memories.

"Ah. A mind reader, this one?" Lazarus asks Crowe. He presses one finger to his forehead, then my view of his thoughts is violently disconnected, and I'm left with an overwhelming sense of vertigo.

"She's new," Crowe murmurs. He shoots me a disappointed look. "And she's in the process of learning what it means to be polite."

Shell-shocked, I stare at Lazarus through wide eyes. "Sorry."

Lazarus smiles in a way that reminds me of the way my grandfather used to when he'd tell a story he was rather fond of. "You're forgiven," he says and steps aside. "Come in out of the cold."

Crowe leads the way inside, and I take it all in. Lazarus' home smells of parchment and herbs, which reminds me of the Sage's room, though this building is tiny in comparison to Headquarters. The main room features a door that leads to a bedroom and the door behind us that leads outside and contains a large table, a handful of chairs, a couch, a fireplace, and a rack filled with herbs and flowers.

"It's been ages since I last saw you, boy," Lazarus says. He sits beside the fireplace, where a large black cauldron sits neatly over the flames.

"I know. Unfortunately, things have been sort of hectic at Headquarters. Doesn't give us much time for anything besides work," Crowe says. He drags a chair from the table to sit next to Lazarus.

"How's Lynx handling his training?" Lazarus asks and picks up a bit of root from the table. He plucks a few thin growths from it before tossing it into the cauldron.

"He's adjusting to everything quite well."

"How's his magic?"

"Very good. Direct," Crowe says, and like me, he's thinking of Callista who remains on the brink of death. Lynx is the only thing keeping her from making the leap.

"Magical damage?"

"We'll… see," Crowe says. Some of his confidence is bleeding away. "There's a patient at Headquarters who's depending on his magical healing to get better."

A knock on the door stops the flow before Lazarus can say anything. I'm the closest to it, so Crowe and Lazarus look at me. I stiffly pull it open and find Flora. Her wide, brown eyes peer at me over the armful of plants she's struggling to hold onto.

Swallowing, she says, "H-hi. I-is Lazarus here?"

I step aside so she can see him by the fireplace, and she scurries past me to the table at the back of the room.

"Flora, were you able to get those herbs?" he asks her.

"Y-yes, sir," she manages, then dumps the bundles on the table before pushing her glasses up the bridge of her nose. She holds one up for him to see.

"Good. Sort those for me please, if you don't mind," he commands. His eyes are drawn to the cauldron by a crackle of the liquid.

Flora spreads out the herbs and stacks them in orderly piles. To me, they all look the same. The more I think about it, the more amazed I am by the information each Coven knows and no other seems to duplicate.

Lazarus watches me fidget and points to the empty chair beside Crowe. "Take a seat, girl."

Radiating pains shoot up my leg, but I don't realize how

badly it hurts until I sit. I clench my teeth, try to rub out the worst of the pain, and look at Crowe. His eyes aren't dull with exhaustion.

How does he do it?

"You should get some rest," Crowe suggests. "Your limp got worse today."

Lazarus watches me intently. "Bad leg?"

I'm too exhausted to explain. Lazarus must sense it because he passes Crowe the herbs he was shredding. Slowly, he presses against the wall, stands, and shuffles across the room. He digs in some cubbyholes and tosses me a green bundle. I catch it and inhale the scent of strong herbs, then look back at him. This parcel reminds me of the chew Fern gave me, but it's different somehow. Stiffer and stronger.

"Tear off pieces and swallow them. It'll be bitter, but it will help keep the pain away. A few leaves at a time oughta do you fine," he says and plops back down on the floor beside Crowe.

"Thank you," I say as I stroke the leaf bundle in my palm.

"My bedroom is right through that door," Lazarus says and stirs his potion. "Feel free to use the bed and facilities."

I'm not used to a lot of kindness; it makes me uncomfortable. Tears threaten to bubble up, but I keep them down by granting Lazarus a real heartfelt smile, then I make my way to the door. Flora keeps her gaze down as I pass her.

I set my hand on the doorknob before pausing to look at Crowe. "Are you gonna get some sleep?"

"I will in a bit," he says. He stares into the fireplace.

There's an odd bit of emotion in his voice that I can't identify. If we were alone, I'd ask him about it, but with Lazarus and Flora in the room, I don't. "Okay."

I enter Lazarus' room and immediately note the difference in temperature between the front room and this one. My eyes land on a large bed with green covers that takes up the majority of the space. I hobble to it and collapse on the soft bedding. After the long day of exercise and sleeping on the floor the previous night, my body soaks in every ounce of comfort.

I roll onto my back, dig the leaf bundle out of my pocket, and tear one of the delicate leaves free. "Bottoms up," I tell myself and pop it into my mouth.

I pucker, ready to spit it out, but somehow, I force myself to keep chewing. Sharp bitter liquid settles on my tongue like needles before I finally manage to swallow it. My stomach rumbles uncomfortably, but the pain in my leg disappears. I sit up and rub the skin where it had hurt so desperately only a minute before. Nothing.

A small smile crosses my face, and I lie back in the bedding. Before I know it, I drift off into a dreamless sleep that's so deep, I may as well be in a coma. It seems as if no more than a second has gone by before someone's shaking my arm. Cold fingers prod my face, and I groan as a voice mutters incomprehensible words.

I open my eyes and squint through the darkness. "Crowe?" I ask, oddly disoriented. I prop myself up on my elbow. "Is it morning?"

"No, but I, uh, I need to talk to you," he says and kneels so he's eye level with me.

His tone is enough to clear away the rest of the haze from my mind. I sit up and rub my eyes. "What's wrong?"

"There's something I didn't tell you back in Aquais," he admits. "Something kind of huge."

I'm not surprised by the admission. I'd suspected something was wrong, but I don't mention that. I stare at him and wait for him to continue.

"My friend Katrina. The one with the drowning powers I told you about. She... she... well, she was gone."

I wipe a lock of black hair from my face and lean toward him. "Gone as in dead? Or gone as in disappeared?"

"Disappeared."

"Uh-oh. Do you think she—"

"Joined the Elementals?" he guesses. His tone is thick and strained, and he picks at a loose piece of skin on his thumb. "Yes, I do."

He's trying to avoid eye contact, and it's hard to tell what he's thinking from his expression alone. I wipe my mouth and, without conscious thought, plunge into his mind. A series of memories comes to me. Crowe and Katrina talking, laughing, kissing. Understanding dawns on me as I back out of his head. This witch isn't simply his friend; he's in love with her.

"Why would she do that?" I ask. I hope he doesn't know I just probed his most intimate memories.

"She was jealous of me. Jealous of what I can do. She wanted me to teach her how to shapeshift like she thought it was something that could be given like-like a disease. When I explained to her it wasn't possible, she called me a liar." He pauses long enough to wipe his face with the back of his hand. "I know she's always wanted to be part of the Council, and when they chose me instead of her... let's just say she didn't handle it well."

"No offense, but that's wrong of her. It's so—"

"Petty?" he answers with a short, dry chuckle.

"Well, yeah," I say. "What are you going to do? Are you going to tell the Sage?"

"I don't have a choice, do I?" he asks. He sinks down on the edge of the bed beside me. "I mean, what would you do if it was your friend in the crosshairs?"

I hear the hurt in his voice. For the first time since I met him, he's wearing his heart on his sleeve, and I'm unsure how to process his vulnerability. If Helena or Clio decided to join the Elementals, I wouldn't tell anyone because my loyalty doesn't lie with the Council. It's with Ignis. With the witches I was forced to leave behind. The Council hasn't treated me as if I'm truly one of them, and part of me doubts they ever will.

Hyacinth has treated me the best since my arrival, but I have a nagging suspicion it's because she wants me to keep my mind open so she can pass along my thoughts and feelings to the Sage.

Life's not fair, I think, and I almost say it to him, but doing so won't solve anything.

Despite his confession, I know which side he's fighting for, and that only further complicates things.

What the hell does he expect me to say?

"You saw what I did for someone who wasn't a friend," I say at last. "If it was for someone I loved? I would go to the ends of the Earth before giving up."

Crowe sighs. "Do you want my honest opinion?"

"Of course."

"I could be executed for saying this," he says and looks

around the room as if he expects there to be witches in hiding, waiting for the moment he speaks to spring out and arrest him.

My expression doesn't change.

"I want to let it go," he says in one great whoosh of breath. More slowly, he adds, "I want to let her do her thing because I know her. She's smart. She wouldn't let herself be tricked into following some manic cult for the hell of it. There's some reason she did this, and maybe I don't have all the pieces, but it doesn't seem right to sentence her without talking to her first."

"Then don't."

"This is my fault. I drove her to do this," he adds softly. "I should be the one facing punishment."

"You didn't make her do anything. She's a big girl who made a big decision all on her own."

"What if she gets sent on one of their missions, like Iris or the girl who poisoned Callista? What if I have to face her in a fight? I can't hurt her, Lilith." He looks up through eyes that are glossy with tears. "But if I let her go, I'll die. The Sage will see to it."

"I think you're being a bit dramatic," I say. "She didn't kill me after either of my faux pas, though she had plenty of reasons to. I think she'd give you a chance to explain yourself."

Crowe frowns at the floor. "I've never been conflicted like this before. Is this how you felt when you were recruited, or rather, how you still feel?"

I open my mouth, ready to spill my heart, when I pause. This could be a test from the Sage. Crowe has been borne and raised to care for them like the rest of his family. Except the hurt in his eyes is real. I trust it. "If we're being truly honest with each other, then yes. I don't think I'll ever feel comfortable with the Council after everything they put me through." I lean a little bit closer to him. "I will never blindly obey every Council order, and you shouldn't either. Don't let them shape you into some kind of heartless monster. Don't let them turn you against the people you love. If you think it's best to keep the information about Katrina to yourself, then do it. You didn't even have to tell me."

"You would've come across it in my thoughts, eventually, I'm sure."

I think of the haze that filled his mind in Aens. "You're better at hiding your thoughts than you think."

Crowe peers up at me with guarded eyes and twines his thumbs together. "I should be mad at you for saying that, but it actually makes me feel better."

"Good," I say. "I'm glad I could help." And I am. This feels like the first real moment of comradery between us.

His gaze trains on my earring. "For what it's worth, I'm sorry about everything."

Some of the warm feelings simmer away. I don't want to rehash any of my hurt. "It's over and done with."

"Okay," he says and stands. He paces to the window as if he senses my unease. "You get enough sleep?"

"I feel pretty rested," I say. "Want the bed?"

He shakes his head. "I want to get moving as soon as possible. Goal is to make it to Mentis by dawn."

"You want to leave in the middle of the night?" I ask, dumbfounded.

"We're wasting time here," he says. "This Coven sends its members wherever they're needed. That means we can't trust them. Even if we do a survey, some of them won't be here because they're scattered across the Land of Five. If they are passing messages to the Elementals, we'd be none the wiser."

"I suppose you're right," I say and stifle a yawn.

I think of Ambrossi's disdain for the Council. At the time, I'd assumed the anger came from concern for me and my injury, but now, I wonder if there is a deeper meaning to it.

He was assigned to you from the moment of your accident, I tell myself.

One of us, Iris' voice bounces around my head.

There's no way Ambrossi is one of them, I argue, but a pit of uncertainty opens in my stomach.

A new, slightly worse thought comes to me. "You don't think Lynx is a double agent, do you?"

"Lynx? Why?" He scrunches his face as if the question is one he's never considered.

I shrug. "He's not allowed to leave the Grove, so it seems there's more to his story than the Sage says."

"If he were truly working for the Elementals, he wouldn't have rushed to Callista's side the way he did. I could see the devotion in his eyes. He's not going to sleep until she recovers."

"He could've easily been ordered to act that way to keep suspicion off him," I point out.

Crowe presses his lips into a tight line. "I know you're right, but I don't want to believe it about one of our own, especially Lynx."

If the Land of Five is really on the verge of war, everyone will have to choose a side to fight on.

I'm not sure which direction I should go.

Hell, I don't even know who I really am.

What I do know is that I don't truly trust either side, and in the end, that needs to change. I'll have to make the hardest decision of my life because I suspect it won't be much longer before the Council corners me about where my loyalties lie.

Chapter Twenty-Seven
Mentis

AS WE TRAVEL through the forests of Alchemy in the darkness of night, Crowe is again on edge. I feel the same as I pull my cloak, given to me by Lazarus, tighter around me to block out the chill. He'd been confused by Crowe's sudden insistence to travel, but once he figured out he wouldn't be able to change his mind, he gave us some supplies and wished us safe travels. If only it could be that simple.

Crowe's gaze is trained on the ground. It's a wonder he hasn't crashed into any of the trees.

"Are you okay?" I finally ask him.

The shadows hide his eyes as he says, "I have a feeling Mentis isn't going to be very friendly toward us."

"Why?" I barely resist the urge to remind him that's how he's felt about *all* the Covens so far. I think of Dawn. The Mentis Adept hadn't seemed particularly different at the Arcane Ceremony… no Mentians had.

"Think about the Elementals' gifts so far. All of them seem to have some sort of mental power. That gives us a disadvantage if any of their gifts have allowed them access to information they shouldn't have."

"So what? That doesn't mean they're all gonna be hostile. If they were, they would've helped Iris attack Tarj when he was down," I point out. "They were right by our side to try to stop her."

"Maybe, but something tells me the Mentis Elementals won't run like the others did. I think they'll stay to face us," he says.

I stop walking, causing him to stop and turn back to face me. "If you really think that, we should get backup then. Going ourselves sounds like a bad idea."

"The Sage insisted we do it alone, remember?" His tone makes it obvious he's on my side on this issue.

"Yeah, I remember," I say darkly. It's hard to forget the few interactions I've had with her. They've all been so strange.

Just when I think that the conversation is about to fizzle out, Crowe asks, "You ever hear stories about a girl named Willow?"

My heart speeds up at her name, and I almost trip over my foot. The story Tarj shut down. Does Crowe know he's not supposed to mention her? *Why is he thinking about her now?* "She's the woman who was executed by the Council for having multiple powers right?" I ask innocently. I try to downplay how desperate I am to hear the rest of the story.

"Yeah. She was from Mentis," he begins. "Some witches here still remember her."

That makes sense. "The Sage knows this?"

"Of course," Crowe says.

"Why was she executed?"

Crowe draws his lips sideways as if he's considering shutting me down like Tarj did. "From what I heard, she was the leader of the Elementals. When the Sage was new to her position, she recruited Willow into the Council. Supposedly, Willow used that link to her advantage and tried to wipe out every other member. The Sage caught on before she could go through with her plan and arrested her. Willow was executed because the Sage believed the Elementals would disband without her leadership."

"Willow let them?" I ask, shocked. If she was as powerful as everyone has made her sound, I can't imagine why she would go gently into that good night. "I thought she had a crazy amount of powers."

"No idea if she really had them or not," Crowe admits. "A lot of the stuff about her isn't clear. Details of that day are pretty hush hush. I learned what I know from Hyacinth, so take the information with a grain of salt."

It's as close to the truth as I've gotten so far, and I'll accept it. After all, Hyacinth has a direct link to the Sage's mind. "It's more than I was able to get out of Tarj. Thank you."

He grunts in response. "I'm telling you this so you understand why I'm worried. If the rumors are true about her, she will have the strongest following here."

We fall silent as we cross the border between Alchemy and Mentis. The trees stop, and the dirt beneath our feet turns to sand. Tropical foliage appears. Beads of sweat gather on my skin, and the cloak that kept the chill away in Alchemy now holds in the heat. I squint and try to see through the soft darkness.

From what I can tell, there's a good amount of territory left between us and any Mentis witches. Even in the early morning hours, the air in this Coven is so hot it's suffocating. Palm trees loom over us as we cross the sand, and all I can think about is how much I'll dread the heat in the middle of the day.

"If there wasn't so much humidity, I'd almost think I was

in Ignis," I say and wipe the moisture from my forehead.

"Is there really a difference? Heat is heat," Crowe says while trying to blow his wet bangs off his forehead.

"Dry heat and wet heat are two very different things."

Crowe snorts. "Desert Coven problems."

"You know it," I say, chin raised high. "How much longer do we have until we get to wherever it is we're going?"

"Tricia's brother lives around here," Crowe says. He gestures to the outlines of houses nestled into the tropical undergrowth that lines the path ahead. "We can get something to eat, and honestly, I'm hoping I can sneak in a quick nap. I'm already regretting not catching a few hours in Alchemy."

"Sounds fine to me," I say and hold a hand over my growling stomach. "As long as Mentis proves to be less hostile than you think it's gonna be."

"Let's hope so," Crowe says and scans our surroundings. "So far, so good."

Crowe hasn't gotten over the anxiety he'd shown at the beginning of the trip. He's gotten better at hiding it. I consider passing him Ambrossi's amulet, except his anxiety is giving *me* anxiety.

The sand beneath us gives way to dirt around the same time the sun begins to peek over the horizon. It sheds light onto the buildings that had been encased in darkness. These homes are bigger than the shacks, cabins, and bungalows of Aens, Alchemy, and Ignis. The detached houses stand beside each other in small groups which are scattered as far as I can see. They vary in color, though their box shape seems to be standard. The most fascinating part of these houses is the artificial light shining inside.

"It's a shame they can't share their technology with the other Covens," Crowe says. "We'd really benefit."

"I'm sure they could learn something from the other Covens as well," I say, thinking of the weather capabilities of Aquais and Aens. Rain and wind would no doubt bring them relief on the most sweltering days.

We walk up to the nearest house, and Crowe bangs on the door with the side of his fist. I bundle my cloak while we wait for someone to answer. A tall, older teenager with short, brown hair and a hefty build answers the door. I recognize Tricia in his features.

"Crowe and Lilith." He greets us with a heartfelt warmth that was missing from the others' greetings.

"I take it Hyacinth let you know we were coming?" Crowe asks.

"Hyacinth can hear this far from the Grove?" I ask, amazed.

"We're closer than we've been in days," Crowe says.

Lilith! I've missed you too! Hyacinth's lilting voice drifts through my mind.

Hyacinth, good to connect again, I say, though it's hard to tell if I mean my words.

"Sure did. Everything is ready for your stay," he says to Crowe, then looks at me. "I'm Quinn if Crowe hasn't told you already."

"Nice to meet you," I reply stiffly. I don't get along well with Tricia, so I'm not sure what to think of her family.

If it's any consolation, Tricia's sorry for what she did, Hyacinth informs me.

I conjure a thumbs up in my mind to project back to her. Being sorry now doesn't excuse all that's happened.

"Come on in," Quinn says and steps aside to give us room.

I stay behind Crowe as we enter the large living room. Technology is scattered around, and I'm not sure what half the things do. Artificial light radiates from the lamp beside a soft-looking chair, and I have the urge to plop down in it and take a nap. A cool breeze tickles my sweaty skin and refreshes me as I wander deeper into the room. Mentis witches live very different lives from those in other Covens. Even the poorest of them live a plush lifestyle.

"It's called air conditioning," Quinn says. He has a pleasant smile on his face.

"It's nice," I murmur. I take a step to the right, and the blast of cold air is stronger, more direct.

"Doesn't Ignis have something like it?" Quinn asks. He runs a finger down the spine of a book on the table beside him.

I shake my head. "No. Our homes are built small to help regulate the air flow naturally."

Quinn juts out his bottom lip. "Huh. Okay. Learn something new every day, I suppose. Would you two like some breakfast?"

"I'd like to sign up for a nap," Crowe says after raising his hand like he's in school.

The smile returns to Quinn's face. "You do look ready to drop." He jerks his thumb over his shoulder. "Down that hallway, you'll find a few spare rooms. Pick whichever one you want."

Crowe dips his head, and I catch the slight smile on his face as he turns away. He seems to be glad to be in a place of comfort.

So greedy.

Everyone has their flaws! Hyacinth offers.

Crowe disappears from the room, and my stomach growls again. "Can I take you up on that breakfast offer?"

Quinn lets out a short laugh. "Of course."

In the kitchen, the artificial light bouncing off the white walls and tiles makes the room almost too bright for me to bear. I sit at the table and listen to Quinn moving around in the next room. He brings me a cup of sweet, red juice, then disappears again. I sip the drink until he comes back a few minutes later with a few plates of food. Quinn sits across from me and watches me for close to a minute.

Uncomfortable with the stare, I swallow and say, "This is good."

"Thanks." He props his head on his hand as he watches me. "It's always interesting to meet the new members of the Council. You're all so different from each other."

That's something I can agree with. Even Hyacinth is on the same page.

I take my time chewing my next bite, and Quinn continues, "Want to go for a tour around the Coven when you're finished eating? Crowe will be down for a while."

"That sounds wonderful." I nearly beam at his hospitality. *And Crowe said they would be hostile.*

You haven't met the actual Coven yet, Hyacinth reminds me.

My most recent bite sticks in my throat, and it's hard to finish my meal with Hyacinth's words of wisdom bouncing around in my head. She's right. Quinn has an obligation to treat us with kindness that the rest of the Coven will not.

I clean my plate and hand it to Quinn. "It seems like forever since the last time we ate."

Quinn takes my plate to the sink and rinses it off. "My Momma used to tell me the best way to get to someone's heart is to feed them or make them laugh. So now, I try to do both whenever I can."

"She sounds like a wonderful woman," I say and stick close by him as he leads the way outside.

The suffocating heat just outside the door hits so suddenly, it feels as if it's stealing my breath. Thinking of the cool air in his house, I momentarily reconsider the tour.

"How do you do it?" I ask as we stroll through the golden sand a few feet from his house.

Quinn raises an eyebrow, genuinely confused. "Do what?"

"Stand the heat. I feel like we're in the ninth circle of Hell!"

"We wear light clothes." He gestures at the shirt and shorts he's wearing.

"This outfit is cooking me," I say. I had left Lazarus' cloak in the house, but the clothes from Aquais aren't meant to breathe—they're stiff and waterproof and hold heat.

Quinn studies the outfit. "Come on. I'm sure we have some clothes you can wear."

I don't protest as we go back inside. I inhale the air conditioning as if my life depends on it. Quinn wanders down the hall, and when he reappears, he's clutching a shirt and shorts similar to his. "These are Tricia's so they might be a little big on you, but better than nothing."

I murmur thanks and make my way to the bathroom where I dress and pop the last bite of Lazarus' herbs in my mouth. I give them a second to take effect, then I clean my face in the sink and pull my fingers through my knotted hair. I tuck Ambrossi's amulet into my pocket before meeting Quinn outside.

"Better?" he asks.

"Yes, thank you."

Walking through the Coven feels like walking through a dream. There's no order to the way it's set up. The houses aren't in line with each other, and I can't figure out where the center is.

"It's cooler toward the center of the Coven," Quinn says. He squints at the path ahead. "That's where the water used to be."

"Used to be?" I echo.

"It was an oasis of sorts, but we had a drought a few years back. It dried up, so we moved the meeting place there since it's more convenient. The Council delivers our water now." His tone is stiff, and there is more under the surface than he wants to say.

I narrow my eyes, confused. "Why don't they just refill the oasis?"

Quinn's eyes close to slits. "You say *they* as if you're not one of them."

He's suspicious of me. For the first time in a long time, I feel as if I'm in a corner all on my own. I'm not connected to the Council, but I'm not on the same level as normal witches anymore either.

"Look," I say slowly. "I don't know if you saw what they did to me at the Dedication Ceremony…"

A sympathetic gleam flashes through his eyes. "The Council is all about showmanship."

"Yes, they are," I say. "And they care very little about the consequences of their actions."

"That's their fear, you know? That one of the Covens will learn to take care of itself. If that happens, we won't need them anymore."

The more he talks, the more I understand Crowe's concerns about Mentis and worry that he might be right. Quinn is *related* to a Council member and for that reason alone, he has to have some semblance of trust in us, but even that trust is small.

"I think that's the message the Elementals want to spread," I say before I can stop myself.

He pauses as though he doesn't want to say his next sentence, but after a look around to ensure that no one else is listening, he says it anyway. "They're not...*wrong*. That treaty—that Godforsaken treaty—hurts us all in some way."

I can't think of anything to say besides the truth. "I know."

Chapter Twenty-Eight
Larc Dupree

QUICKER THAN I'VE ever done anything before, I cloak my thoughts from Hyacinth. This is a conversation that could land me in hot water if the wrong people overhear. I don't know whether she can be considered a friend or an enemy, and I don't want to choose wrong in my assumption.

As we near the center of the Coven, we pass a few Mentis witches going about their day. I try to smile and appear pleasant, more than I did with the other Covens. It hasn't left my mind how close I'd come to becoming a permanent member of Mentis.

"How do you tell them apart?" Quinn asks. "The Elementals from the normal witches?" There's a darkness in his eyes that makes me shiver as he watches a pair of his Covenmates pass by.

If Hyacinth can read my thoughts, she can probably read his as well. If there's something I need to know about him, I'm sure she'll tell me.

"Not sure," I say. I'm glad I haven't had to face any of them. "Most of them split before we could find them. Aens was hit the hardest."

"Almost sounds like they're planning something big," Quinn says. "If not, they'd have no reason to leave."

"Stakes are higher now. They know if they're caught, they'll be executed, like Iris." I stare into the dip of the old oasis then at the buildings on the other side. A new thought comes to me. "Where's Dawn?"

The other Adepts had quickly appeared when they caught wind of our arrival, but I haven't seen so much as a glimpse of the girl who caught my eye at the Arcane Ceremony.

Quinn shrugs. "She hangs around the Healer's den sometimes, or she might be handling some of her Coven duties. I can introduce you to our Healer, Lavina, if you'd like. She might know where Dawn is."

I consider the offer. The four Healers I've met have all been vastly different. I can't help wondering what Mentis' will be like. "Yeah, sure."

"Wait here for a second," he says and disappears into a nearby house.

"Oh, okay," I say and stare after him.

I assume he'll only be gone a few seconds, so I stay put. But after a few minutes pass, and he doesn't emerge, I content myself with studying my surroundings, starting with the outlines of the palm trees in the distance and ending with the dirt pit of the old oasis. It's so dry and cracked, it's hard to believe there was ever water there. A large rock, similar to the one in Aens, sits at the center. I slide down the side of the dried hole and run my fingers over the smooth stone. I lean against it and revel in the rest for my painful leg. I wish I would've had the willpower to wait to finish off Lazarus' herbs… or I had been brave enough to ask for another dose before we left Alchemy.

You're being watched, Hyacinth warns.

My eyes shoot open. A girl with short hair stares at me from a little way away. She's half-hidden in the shadows of a red house, and almost impossible to see with the way the sun glares in my eyes.

Does she know I'm watching her? I ask Hyacinth.

No response.

I stretch, uncomfortable under her glare. It doesn't seem to matter that I'm openly staring back. She's not reacting. Just as Crowe predicted. I consider blasting her with my powers to get her to stop; instead, I blink and, when I open my eyes again, she's gone.

"Hey there, beautiful. You look a little down," a voice says, and all thoughts of the girl leave my mind.

I jump and hold a hand over my heart as I whip around to see who spoke. A male with an elliptical face, small brown eyes, and a tough jawline stares back at me. He looks to be easily thirty-five.

"I-I uh… I'm okay," I stutter. I look back at the door Quinn disappeared through, wanting him to emerge and come to my rescue.

"It's a shame to see you all alone," the man says. He stalks around the pit and grips my hand, then plants his lips against my skin much the way Kieran did in Aquais, but there's something different about it. It's off-putting. I rip my hand from him and stagger backward a few steps. I bump into the edge of the pit, and when I realize I won't be able to climb out on my own, I lift my hand to strike him with whatever power comes first.

"Look, you're coming on really strong, and I'm about to hex your ass into oblivion if you don't back off," I snarl. I don't care that I'm openly threatening a civilian. I just want him to go far away… even if I have to blast him there myself.

He grins, takes a step backward, and raises his palms defensively. I notice his limp. "Fiery, huh? Just like Ivy. You look like her too."

"Look, I don't—"

"Is everybody okay?" Dawn's voice calls out behind me.

She climbs down into the pit and grasps my elbow, pulling me from the battle stance I'd unconsciously taken.

"No… that guy," I say and point him out.

"What's going on?" Quinn asks as he finally emerges from the house. He slides down the path Dawn had taken and hurries to my side. With her help, he tries to get me back up the slope.

"Him! That guy." I spot the man leaning against the rock. He winks, not the least bit ashamed of himself. Shuddering, I turn back to Quinn. "He's a pig, and I was about to cook him."

"Ugh, I know," Dawn scoffs as she helps me steady myself. Judging by the haunted look in her eyes, I assume she's had similar experiences.

Poor girl.

"That's Larc Dupree," Quinn says with a grimace as he joins us. "Coven drunk. Huge creep."

"I got that part." I shiver again and wonder if I can have him executed for leering at me.

You can't execute someone for being disgusting, Hyacinth reminds me. *Unfortunately.*

"It's a good thing he's UnEquipped. I'd hate to see the kind of havoc he'd wreak if he weren't," Quinn mutters.

It's not very often witches make a strong point in an UnEquipped's favor. "If he's that much of a problem, why doesn't the Council exile him, like they supposedly did to Iris?"

"You tell me."

Well, Hyacinth? I prompt, but she's silent again.

Quinn leads the way to the Healer den. A blanket hangs over the entrance rather than a traditional door. I have the feeling that, despite Mentis' technological advances, the Healer lives her life as closely as she can to the way it was in Alchemy. Thoughts of Larc slip away as I follow Quinn inside.

The den smells the same as Lazarus' house. The artificial lights are off, and a candle sits in the middle of a table with a cauldron on one side and a pile of herbs on the other. Bookshelves take up one corner of the room, each shelf stocked with hefty medical books. I want to ask if I can read one, though now is definitely not the time or place for my curiosity.

A dark-skinned woman with silky, raven hair and warm eyes approaches. She smiles at me. Her gaudy, blue robes billow behind her, and the air around her has a calming effect that most likely comes from her powers.

"Name's Lavina. It's nice to meet you," she says. She clutches one of my hands in hers.

I smile back at her. "I'm Lilith."

The Healer gestures for me to sit on the loveseat on the west side of the room, and I obey. Dawn plops down at a table, chopping some of Lavina's herbs. Part of me wonders if she has some sort of healing ability or reason why she's so drawn to the Healer's Den. If she does, then that means she's got multiple powers like I do. Given the way she nearly beat Clio at the Arcane Ceremony, it's a possibility.

Yet, she disappeared at the first sign of Iris' attack.

You noticed too? Hyacinth asks.

Yeah. Should I pry into her mind?

You can certainly try, but it's done me no good. Most Mentis people are hard to read. They're used to mind readers poking around in their intimate thoughts, so they've learned to cloak themselves.

We can't catch a break, huh?

"Lilith?" Quinn asks. He nudges me in the ribs with his elbow.

"Huh?" I blurt out, realizing I've missed an entire chunk of conversation.

"Quinn tells me you're searching for Elementals?" Lavina asks. She doesn't seem upset that she has to repeat herself as she slips into the chair across from me.

"It's been a pretty fruitless search so far," I admit, though it's hard to forget the girl who'd been watching me before Larc's interruption. "Have you seen anything suspicious lately?"

She presses her lips together and glances at Dawn. The Adept shakes her head, and Lavina says, "Most of the Coven has kept to themselves since the Arcane Ceremony."

"Have there been any injuries since then?"

Lavina clasps her hands. "The usual scrapes here and there. Nothing major. For the most part, it's been quiet. To me *that's* suspicious."

"Definitely," I say. Even if it's minor, witches occasionally get hurt doing something as regular as Coven duties.

"It's almost like this entire Coven is walking on eggshells," Quinn says.

Dawn sets down her knife and looks at me through dead, amber eyes. "I don't know if this counts as strange or downright frustrating, but many witches are refusing to participate in battle training. They either sleep through the lessons or talk back when given orders. There's no sense of Coven Pride anymore."

"Have you told anyone this?" I ask and watch the way she squirms under my gaze.

"Who am I going to tell? I'm supposed to take issues like this up with y'all. And you're here."

"Sounds like something your clairvoyant should scope out," Lavina interjects. Her dark eyes dip downward, and she takes in the full extent of my bad leg. I'd been so swept up in the conversation, I'd forgotten the shorts Quinn lent me left the worst of the damage exposed. "Your leg. How'd you hurt it?"

"Childhood accident," I say reflexively and pause. "Ambrossi's tried to heal it, but he says the magical damage is too deep."

"May I see it?"

I stretch my leg out. Lavina rises, crouches beside me, and sets her fingers against my skin. She's silent for so long, I start to grow uncomfortable. I shift subtly and hope the movement will spark a conversation.

"What are your powers?" She doesn't take her eyes off my leg.

I feel uncomfortably exposed, as if she's looking into my soul. "Telekinesis mostly."

"Mostly?"

"Also, some mindreading."

"No pyro?" she asks as she stands.

"One time when I was really tired. Why?"

"I believe the damage is so deep, it's spread to your blood and worked its way into your abilities, thus changing the very root of your magic."

I don't like the sound of that. "So, what are you saying?" I ask. My voice is strained. "D-does that mean I wasn't supposed to develop pyro powers?"

"Judging from your initial magic, I'd say not. It seems somebody didn't want you to know that."

The air leaves my lungs, and I'm on the verge of fainting when I remember my parents' hesitation to tell me the truth about my accident. Could they have had something to do with it? Could the Sage?

The *what ifs* bounce around inside my head again and nothing else matters. Hyacinth tries to whisper reassuring words, but I can't focus over the beating of my heart. The blood rushes to my head and pounds in my ears, and before I know it, I collapse, slipping into unconsciousness amid a chorus of concerned shrieks.

Chapter Twenty-Nine
Chastity

I BARELY HEAR Lavina, Quinn, and Dawn urging me back to consciousness. Their words flow in one ear and out the other. Someone puts a hand on my forehead, possibly to gauge my temperature. They're faceless as they grab my arms, help me off the ground, and somehow sit me back on the couch. I don't take my eyes off my leg, consumed with a darkness that refuses to clear. Everything I've learned over the course of the past week and a half flood through my mind.

One. Since I was little, my parents have lied about what really happened to my leg.

Two. I'm not the one who injured myself.

Three. The fire damage was bad enough that my other powers stepped in to heal it, holding the magic in place.

Four. Whoever did it hurt me bad enough to potentially change the root of my magic.

Five. If Mentis powers were my original magic, then that means I most likely am from Mentis.

Six. If I came from Mentis, then my parents are not my real parents.

Who am I?

"Lilith?" Quinn asks. He leans close to me and shakes my arm with his large hand.

"She's in shock," Lavina says.

Dawn crouches before me. Her hands rest on my knees as she stares into my eyes, looking for some sign of life. "Lilith? Lilith, are you there?"

"Huh?" I blink.

"She's back," Dawn says and takes a step back.

"Are you okay?" Quinn asks slowly, as though he's not sure I'll be able to follow.

Slowly, I nod. I wince at the slight taste of blood in my mouth and poke the fresh wound in my tongue.

"Let's go back to my place," Quinn says. "Crowe is probably awake by now."

"H-how long was I out?" I ask, holding my hand to the side of my head.

"A minute or two," Lavina answers. She offers me a sympathetic smile as if she can guess how overwhelmed I am. "Are you okay?"

To me, it feels as though fifty years have passed.

"Yes," I murmur and try to stand. "It was… nice to meet you." I don't meet her gaze because I don't want her to see the haunted look in my eyes. To know just how rattled this entire situation has made me.

Dawn stands a pace behind Lavina and silently watches as Quinn helps me stand. I pass them, and Lavina grasps my arm gently.

Her thin fingers knead my skin. "Be careful out there, child."

I don't know how to respond, so I don't. I follow Quinn through the door, and I'm instantly aware of the Mentis heat. Sweat runs down my face, and with any luck, I won't faint again.

I mistakenly glance toward the dry oasis. Larc sends me a creepy glance in return.

"Doesn't he have anything better to do than stand around in the middle of the Coven and hit on unsuspecting girls?" I grumble, hoping Quinn won't ask me any questions about what happened in Lavina's.

"He's unemployed and UnEquipped, so I'm gonna say no," Quinn replies. He sticks his hands in his pockets as we make our way down the path into the tropical foliage.

I shiver and hope we won't have to come back to this part of the Coven when Crowe wakes up.

"So, can't ignore what happened back there," Quinn says slowly. "Are you okay? Like…truly?"

I stop and look at him knowing I won't be able to keep my thoughts to myself. "My entire life, people have pitied me because of my leg. They thought I'd never measure up to my classmates. They didn't think I'd graduate. Hell, some of them thought I might struggle to keep up with even the UnEquipped. I've always been thought of as lesser than. To think this was done on purpose, that someone wanted me to live like this, boggles my mind. I want to go home and call it quits, but nowhere feels like home anymore." To make things worse, tears start to swell in my eyes, and I want to cry. Nowhere feels safe. No person does either. I don't have a home at Headquarters yet, and if what Lavina said is true, I don't have a home in Ignis with Raya and Haze either. "So, to answer your question… no, I'm not."

Quinn sighs lightly, tilts his head backward, and lets the sunlight hit his face. I take in a breath, preparing him to unload some bucket list of cliches on me. "You know what people used to tell me when I was growing up in the shadow of Tricia's gift?"

I sniffle and wipe my eyes. "What's that?"

"They told me all my hang-ups and doubts, they were all in my head. At the end of the day, I'm my own person, and I'm unique. Pain and anguish are part of the experience. The more you go through, and the more experiences you have, the stronger you become."

I let out a dry laugh. "Then I must be the strongest person in the world!"

"If you're on a journey that's only just begun then I'd say it sounds like your strength will only increase from here," Quinn says.

I don't believe him, so I change the subject. "How long has Lavina been a Healer?"

"Quite a few years." He glances at me out of the corner of his eye. "Why do you ask?"

Some part of me hopes she's wrong. That maybe I'm blowing things out of proportion. "She looks so young."

"That's not why you're asking," Quinn says after a minute of carefully studying me. "You want to know if you can trust her word, don't you?"

I let out a slow breath. "Of course I do. What she told me could change everything."

"Who says?"

I hold in the ironic chuckle that wants to fall out. This conversation reminds me of the one I had with Crowe about Katrina except I'm not composed this time. I take shallow breaths and realize I'm having an existential crisis, and I have no idea how to solve it.

"You were there, weren't you? I mean, she was hinting I'm not from Ignis, right?" I say. "Or at least that's how I interpreted it."

"That's what it seemed like," Quinn says. "But either way, why is that such a big deal? You're still *you*, regardless of what Coven you came from."

The question is so casual, it catches me off guard. I can't put into words exactly what this revelation means, only that's huge. I gather my thoughts as carefully as I can before I say, "I've always been suspicious about my accident, especially recently. The things my parents told me didn't add up. It never occurred to me someone might have done this on purpose."

The slightest bit of sadness crosses his face. "If I were you, I'd talk to my parents."

I force out another laugh. "I tried, and they won't say a word. Even if they do, how do I know I can trust them? They made me believe I did this to myself... that I used pyrokinesis when I was little. I had no reason to suspect they were lying until... until Iris..." I trail off. I've spoken for far too long and said far too much.

"It sounds like you already have your answer."

Hearing it from someone else solidifies the information in a way that's not easy to ignore.

"You'll find the answers you're after sooner or later," Quinn promises. "A secret this big will eventually come to light. They always do."

I want to believe him, but I can't. I hold my tongue for the duration of the walk through Mentis. Back at Quinn's house, Crowe is seated at the table, eating a watery bowl of oats. His hair is disheveled from sleep, but other than that, he looks like he's ready to go. He looks up as we enter.

"Where'd you two go?" he asks and sets his spoon down.

"I took Lilith for a little tour around the Coven," Quinn replies.

"Oh?" Crowe says and looks at me. "Learn anything?"

"Lavina says things have been odd," I say, then summarize the trip in the most compact way I can. "They think we should have Hyacinth sort them out."

Already told the Sage. Hyacinth cuts in at the mention of her name.

Thank you, I tell her. To Crowe, I say, "Hyacinth has alerted the Sage."

"Fast but expected," Crowe says and stands. "So, you gonna tell me what else happened? I'm sensing there's more."

I don't answer him, so he hits Quinn with the same question. He doesn't answer right away, and Crowe huffs.

"Lilith, would you mind leaving me and Quinn alone for a bit? I need to talk to him in private."

"Of course," I say and move from the bliss of the air conditioning into the nightmare of the heat outside.

I'm tempted to eavesdrop on their conversation, but it wouldn't be right. Plus, I'm sure it's going to be about what happened at Lavina's, and I don't want to know what either of them really think of me. So I breathe in the humid air, walk along the sand, and try to calm my frazzled nerves. I keep telling myself everything will be okay. I've made it this far; this is just one more obstacle to overcome.

Be on your guard, Hyacinth warns me before I hear

footsteps.

I pause, look up, and see a girl with red hair watching me. It's the same person I spotted before Larc distracted me. Slowly, she approaches. The only part of me that moves is my heart—it pounds with a surge of adrenaline. My breathing is erratic and difficult to control, and although I tell myself to hold my ground, I don't.

The anger takes hold of me, and I storm toward her, jabbing my finger at her. "Why are you following me?" I demand. I'm wary of her even though I'm taller by at least half a foot. Up close, she looks younger than I guessed. Maybe fifteen at the oldest.

"Your resemblance to Ivy is uncanny," she murmurs and stares at me with beautiful, ocean-blue eyes.

I'm as confused this time as I had been when Larc said it. Who is this Ivy person, and why do they keep comparing me to her? Unlike the incident I had with the witch who poisoned Callista, I'm determined not to fail this time. "Who's Ivy?"

"My idol," she says.

I'm as uncomfortable with her as I was with Larc. "I must inform you that you're in the presence of an active Council member. I can arrest you!"

She smiles. "For what exactly?"

Flustered, I can't think of a response.

The girl beams at me. "Fleur was right about you. Just from the tiny encounter you two shared, she could tell something was special. You have a very strong presence."

Though her words are praises, I perceive them only as threats.

She doesn't seem put off by the lull in conversation. "What would it take to influence you?"

"Influence me to what?"

"To join us. The Elementals."

My mouth goes dry at the casual mention of the name.

When I don't speak, she continues, "You're one of us, you know. Why do you fight so hard?"

I glance over my shoulder, hoping to see Crowe and Quinn coming to help me. She's a self-proclaimed member of the Elementals which means I need to do *something*, but I'm shellshocked. "B-but I'm not."

"Iris was meant to capture you that day. Problem is none of us thought you'd choose to protect him, to protect *them*, after all they'd done to you."

My mouth hangs open as I process her words. *Capture* me? Hadn't Iris promised she meant me no harm? My head swims with information, and I struggle to breathe.

I take a step backward and frantically try to figure out what to do next. "Stay away from me," I growl, hoping I sound fiercer than I feel.

Calm drifts over my mind, and I recognize the feeling from Tricia's attempt to control me at the Dedication Ceremony. I jump backward a few feet, concerned this witch might have gained control. Rapidly, I push the sensation away, lift a hand, and pump out an invisible blast of power that sends her flying. She lands on the ground a few feet away. As soon as eye contact is broken, the tendrils of her power loosen.

One moment.

That's all I have to decide what comes next. Being a

member of the Council means I have the authority to arrest her, but what happens if she's not truly alone? What if, the minute I have her in my hands, another Elemental appears to grab me?

Hyacinth is stumped too.

I take one more step backward and wobble on my bad leg. *Please, Goddess, not now!*

Desperation claws at me like a panicked animal, and I growl at her before sending another blast of energy out. It turns to fire that lights the front of her robes. She rushes to put it out when I hear a voice hollering at me across the beach.

"Lilith!"

It's Crowe.

My eyes stay on the girl as she rises from the ground and brushes the dirt away. I expect anger, but her eyes are still filled with that odd admiration.

"S-she's one of them!" I call to Crowe. I don't turn to see how far away he is, to see how far away *help* is.

A second later, I find out. He lunges toward her and wraps his arm around her neck to hold her in place while he slips a heavy pair of bindings on her wrists. Only when they're secure do I let myself relax. The cuffs will not only physically incapacitate her, but they'll also cripple her powers.

Quinn arrives next to me, bends over, and places his hands on his thighs as he struggles to catch his breath. "Well, that was close."

The girl in Crowe's arms gnashes her teeth and tries to lunge toward me, but Crowe holds her back.

Quinn flinches and looks me over. "Are you okay?"

"Yeah." Nervously, I reach across my body to clutch my

elbow. She didn't hurt me, but I'm still rattled. How much worse could the situation have gotten without Crowe's help? "Let's get her back to Headquarters," I say. I hope my tough act will hide how bothered I am.

"I see a swift execution in her future, like Iris," Crowe says and tightens his grip on the girl. He uses his hold to turn her toward him. "You, what's your name?"

She bats her eyelashes as she looks up at him. "Chastity."

She has no fear. *They* have no fear.

When her gaze returns to me, her eyes are like hardened sapphires as if she'd heard my thoughts. "This doesn't end with me. There will be others."

"What does that mean?" I ask and take a small step closer. "What doesn't end?"

"You can run, Lilith, but you can't hide!" Chastity squeals in a sing-song tone. She's toying with me.

Crowe realizes it too because his face goes tight with anger. "You are to remain silent," he says and pulls the handcuffs tighter behind her back.

She opens her mouth, but she's bound to silence.

* * *

IT'S A LONG walk back to Headquarters with Crowe leading Chastity ahead of me. We use a wyrm to cover some of the distance, but it's still a long trip. Chastity's last words before being silenced are haunting, and I play them over in my head. I don't dare get close to her. Even with her bound, I'm frightened by what she might be capable of.

Her red curls bounce with each step. Why would someone so young would get involved with the Elementals? Was she born into them? How long have they been around?

And how does that involve me?

I stare harder at the back of Chastity's head. If they really wanted me to consider everything they'd said, they would answer my questions, not tease me with tidbits of information.

Are you really baffled about why the bad guy would lie to you? Hyacinth's sardonic thought bites me when I'm most vulnerable.

Oh, Hyacinth, good to hear you have advice for my private reflections, but not when my life is in danger, I shoot back.

I have responsibilities other than watching your back twenty-four seven, you know.

Then get out of my head.

Try quieting your thoughts every now and then, and I might be able to pull it off.

I put up a wall inside my head. I don't need to hear her right now. I don't need to hear *anyone*.

Except you, I think. I stare at Chastity, again, and try to poke into her mind, but she successfully keeps me out.

At Headquarters, Crowe passes Chastity off to Tricia without so much as a goodbye, and we head into the Sage's office. The elderly witch looks up at us from behind her desk. Her pleasant smile masks the concern in her eyes.

"You're back, and with a prisoner no less," she says.

"She attacked Lilith in Mentis," Crowe informs her. "Tried to capture her."

"Lavina thinks activity in the Coven has been odd for a while. Dawn too. They want Hyacinth to scope things out," I add.

"I'll send her immediately, but first, how are the other Covens?"

"Aens was nearly abandoned. Aquais was business as usual, and Alchemy seems as though they could go either way," Crowe says as he counts off each Coven on his fingers.

"And Ignis?" the Sage prompts.

"That's the only Coven we haven't visited yet," I reply wistfully.

"Then that's the first place you'll go as soon as the execution is finished."

I raise my eyebrows, unable to contain my surprise. "You've already decided her fate?"

"Of course," the Sage says. "Attacking one of us? That's treason."

"But she's so young!" I blurt out. As soon as the words tumble out, I slap a hand over my mouth, but it's too late. She's heard them. And so has Crowe.

You're one of us.

As far as the world is concerned, I'm with the Council. This fight isn't mine. I'd protested Iris' execution and let the girl who had poisoned Callista go. What will they think if I stand up for the Elementals a third time?

Chapter Thirty

Everyone Has Secrets

I

T'S HARD TO miss Crowe staring at me. He seems baffled, as if he doesn't understand my concern. Hell, I barely understand it, but I know enough to speak out when something's wrong. If the Council is willing to execute children in the name of peace, is anyone safe?

A gleam in the Sage's eyes tells me she's read all of my thoughts, unfiltered and in full.

"Crowe, you're excused. I need to speak with Lilith alone," she says.

"Thank you, ma'am. I'll help Hyacinth prepare for her mission," Crowe says. His eyes dart between me and the Sage before resting on me again. There's a pleading look in them.

Please, he thinks. He's worried I'll spill his secrets, the things he told me in Alchemy, but I'm more worried about keeping my own actions under wraps.

I meet his gaze. I don't know what he sees in my eyes, but the gleam in his turns to gratitude, and he takes his leave. I watch him go, then turn back to the Sage.

"You don't believe the girl should be executed?" she asks in an even tone.

"No," I say, and I'm stunned by my honesty. "She must have been brainwashed to do what she did. She's so young."

"Lilith, you'd be surprised what horrors people, even the

young, are capable of. Age doesn't matter in the face of evil," she says.

I flinch, unsure where the conversation is going. Has she successfully probed Chastity's mind and unraveled her true motives? I fidget, unable to get the worst of the tremors under control. In her years presiding over the Land of Five, what has she seen? It can't be easy to read everyone's minds and know all the evil that lies in their heads.

I'd never be able to trust anyone ever again, I think.

"What I'm about to tell you is something that must not be shared with anyone else. Even Hyacinth needs to be kept out at all costs."

At all costs? What could the Sage possibly have to tell me that no one knows about? Is it something about Willow? *Me?* Her voice is timid, almost afraid. Not at all like the Sage.

"I support the Elementals and their beliefs."

All the air *whooshes* from my lungs, and my legs buckle. Thankfully, I'm standing in front of a chair, though I doubt I would've noticed if I fell directly to the floor.

"Wh-what?" I ask. It's as close to a comprehensible sound as I can manage.

"The treaty. It hurts us all," the Sage says and rises from her seat. She walks over to her bookshelf and runs her fingers over the books' spines. "You saw as much yourself."

This is a trap, I tell myself. A trick of some sort. I keep my mouth shut.

The Sage turns her back to the bookshelf and continues, "If I could curse the witches who crafted it, I would. The Land of Five was never meant to be split. The Covens are supposed to help each other. Witches work best when their powers are mixed."

"The treaty keeps us safe. Functioning." I say the line I'm most positive will get me out of this—the official party anthem I'm finding I believe less and less as time passes.

You're standing on a cliff. Feelings are irrelevant, I remind myself. *One wrong move, and you'll go over.* Problem is, I don't know what that wrong move could be.

"That's what you've been brainwashed to believe," the Sage says. She plucks a thin book from the shelf, opens it and flips through a few pages before she sets it on the desk. It discusses the writing of the treaty and the witches who composed it. "Things around here have a tendency to function on pretty lies because the ugly truth would destroy them."

"What is the ugly truth?" I manage to ask, looking up from the page.

"That the main purpose of the treaty is for the Council to manipulate the Land of Five as it sees fit. Under its decree, everyone is suffering."

I can believe that when I think of the drought in Mentis that could easily be fixed using the abilities of a witch like Kieran. The food shortage in Aquais that could be easily fixed by the crops the witches grow in Aens. The absolute necessity of an Alchemy witch Healer in every Coven.

The room threatens to spin, and I'm glad I'm sitting. I rest my head on the back of the chair and stare at the ceiling. Of all the people to suspect of having Elemental ties, I would've never guessed the Sage.

And that's why you should always expect the unexpected. Misty's ironic phrase from the last day of school runs through my head.

"I-I don't understand," I finally blurt out. I'm looking at her from such an odd angle, it almost hurts. "How can you believe any of this? You're the leader of the Council. These people want our blood."

"You're not a close-minded person, Lilith," the Sage says, calmly, coolly. "Don't tell me you've never had a single doubt about the Council. That there's never been a time when you wished the treaty didn't exist."

"Forgive me because I mean no disrespect, but nothing about this makes sense! What exactly are you trying to say? That you're not on either side of the war? That you want the Elementals to win? If that's the case… why kill Iris? Why order Chastity to die as well? For that matter why not abolish the treaty yourself and end this war before it can begin?" I ask, dumbfounded. "Why did you send us out there to find them?"

"Politics and human nature are not simple things to fix, my dear."

After my speech, I'm too winded to speak. Even if I could, I doubt I'd have a proper response.

"It's time for me to tell you a story, Lilith," she says and clasps her hands together, resting them on the desk beside the still open book. "When I rose to this position, I was young. Maybe a year or two older than you are now. There were no Elementals, just five Covens trying to heal after the shock of a century-long war. When the treaty was put into place, I was a little girl. It was held in high esteem until my Dedication Ceremony. The creators of the treaty truly believed keeping the different types of magic apart would be the best way to keep more wars from breaking out. And for a while it did exactly that."

"So, what changed your mind?"

"Being here, meeting witches from all over the Land of Five, I started to see the world for what it was. The way it could be. The treaty harmed those it was meant to protect. I wanted to create a new way of living, one that would make the treaty obsolete. Turns out, accomplishing that task is harder than I ever imagined. In my time as the Sage, the most I've accomplished is the Coven crossover from Alchemy."

The most powerful witch in the Land of Five is pouring her heart out to me, and I can hardly process her words. "You're the Sage," I say in a breathy whisper. "Your word is law. These witches… they have to obey you regardless of your decision."

"It's not that simple, Lilith," she says. "One person should never decide the fate of the majority. The Council was created with that idea in mind. While I have absolute say over the way the Grove is run, it's a collaborative project with the rest of the Land of Five. Many witches, especially the older ones, know others who were directly affected by the war. They know what can happen when witches go against one another, and they fear it. Making such a drastic change now, even in the name of good, could lead to some bad results."

"Is that why you wanted us to find Elementals? So you could recruit them to the Council and use them to influence the naysayers?"

"That would never work," the Sage says. I wonder if it's something she's tried to do in the past. Is it why she recruited me?

"Why are you telling me this?" I manage to ask. This is a heavy secret, and with the weight of my own still dangling over my head, I worry I can't handle it.

"It's a delicate situation, Lilith," the Sage concedes. "You would've found out the truth sooner rather than later. I'm certain of it. You're inquisitive and smart. It seemed only fair."

"This is information the senior members of the Council should know," I argue. "Not me."

"I don't want them to," the Sage says. "They lack a certain level of understanding, and I'm out of time. I'm growing old, Lilith. You believe you are alone because of the events that have shaped you into who you are today, but I believe they have only connected you more. I must name a successor. Someone who can walk in my footsteps. Someone who can understand me on a personal level and can pass my beliefs onto the next generation."

Air no longer wants to fill my lungs, and I struggle to say, "Me?"

The tiniest hint of a smile shows as she says, "When I first heard about you and your actions at the Arcane Ceremony, how the Elementals are drawn to you, I marveled at how perfect it all was. Call it intuition, but I sense something in you. You're a strong witch, Lilith, whether or not you're willing to believe me. And that strength is going to do a lot of good for a lot of people."

I want to scream at her that she's insane, that maybe the Elementals got to her too, and they're using her as a puppet somehow. None of this can be real. "All my life, people have doubted me. How in the world do you expect me to have faith in myself?"

"Because they're wrong. You, and you alone, know all that you are truly capable of. Think about all you've accomplished in the short time since your Arcane Ceremony."

I've never been good at taking compliments, but now,

when the stakes are so high, it's worse. She can say whatever she will about what I've accomplished, but I've hit a wall. None of it feels like enough.

"You can live your life as is, continuing to feel like an underdog, or you can step up, be someone who matters, and make a change."

I don't hesitate to make eye contact as I say, "What makes you think I'll be able to do much more than you?"

The Sage's smile grows. She's not at all put off by the barb in my tone. "A rebellious spirit is not always a flaw. At first, with your quick tongue and impressive powers, I thought you might be an Elemental. Now I see you as you actually are, and I want you to see it too."

A knock echoes down the corridor. The Sage looks at me apologetically as she rises from her seat. "That's Lynx with an update on Callista. I'm sorry to leave you like this, but duty calls, my dear," she says and disappears into the darkness before I can stop her.

Chapter Thirty-One
Labyrinth

I STAY IN the Sage's office well after she leaves trying to pull myself together. I urge myself to get up, to move, but I can't. Nothing matters.

Chastity's execution will be the first one I attend as a member of the Council. Agree with it or not, I have to pretend to pledge my loyalty to them because of the dark secret that binds me to the Sage. I'd already felt as if I were in danger, but the feeling is worse now. At any time, the Sage can decide I've done some taboo and must be executed as a means of saving her secret. By the time I finally stumble into the Common Room, so much time has passed, the room is empty.

Tricia took Chastity somewhere for holding—I make a mental note to find out where when things have calmed—and Crowe most likely escorted Hyacinth to Mentis at the Sage's request.

With a shuddering sigh of relief, I collapse into the nearest chair. I'm so tired I don't even put up a block in my head. How can the Sage possibly think I'm capable of following in her footsteps?

"You seem tense," Tricia observes. Too late, I realize she's come back and seated herself in the chair beside me. Her chin is cupped in her palm, watching me.

I don't know how much to tell her about the trip, about

what I've learned. Had Crowe told her what happened in Mentis? Had Hyacinth? "I've taken a long… look at myself recently," I admit with a grimace and stare down at my bad leg.

"Oh?" she prompts, clearly surprised I've decided to open up to her. I am too. I wish I could talk to Clio and Helena, but until I see them again, my options are limited. If I have to hold onto this information any longer, it'll consume me. "What about it?"

"In Mentis, Lavina told me someone might've hurt me… on purpose."

Tricia's eyes narrow to slits, and I can't tell what emotion causes it. "Why would they do that?"

"To hide the truth of who I am," I say. I remember the look on Lavina's face as soon as she'd finished studying my leg. "According to her, the severity of the burns actually gave me pyrokinetic powers. Without the injury, I would've never had them."

"So, where are you from if not from Ignis?"

"Mentis makes the most sense." If any of this does.

Tricia considers my words and nods slightly. "If you truly are from Mentis, how'd you end up in Ignis?"

It's a good question. One I'm scared to learn the answer to.

"I suppose I'll have to ask." Until now, I'd given myself a dozen reasons, excuses, about why I should overlook everything my parents said and did. I can't do that anymore. This secret has turned into something much larger than I could've possibly imagined.

Tricia simpers, and I try to prod her mind, to see what she

thinks of the bomb I've just dropped on her but her mind is veiled.

I wipe my face and try to bury my emotions deep, wishing I could take back the last five minutes. I feel better now that the information is out there. Problem is, I don't know what Tricia will do with it.

If the Sage can learn to trust people after all she's been through, you can too, I tell myself.

In an attempt to change the conversation, I ask, "How's Callista doing?"

"She's stable. You can go see for yourself if you want, but Lynx might be a little surly. He's been at her side for days. I doubt he's even slept."

"I think I'll go say hi. I worried about her while we were away," I say and stumble to my feet, glad for the excuse to slip away.

Tricia doesn't offer her own goodbye. Her gaze scorches me as I walk across the room, and I wonder exactly what Quinn told her about my time in Mentis.

As I walk through the Council's elaborate garden, I'm glad for the pain in my leg. It centers me and reminds me of my task even when my mind wants to take me elsewhere. I move slowly and carefully through the night as I follow the river to the tiny hut on the bank. It's not far from Thorn and Callista's home in the reeds. I smell the herbs before I announce my presence.

"May I come in?" I ask through the blanket hanging over the door.

"Lilith?" Lynx replies, sounding almost surprised. "Of course."

I push into the house and narrow my eyes to better see in

the dim candlelight. There's a small bed pushed up against the wall. Callista is spread out on it. Her wings are parted to create a pink layer between her and the sheets, and there's a noticeable absence of emotions on her usually cheery face.

"Hi, Callista, how are you feeling?" I ask as I take a small step into the room.

She struggles to sit, then props herself up on her elbow. "I've had better days, Lilith."

Remembering that I let the girl who did this go stings me all over. "I-I'm sorry about—"

She holds up a tiny hand. "It's okay. The Sage explained what happened. You were new and unprepared for their tricks. No need to apologize."

Accident or negligence? "If you say so," I murmur, not at all convinced.

"Something wrong?" Lynx asks.

Can everyone tell I don't feel like myself?

"No," I say honestly. The word leaves a weird feeling in the pit of my stomach that I don't altogether care for. "I-I need advice."

"I'm happy to help," Callista chirps and tries to sit up again though my request had been directed at Lynx and not her. A pitiful groan leaks from her, and she flops back down on the bed. "As much as I can anyway."

"Oh, my Goddess, are you okay?" I take a hesitant step forward. Pain stretches across her tiny, beautiful face, and I have the sudden desire to leave. How selfish am I for coming to bug her with my problems when she's nowhere near healed?

"She's fine. She'd be better if she'd stop trying to push

herself to heal faster than her body can," Lynx says with a pointed frown at Callista.

She sighs in defeat and relaxes against the mattress. "I'm sorry, Lilith. I don't like being bedridden."

"I understand."

Lynx rises from his seat and walks me to the door. "It's gonna take some time for her to heal. She's determined to fight every step of the way, and company doesn't help. I know you wanted to visit, but as far as advice, I think you'd be better off asking Thorn until Callista's fully recovered."

I stiffen at the thought of the brusque fairy and look up at Lynx. His aquamarine eyes are glazed over, and he has purple half-circles beneath them showing the extent of his exhaustion. Callista needs to heal, not just for herself, but for Lynx as well.

"Let me know when she's better," I say before calling to Callista, "Hope you get better soon!"

"Thank you," she says. She sounds as though she's on the verge of sleep, as if the little bit of movement zapped her of every ounce of energy.

As I leave Lynx's den, I stare across the river at the Advisory Council's home in the reeds. I'm unsure whether Thorn will be there or out somewhere else covering Callista's duties. A breeze blasts through the trees, and I shiver. I'm still dressed in the thin Mentis clothes Quinn gave me, and in the excitement since returning to the Grove, I hadn't thought to change out of them.

"Thorn, are you here?" I call into the darkness. I listen to the gentle burble of the river passing through the plants as I wait for an answer.

A glint of silver around black wings catches the moonlight as she flies from the water. "Lilith, this is a surprise," she says and lights down on the grass beside me.

"Thought I'd come say hi," I say and plop down beside her. "I visited Callista a few minutes ago. She's doing well." Or at the very least, better than she was before Crowe and I went on our trip.

"She'd be a lot better if she'd let herself relax. Damn her enthusiasm," Thorn says with a shrug. "I hope you didn't get her too worked up."

"Of course not," I say. I remember how Lynx had pretty much told me the same thing.

"So, what's really going on?" Thorn asks with a pointed glare. "You didn't come to shoot the breeze."

Her words send a bigger chill down my spine than the cold night air. Am I making a mistake seeking her help? This is my issue, after all. What could anyone possibly do or say that would make any of this better?

"I need advice, and I don't know who else I can turn to," I admit.

Her frown eases a bit, and I realize how truly similar we are. We wear hardened masks on the outside to hide the fact that inside we care… probably too much.

"What's going on?" she asks.

"I-the Sage talked to me about something important, and I don't know who to tell."

Thorn raises her eyebrows and waits impatiently for me to get to the point.

"She discussed the possibility of my becoming her

successor." I force the words out.

The expression on Thorn's face doesn't change. "Well, that's good news, isn't it?"

"No," I state bluntly. "I can't do what she does. I barely have any control over the things I can do."

"Crowe says you're able to access powers from Ignis and Mentis. That's a start." She looks down at her fingernails as if losing interest in the conversation.

"It would be if things weren't so complicated. According to Lavina, I shouldn't be capable of pyrokinesis. She thinks that whoever burned my leg imbued me with the ability, possibly to hide the fact that I'm from Mentis, which would explain my telekinesis and mind reading abilities. If that's the truth, I'm an average, Equipped, Mentis witch. I'm not the powerhouse everyone thinks I am."

Thorn doesn't speak, and I appreciate the silence. She takes a moment to allow the words to work their way through her mind before responding.

"Did you tell the Sage this?" she asks at last.

I shake my head. "I'm sure she knows."

"If she knows, and she is still telling you these things, she isn't blowing smoke. She has a plan. You should feel honored to be chosen for this. Or at the very least considered."

I snort. "Like I should've been honored to be nominated for the Council?"

She gives me the stink-eye.

"I can't do it."

Thorn grunts, clearly annoyed, and flaps her wings. "I get it's hard to have faith in yourself, but you have a duty to fulfill. If the Sage has chosen you, then your fate has been decided. You don't have a choice, and to pretend you do only makes this harder on you and those around you."

"I thought you were supposed to be helpful. You're just repeating what Tricia told me," I reply, equally frustrated.

"Then it sounds like you should've listened to her," Thorn says. "Would've saved us both some time."

"Okay." I painfully rise to my feet. "Seems as if I made a mistake coming down here."

"Before you run off butthurt, let me ask you a question. Have you gone back to Ignis yet?"

I pause and frown. "No, we're supposed to go when Crowe gets back. After the execution."

"Good. May I suggest you use your time there wisely. Get to the bottom of your mystery. The sooner you tackle that issue, the sooner you can work on feeling better about yourself and putting your heart and soul where it belongs."

"But—"

"That's enough buts, Lilith. You have power you didn't have before. Everyone, your parents included, must respect that and you. Stop acting like a scared child. You're strong, and you'd be even stronger if you'd show it. If you demand the truth from your parents, they will be bound by an oath they cannot break. Do you understand?"

This was information I hadn't heard before. "Really?"

"A gift for the role."

About the only gift I've gotten from the Council. "Thank you for your advice."

Her lips pull into a tight smile. The first real one I've seen her wear. "That's why I'm here. Now, do you need anything else, or can you take it from here?"

"If you could give me courage, that would be splendid."

"I'm not a genie," she replies. Her eyes are half-lidded with a lack of amusement. "Remember what I said about finding your confidence, your inner strength. It's a power all witches have but very few learn to utilize properly."

"Right," I murmur. I feel a pit open in the depths of my stomach. The only one capable of building myself up is me, and it seems all but impossible.

Chapter Thirty-Two
Duty

THE SCENE FEELS all too familiar as groups of witches gather at the Ceremony Grounds to watch the execution as if it's the next chapter of their favorite spectacle. Only this time, instead of Iris, it's Chastity tied to the stake. Council members, me included, are spread out across the field. We stand out from the crowd in our blue and black, hooded robes.

Witches from our home Covens gather around their representatives, and I'm uncomfortable standing among the witches I'd grown up with. Witches with whom I had one time played hide-and-seek. Witches with whom I'd imagined a very different life.

My hood pushes some of my blue-black hair into my face, and I'm glad for the shelter it offers. Not everyone from my Coven misses me. Some eye me with disdain, and I'm not quite sure of the reason for their hostility.

Upon arriving, I seek out Clio and Helena, but to my disappointment, they aren't here. Against the sun's blinding glare, I stare up the hill at the spot that, in a few minutes, will be Chastity's final resting place. While Tarj controlled the last execution, Tricia leads this one. She stands proudly beside the girl tied to the stake.

Chastity looks so much smaller than she really is. With her arms bound behind her, she's nearly as thin as the stake she's tied to. Chastity stares at the first row of onlookers, unintimidated by her fate. If anything, she looks bored. When I try to probe her mind, it's as vacant as the expression on her face.

The longer I watch her, the more conflicted I feel. Is it right for them to execute this girl rather than me? Something in me screams that I should help her. If the Sage is right about my connection to the Elementals, I could very well be looking at my own fate somewhere down the line.

Chasity's gaze rests on me, and I shiver as I remember her ominous threats in Mentis.

"For your crimes against the Council, we find you guilty. As a result, you, Chastity Vines, will be executed this day at the stake. Do you have any last words?" Tricia asks.

The girl doesn't speak. She scuffs the dust beneath her and grins.

Tricia raises an eyebrow. "Is that a no then?"

You aren't gonna do a thing?

The sudden intrusion jolts me, but I hold my place at the edge of the field.

Do something, the voice continues.

It isn't Hyacinth's, and it's definitely not mine. I should be concerned that an unknown witch is intruding into my head, but somehow, I'm not. If they were a threat, Hyacinth would know. She'd pick up on it and warn me. So, I ignore the voice and watch as Tricia covers Chastity in liquid. The girl retains her eerie smile, and I admire Tricia for not being bothered by it.

When the jug is empty, Tricia sets it down and gestures for me to approach. Unsure of my role in the ceremony, I follow her command and walk slowly toward the rise. None of the others had given me a proper rundown of what to expect today. Will I have to testify about Chastity's crimes?

The crowd parts as I stiffly make my way through. Whispers surround me, not all of them kind. I don't make eye contact, worried I'll meet some not-so-friendly eyes. At the base of the rise, I plant my feet and look up at Tricia and Chastity. Tricia gestures again for me to come closer, and a horrible feeling wells inside me. It's amplified when I look at Chastity and her eerie grin.

"What do I do?" I hiss at Tricia.

She doesn't answer with words. The look in her eyes says it all.

Me. *I'm* supposed to be the executioner. I stare at the girl then Tricia with butterflies in my stomach.

I can't do this, I think, and I try to take a step backward. I nearly bump into a nearby witch, reminding me how much is riding on the moment. To walk away without doing the job, without doing my duty will seal my fate.

They'll put you up there with her, that unfamiliar voice jeers.

Something in me shatters. A divide between who I used to be and the person I have to become is finally opening. There is no easy way out of this. I close my eyes and try to center myself. When I open them again, they're wet. Breathing in slowly to keep myself from audibly sniffling, I try to focus on the situation.

To access the pyro powers I shouldn't have, yet still do.

Nothing happens. Mocking comments from around the clearing fill my mind like a swarm of angry bees, stinging and jabbing anywhere they can reach. I have the hopeful thought that I won't be able to access the needed power, and someone else will have to be called upon in my place.

That's my easy out, I tell myself.

I'm ready to tell Tricia I can't do it when fire ignites beneath Chastity's feet. Her eerie smile falters as the pain bites her, but it never fades completely. The flames grow, and she's devoured by them. A sharp piercing wail comes from deep in her belly.

Tricia gives me an approving nod.

"I didn't do it!" I try to tell her, but my words are drowned out by Chastity's screams.

Tricia turns away, and I look at the crowd. None of the other witches heard me.

Chastity's screams dwindle, and she sends one last eerie grin in my direction. It tells me *she* heard me. I can't take my eyes off her as she gradually dissolves into charred clothes and melted flesh. The longer I watch, the more petrified I become.

I doubt I'll ever forget this moment.

She was so young. Too young to sacrifice her life. Other than her name and mission, I know nothing about her. What were her motives? For that matter, what are the Sage's? Why had she been so quick to insist on this execution, when we could've questioned her, probed her mind, and gotten information from her first?

More importantly, who lit the fire?

Quinn, who had moved through the crowd to stand between me and the rest of the witches, offers me a gentle smile. "Relax. You don't have to worry about her anymore."

Except she wasn't who I'd been worried about. Chastity would no longer be a threat, but plenty of other witches would.

She'd said this was only the beginning, and I'm starting to realize she was right.

Hyacinth appears in the distance. Her face is scrunched as she stares at the sky, lost in thought. Is the voice who reached out to me trying to contact her?

Is it telling her something about me?

"Good job," Tricia says. "I know this wasn't an easy choice for you, but you did it."

I barely hear her as I watch her pull remaining bits of stake from the ground. I think about the part of me who no longer exists—the girl who had been so dissatisfied with her life in Ignis.

Careful what you wish for, Hyacinth's voice flits through my mind.

Not wanting to acknowledge the comment, I put up my veil and shift my mind to memories of Chastity's final moments.

That's going to be you, I tell myself. I squeeze my eyes shut in a desperate attempt to block out the scene around me.

"Are you okay?" Quinn asks.

I jump. My disconnecting had worked a bit too well. I clear everything from my face and hope he hasn't seen anything that could be flagged as suspicious. "Yeah, I'm fine."

He smiles sympathetically, and I know he saw every bit of my internal struggle. I might've had the forethought to put a cloak on my mind, but it did nothing for my face.

"Did you know her?" I tip my head toward the rise.

He opens his mouth, then closes it as he considers his words. "Not well. She kept to herself mostly. Really only came out of her house for Coven duties."

"You didn't otherwise notice her around Mentis?" I'm not

sure what I'm trying to get him to admit, but something tells me he doesn't want to say what's really on his mind.

Quinn frowns. "She had a… habit of getting in and out of places unnoticed."

Apparently. If she was part of the Elementals, she was *really* good at it. She hadn't been suspected of anything until she attacked me.

I survey the group of onlookers and note the lack of sorrow. Of any emotion at all. Death is always a grim event, a reminder of the fate we will all face and be unable to escape one day. No one on the Ceremony Grounds sheds a tear over Chastity's demise. Their faces are blank, as if they're unsure of how they feel, or they simply don't care.

How could someone go through their entire life and not be close to anyone? Are Mentis witches less connected to one another because it's a larger Coven? Or are Chastity's loved ones afraid to show their grief because they fear the way their emotions will be perceived by the Council?

Surely someone will miss her.

"Didn't she have a family?" I blurt out.

"Of course," Quinn says. He is seemingly perturbed by the question. "But both of her parents died of some strange illness a few years back. Lavina never could figure out what it was."

"Hmm." I glance toward the smoldering pile of Chastity's remains. If she'd been living on her own for some time, she would have had plenty of opportunities to connect with the Elementals, and no one would have been any wiser.

"What is it?" Quinn asks, eyes wide with interest. "You think she did something to them? Maybe some rite of passage into the Elementals?"

"Nothing like that," I say reflexively then I want to take back my words.

What if that's the truth? Her case is strange, but oddly normal for the times. Several people close to my age are missing one or both parents.

They can't all be accidents, the little voice in the back of my head warns.

With a shiver, I think of Clio. His parents are dead too. *No. No way. Not Clio.*

Quinn continues to stare at me and waits for a response.

"It's definitely suspicious," I force myself to say.

Quinn's shoulders slump as if he'd expected me to say something else.

"Quinn!" Tricia calls him.

We make eye contact for a second longer before he turns away to meet her.

"Everything about the Elementals is suspicious," a voice says behind me.

"Tarj!" I gasp, and I fight the urge to hug him. It isn't necessarily happiness that drives my reaction, but relief. After his disappearing act, I'd wondered what happened to him. No one so much as said his name as if he'd become another taboo subject. It's reassuring to know Council members aren't killed off when they're replaced.

"How's your training going?" he asks.

"Uh, good," I say. I'm too shocked by his sudden reappearance to engage in proper conversation.

"Good, good. Is Crowe here?" He moves as though he's

leaving to search for him. "I haven't seen him yet."

I grab his arm. "Wait. Where have you been?"

"Why?" he asks with a small chuckle as I let go of him. "Have you missed me?"

"I thought something happened." I don't add what, and I hope he doesn't ask.

He places his finger against his ear, and I follow the movement. There's no gem, not even a red stud from Ignis. "I've been dismissed."

"Why?" I ask. My heart thuds in my chest.

Does it have to do with what the Sage told me? Is it possible Tarj had known, or was an Elemental himself, and the Sage had used me as an excuse to send him back to Ignis where he could manage a direct connection in private?

They wanted us to scout Ignis last, I remember. Pieces are fitting together to tell a story I'm not sure I'm ready to read.

"I thought you were the Sage's right-hand man."

"Yeah, well. Things change. After recruiting you, she didn't need me anymore." I can't quite decipher his tone. Bitterness? Shame? Anger?

"I'm… sorry," I say and place a hand over my heart. "I didn't know what my coming here would mean for you."

"I wanted to leave, and I think she knew," he says. "Of all the Council members, I was always the weakest. The others are capable of greatness. And me? I have a typical Ignis power."

I want to protest, but I can't. Pyrokinesis isn't special, not really, and if it's all he can do, he's got a point.

Before I say anything, he continues, "I had my doubts for some time, but it hit me hardest when you saved me from Iris.

You deserve the position a Hell of a lot more than I do."

I don't know if *deserve* is the right word for it.

"I'm glad you hold no ill will against me," I say stiffly. I hope I sound polite as I fight the urge to tell him what I'm really thinking.

"Of course not," he says. "You'll do Ignis proud."

"Hey, ready to go?" Crowe says behind me.

Tarj and Crowe exchange a high five. "Hey, man. What's up? Haven't seen you around lately."

"Yeah, I'm sure you heard the news," Tarj replies. There's a passive gleam in his eyes.

"I did. Tough break."

"How's Ignis been?" I ask Tarj in an attempt to diffuse the tension.

"Business as usual. Your class seems strong," Tarj tells me. "Clio's a great leader. He seems to know exactly what to say to motivate his friends. They do group training just about every day."

Of course he's doing good work, I think. A blush creeps across my cheeks at the thought of him. He's doing so well. If only I could say the same for Helena.

"It's been fun catching up, Tarj," Crowe says, "but we've got to get on the road. The Sage is expecting us to be in Ignis by tonight."

"A mission about the Elementals, I take it?" Tarj asks.

"Is there any other?" Crowe rolls his eyes.

I think not.

"I'll walk with you guys. It'll be like old times," Tarj offers.

Crowe doesn't protest, and I don't either. It can't hurt to

have his insight.

We leave the Ceremony Grounds with Crowe and Tarj in the lead. I follow with heavy feet, wondering what I'll find back home. I should be filled with unbridled excitement at the thought of seeing Helena and Clio again and getting to the bottom of the mystery of my true heritage.

But I'm not.

I'm wary. Cautious even.

All I can think about are the loyalties of the people I grew up with. How many of them are willing to tear others apart in the name of peace?

Chapter Thirty-Three

The Truth

BASED ON THE story Tarj tells during our walk, things have been virtually the same in Ignis since I left. That strikes me as odd. The rest of the Covens had noticeable issues, even if they weren't glaringly obvious at first.

Either way it goes, things *won't* be the same. For me at least. After everything that's happened since my last visit, they can't be. As Thorn noted, I have power—the power to control my loved ones, to take away their free will if I demand it. I don't want such a power, but I can appreciate why it might be necessary.

When I had been first elected to the Council, Helena had barely been able to stand my presence. How will she feel about me now? Will she want to see me? The knowledge that I'm the Sage's apprentice burns in the back of my mind, and I can guess the answer.

But I don't like it.

Just as I don't like the thought of forcing my parents to spill their secrets. How will they react when I confront them with all that I've learned? Will they finally come clean of their own volition, or will they make me bind them to an oath to get them to talk?

If it takes that, maybe I'm better off not knowing, I think darkly.

As the grass from the Grove fades to sunbaked soil, I realize how parched I am. Between returning from Mentis and

Chastity's execution, I hope the Council hasn't forgotten to deliver water to Ignis. I think of the treaty again and what it would mean for it to be abolished.

Crowe summons a wyrm, and I hesitate to climb on. "Where are we going?"

"Tarj's home for dinner," Crowe says.

"I-Is it okay if… I mean, may I travel solo for a bit?" I stumble over my words. "There are a few people I'd like to talk to while I'm here. I think… they may be more willing to talk to me without an audience."

Crowe shoots Tarj a sideways glance as if looking for a second opinion.

"Sounds fine to me," Tarj says.

I'm glad they don't resist. If it had come to an argument, I might've lost my nerve. Now, I can save them for when I really need them. The wyrm takes off, sending puffs of dirt into the darkening sky. I wait until they're gone before moving down a familiar path I've walked thousands of times. The closer I get to my parents' house, the worse the feeling in my gut becomes. The anxiety is overwhelming as I replay images from the last time I saw them.

Will they open the door when they realize I've returned? *They have to*, I tell myself, remembering what Thorn told me. Everything has boiled down to the next few hours of my life. No more hiding or lying.

At last, I spot the house, a structure of stone and mortar. My breath catches in my throat. I thought I was ready to face them, but inside, I feel like the scared, young woman who left Ignis two weeks ago. I lift my hand to knock, and my entire body shakes. Part of me almost hopes they don't answer. My knocks fade away, and just when I think no one is going to open the door, Raya answers.

She stares at me, wordlessly, and it's easy to imagine her slamming the door in my face. She ends the awkward moment when she flies across the threshold and pulls me into the tightest bear hug of my life. Raya has never been affectionate, not toward her husband and certainly not toward me.

"Lilith, honey, I was so worried," she whispers in my ear.

"Hi, uh, Mom?" I ask, uncertainly. She nearly drags me into the house still wrapped in her arms.

"I really thought you wouldn't come back."

I break free. "Wasn't it your idea for me not to?"

She meets my eye, and I can't quite identify what emotion is there.

It's all downhill from here.

"We never wanted that," she says. "We only wanted what was best for you."

"For you or for me?"

"For you, always."

I knew she'd answer the question like that. "If it's for me, then I need you to answer one question, and I'll be on my way." My voice is oddly void of emotion. Panic dances in her eyes, and I sense that she knows what's coming. "Are you… my mother?"

"Haze, get in here!" she shouts. Her eyes are wide and shiny, and she takes a step backward as if she thinks I'm going to physically harm her.

My father runs into the room as though he thinks the house is under attack. His expression softens when he sees me, but the muscles in my face are stuck in an expression that lacks any real warmth.

"Lilith!" he says and stands beside Raya. "What are you doing here?"

What am I doing here? As if I haven't spent the last eighteen years of my life living here, growing here, learning how to be a human here. I lift my hand to let him know I mean business. "This isn't a reunion," I say with full authority in my voice. It's the same tone Crowe uses when announcing our presence in the other Covens. I sound strong, even to my own ears, and if the situation wasn't so urgent, I might've taken a moment to pat myself on the back.

"B-business? You mean this is related to the Council?" Raya stutters, somehow looking smaller as if she's shrinking in on herself.

"My time away from Ignis has taught me some things about myself, about everything," I begin, looking from one parent to the other. "So, when I ask this question, I need an answer." Neither one speaks so I continue, "Are you my real parents?"

The silence in the room would've been overwhelming were it not for the sound of blood pumping in my ears.

Raya stares down at her hands, and Haze glares at me as if I've openly insulted him. Maybe I have, I'm not sure.

Normally, I would lower my gaze, intimidated by the man who raised me, but now the look is aggravating. Why is he so insistent on holding onto his secrets? "Well, are you?" I ask, raising my eyebrows.

"I thought we were past this," he says at last.

"We were. Then the Mentis Healer told me I'm only able

to access Ignis powers thanks to my injury. My powers are native to Mentis. *I'm* native to Mentis."

Raya turns so pale, I wonder if she'll faint in the middle of the kitchen. Haze flushes red and waves a dismissive hand. "You'd believe some stranger over us?"

"Yes. A stranger has no reason to lie to me. Here's my theory. Something happened to my real parents, and you took me. What I need to know is why. What happened?" *Who were they?*

"T-that's that's—" Raya tries to protest.

I talk over her. "And was it before or after my accident?"

"What exactly are you accusing us of?" Haze snaps.

Something wiggles in my gut, warning me that I'm close to the answer, but I'm not going to like it.

"We have taken care of you for most of your life. Does it really matter if we're not your real parents?" Raya finally rejoins the conversation, her voice a mere whisper.

"It wouldn't, no. Except lately, you haven't acted like parents. Not *my* parents anyway. Throwing me out when my life was at its lowest point? That was cowardice. I was afraid. Alone. And you offered me no comfort. No shelter."

"We did what we had to do," Haze says.

"Is that a confession?" My mouth is dry, but I somehow manage to keep my face from changing expression. "Are you officially saying I'm adopted?"

Haze opens his mouth to reply when Raya sets a hand on his arm to stop him. She looks tired and weary, and I suddenly realize she's fought a battle I had no clue existed.

"Yes, you are."

Despite my best attempt to stay strong, tears well in the

corners of my eyes. I thought I'd feel righteous when I learned the truth, but instead, I'm empty. "Why did you never tell me?"

"You were better off not knowing," Haze says.

"I'm not," I say and swallow back the ugly sob that wants to come. "Who are my real parents? And where are they now?"

"We've answered your one question," he says. "But this is where I draw the line."

I don't want it to, but my lip curls into a snarl. "Because you did this?" I ask, shifting my bad leg forward. I don't want to make the accusation, but it slings through the room like an invisible knife, hitting its mark.

Raya closes her eyes and says, "Yes." Her voice is a shaky whisper. Her eyes open, glistening with tears. "We did it a month after you were given to us."

"W-why?" I stammer. I'm finding it hard to keep my balance. I want to stay strong, but inside, I'm breaking. "Which one of you did it?"

Neither one will meet my eye.

"What was…" I stutter, dumbfounded. "How could you do this to me? I may not know who my real parents are, but I would be willing to bet they would disagree with what you did."

Haze opens his mouth, but after the protests he's given so far, I can't stand to hear anything else he has to say.

I swallow down my sadness, knowing I'll drown in it later. *You're not a scared child anymore,* Thorn's voice comes back to me. "I'm appreciative of the life you gave me, the food you cooked for me, the clothes you made me, but I'm afraid this is goodbye," I say then, with a touch of salt, I add, "It's for the best."

I don't want to see their faces as I turn away, and I

certainly don't want them to see the tears that are beginning to flow down my cheeks. I run to the door, desperate to escape from the situation and the weight of the emotions crushing my will to live.

I hurry along the stone path outside, listening to my parents' footsteps behind me. Raya stops at the doorframe and clings to it as if she'll fall without its support. "Wait, Lilith! You don't understand!"

No, I don't.

I've witnessed so much unnecessary cruelness in the world the past few days, I've hit my limit. I'm sobbing as I hurry away from my childhood home to get as far from Haze and Raya as the border of Ignis will allow. The only thing I can think about now is avoiding Crowe and Tarj.

I don't want them to see me like this.

I don't want *anyone* to see me like this.

Chapter Thirty-Four
All on the Table

ON REFLEX, MY feet lead me to Clio's house. My leg aches as I wait on his doorstep, and I hope, against all odds, he'll be as happy to see me as he was the last time I was here.

His eyes light up when he answers the door, and I know I've worried for nothing. About him at least. "Lilith!" He pulls me into his arms and whispers in my ear, "I've missed you."

"I missed you too," I say and melt into his embrace. The genuine warmth that leaks from his touch hits me in a way the hug from my mother hadn't. His words and his gesture are genuine.

Clio grabs my hand, yanking me into his house before he pulls the door closed. "I thought you wouldn't be back for some time," he says and sits on the sofa.

"We're searching for Elementals," I reply and sit beside him. "I'm sure Tarj told you. Crowe and I have traveled through the entire Land of Five this past week, searching for clues."

"Did you find any?"

"Let's just say things don't look too good right now for *any* of the Covens."

Clio's face turns grim. "I heard there was an execution today."

I nod briefly. Flashes of Chastity's burning corpse and eerie grin are stuck in my mind.

"I would've been there, but I couldn't get out of training."

I hardly hear him. After the confrontation with Raya and Haze, I had nearly forgotten my other problems.

"The girl they executed—Chastity—was killed because of… because of me. She was an Elemental," I explain. "And she tried to abduct me in Mentis."

"She didn't hurt you, did she?" He places his hand on mine as if he's searching for physical injuries.

I shake my head. "No, but the entire experience has…changed me."

Clio raises a questioning eyebrow.

I think about the execution, about the fire I couldn't summon, about the flames someone else had. I want to tell him *everything* that's happened, but I can't work up the nerve. So, I decide to drop a different bombshell. "I think I'm… from there. From Mentis."

"What?" he demands in a choked whisper that leads me to believe he meant for his words to be much louder. His grip on my hand tightens, causing my knuckles to crunch together uncomfortably. "Sorry," he says and loosens his hold. "How'd you come to that conclusion?"

"A… long story. My parents… they're the ones who did this to me," I say and gesture at my leg.

Clio is silent, so I repeat myself.

"That's what I thought you said." His face becomes animated with rage. "They *burned* you? With what magic? And for what purpose?"

"Their own magic, I guess. One of them is Equipped. They have to be. And they've been pretending not to for all this time. As for the reason, I don't know." My voice drops to a whisper, and I avoid his gaze. "Just as I don't know who my real parents are or what happened to them."

His expression softens when he realizes how hurt I am, and he pulls me into his arms. "I'm always here for you, sweetheart. If nothing else, know you've got me."

"I do know," I say and relax the slightest bit. This right here is the only thing in my life that I *am* sure of. The tiny bit of quiet in the storm.

He pulls back enough to kiss me. The contact jolts me and scrambles my thoughts. My mind tries to convince me to pull away, to find Crowe and serve my duty to Ignis, but it's a weak urge, which is easily overpowered. After everything I've endured, I deserve this fleeting moment of happiness. I kiss him back and run my fingers through his hair. The Elementals are hunting me, and my life is in danger. For all I know, this could be the last time I see him. From the way he holds me, he must have the same thought.

When we finally part, Clio stares at me, and his eyes search deep into mine. I don't have a clue what he's looking for. I pull completely out of his grasp when I remember the situation.

My parents, the Council, the war.

Clio rises from his chair, stretches, then looks toward the kitchen as if he's considering cooking something. "How long are you staying?"

"Most likely, only a few hours if I know Crowe."

"That's too bad," he says. His genuine disappointment is clear on his face. "I thought about inviting Helena over for dinner. She could use some cheering up."

"You think she'd be happy to see me? She couldn't bear to look at me last time I was here."

Clio crinkles his forehead in thought. "She's... uh... she's changed a lot."

A new, horrifying thought crosses my mind. If the Elementals have infiltrated the other Covens, their influence will be in Ignis too, no doubt. Could they have gotten to Helena? Would they go after her because of our friendship?

Clio notes my horrified expression. "What? You don't think..." he trails off as he comes to the same conclusion I have.

She wouldn't, I want to say, but the truth is, I don't know. Every time I see her, she pulls away more and more. I remember Crowe's face in Alchemy telling me about Katrina, his disbelief and fear.

Everyone is suffering, the Sage's words come through my mind.

I run a hand down my face, trying to get my mind to slow down. It's been a heavy day, and it's far from over. Maybe it would be a good idea to visit Helena. This time of day, she would most likely be doing coven duties. Since she's taken over my position with Angel, there's a good possibility that she's hanging out in Ambrossi's den.

Ambrossi. He's taken care of me since my leg was injured. Does he know my adopted parents did it? Does he know who my *real* parents are?"

Two birds, one stone, I think and stand up so quickly that Clio flinches. "What's wrong?"

"Nothing. I just...I need to talk to Ambrossi."

"About..." Clio begins and looks at my leg.

I nod.

"Do you want me to come with you?"

I can't imagine a situation where I'd need emotional support more than this one. "If you don't mind."

"Of course," he says, and we step outside into the fading warmth of the Ignis evening.

We start to walk, but Clio looks uneasy after a few steps. I'm about to ask him what's wrong when I notice it too. The world around us is eerily silent. No sounds from birds or wildlife. We exchange looks but say nothing. If something were amiss, surely Crowe or Tarj would've sought me out.

As we approach the heart of Ignis that heavy feeling doesn't go away. If anything, it becomes more apparent. As we crest the rise and the dirt underfoot changes to rock, I see something that makes my heart fall to my stomach.

Clio sees it at the same time as me. "Is that…*smoke?*"

Fire isn't anything unusual in Ignis, but in the wrong part of the Coven, it can be dangerous. Like Mentis, our water is delivered by the Council. With the exception of the oasis, the amount on hand is limited. That's why my covenmates have an understanding that fire gifts aren't to be used in the heart of Ignis.

Seeing smoke here in the most populated part of our Coven is cause for concern. Clio and I move faster. A sinking feeling in my stomach tells me what I'll see before we round the bend, and it comes into view just as horrific as I imagined it to be.

Ambrossi's Den is on fire.

The Elemental Coven
(The Witch's Ambitions Trilogy Book Two)

Held by the Enemy in a Land Far, Far Away…

The Land of Five is being systematically torn apart by war, and witch Lilith Lace has a number of problems. First—having been captured in the Battle of Ignis by the Elemental Coven, she's now being held… well, she really has no idea where, so getting back home again is going to be hard, if not outright impossible. Especially since she has to cope with the deaths of everyone she's ever loved while being held captive.

Unable to decide between escape and giving up completely, Lilith is presented with a new challenge when she learns that the infamous rouge witch, Willow, is not only alive and well but played a larger role in Lilith's childhood accident than she ever imagined.

Everything Lilith's ever known is in flux. Friends are becoming enemies and enemies are becoming friends. Will Lilith finally get to the bottom of her past among the ranks of the Elemental Coven, or will she instead get hurt worse than anything she's encountered so far?

About the Author

Raised in Michigan but moved to Texas and has experienced the best and worst of both. Kayla has interests in the dark and macabre. She enjoys '80's music and movies. A little neurotic and a huge lover of Halloween, creepy stories and cats are totally her jam.

www.ingramcontent.com/pod-product-compliance
Lightning Source LLC
Chambersburg PA
CBHW060649190726
48289CB00002B/332